Trained together at the Athena Academy, these six women vowed to help each other when in need. Now one of their own has been murdered, and it is up to them to find the killer, before they become the next victims....

Al
This forensic scientist c
PROOF, by Ju

Darc
A master of disg
any ~~crime scene.~~
ALIAS, by Amy J. Fetzer—August 2004

Tory Patton:
Used to uncovering scandals, this investigative reporter will get to the bottom of any story—especially murder.
EXPOSED, by Katherine Garbera—September 2004

Samantha St. John:
Though she's the youngest, this lightning-fast secret agent can take down men twice her size.
DOUBLE-CROSS, by Meredith Fletcher—October 2004

Josie Lockworth:
A little danger won't stop this daredevil air force pilot from uncovering the truth.
PURSUED, by Catherine Mann—November 2004

Kayla Ryan:
This police lieutenant won't rest until the real killer is brought to justice, even if it makes her the next target!
JUSTICE, by Debra Webb—December 2004

ATHENA FORCE:
They were the best, the brightest, the strongest—women who shared a bond like no other....

Dear Reader,

We're thrilled to bring you another exhilarating month of captivating women and explosive action! Our Bombshell heroines will take you for the ride of your life as they come under fire from all directions. With lives at stake and emotions on edge, these women stand and deliver memorable stories that will keep you riveted from cover to cover.

When the going gets tough, feisty Stella Valocchi gets going, in *Stella, Get Your Gun,* by Nancy Bartholomew. Her boyfriend's a lying rat, her uncle's been murdered and her sexy ex is back in town, but trust Stella—compared to last week, things are looking up....

Loyal CIA agent Samantha St. John has been locked up—for treason! With the reluctant help of her wary partner, Sam will hunt for the real traitor—who bears an uncanny resemblance to Sam herself—in *Double-Cross,* by Meredith Fletcher, the latest adventure in the twelve-book ATHENA FORCE continuity series.

Don't miss the twists and turns as a former operative is sucked back into the spy life to right the wrongs done to her family, in author Natalie Dunbar's exciting thriller, *Private Agenda.*

And finally, a secret agent needs a break—but when her final mission goes wrong, she's pushed to the limit and has to take on a rookie partner. Luckily she's still got her deadliest weapon... it's *Killer Instinct,* by Cindy Dees.

When it comes to excitement, we're pulling no punches! Please send me your comments c/o Silhouette Books, 233 Broadway, Suite 1001, New York, NY 10279.

Sincerely,

Natashya Wilson

Natashya Wilson
Associate Senior Editor, Silhouette Bombshell

DOUBLE-CROSS

MEREDITH FLETCHER

Published by Silhouette Books

America's Publisher of Contemporary Romance

Special thanks and acknowledgment
are given to Meredith Fletcher for her contribution
to the ATHENA FORCE series.

 SILHOUETTE BOOKS

ISBN 0-373-51328-3

DOUBLE-CROSS

Copyright © 2004 by Harlequin Books S.A.

This edition published by arrangement with Harlequin Books S.A.

® and TM are trademarks of Harlequin Books S.A., used under license. Trademarks indicated with ® are registered in the United States Patent and Trademark Office, the Canadian Trade Marks Office and in other countries.

Visit Silhouette Books at www.eHarlequin.com

Printed in U.S.A.

MEREDITH FLETCHER

doesn't really call any place home. She blames her wanderlust on her navy father, who moved the family several times around the United States and other countries. The one constant she had was her books. The battered trunk of favorite novels followed her around the world when she was growing up and shared dorm space with her in college. These days, the trunk is stored, but sometimes comes with Meredith to visit A-frame houses high in the Colorado mountains, cottages in Maine, where she likes to visit lighthouses and work with fishing crews, and rental flats where she takes moments of "early retirement" for months at a stretch. Interested readers can reach her at MFletcher1216@aol.com.

Chapter 1

Late August
Munich, Germany

"Your target is at three o'clock, Sam. Coming down the stairs. Can you confirm visual?"

Shifting amid the throng of celebrants gathered around the nearest open wet bar, Samantha St. John turned to her right and looked up the long winding stone staircase that connected the elegant ballroom to the castle's second floor. Considering the ceiling was almost forty feet high, the staircase had plenty of meandering room. Other heads started to turn in the direction of the staircase as her target descended. Konrad Steiner loved to make an entrance.

"Sam?"

Riley McLane's warm voice echoed in Sam's ear as if he was standing right beside her. He'd caught her off guard even though she'd been expecting the audio contact through the micro ear transceiver she wore. She'd been standing idle, making the party scene with small talk for almost two hours without seeing her target or hearing much from Riley. She was good at waiting, but she didn't like it.

Sam's partner on-site had met with the target briefly outside and had managed to tag Steiner with an ultraviolet mist that showed up on the thermal-imaging surveillance systems the support team was using through a geosynchronous weather satellite the Central Intelligence Agency had gotten access to. Riley and the support team in Langley, Virginia, back in the United States had followed the man through the castle, once the tag had been made.

Only five feet, three inches tall, Sam had to peer over the crowd of guests around her. The spiked heels she wore gave her a boost. Of course, if she got into a footrace, she was in trouble.

The plan is not to get into trouble, Sam reminded herself. Get in, install the computer program on the target's computer and get out. Simple and trouble free. Stick with that. No trouble.

Steiner, the party's host and an international crime figure, although most of the attendees didn't know that, descended the stairs with a svelte redhead on his arm. She trailed a hand down the wrought-iron banister, the movement as suggestive as her rolling hips. Her proximity staked her claim on the man at her side for every other woman in the ballroom. And perhaps that message was intended for some of the men, as well.

Steiner was in his early fifties, but only the mission background Sam had read on the man gave that away. He took care of himself, and obviously considered his image one of his best attributes. His black hair was expertly groomed and his short-cropped goatee stood out proudly. A cruel smile curved his generous mouth. The dark blue tuxedo he wore fit him like a glove, delineating the broad shoulders and narrow waist.

The man looks like a medieval lord, Sam thought as she watched Steiner. The castle suits him well. But then, he knows that, doesn't he?

Balloons and festive party decorations covered the walls. The chandelier in the ballroom glittered with a thousand points of light.

The castle outside Munich, Germany, along with the landscaped grounds inside the walls and the forest beyond, was a recent acquisition that Steiner was showing off. He was also showing off the woman at his side, another recent—although more temporary, judging from past behavior—acquisition. His relationships with women tended to be perishable in all senses of the word. Tonight the castle and the woman both were intended to intimidate those Steiner planned to do business with.

His slender companion was less than half his age. She wore a shimmering dark green evening gown that left little to the imagination. She clung to Steiner's arm, dwarfed by his height. She laughed and talked freely, patting Steiner on the arm.

Steiner paid polite interest to the young woman, but his sharp hazel eyes roved over his guests like those of a hawk swooping toward a nest of field mice. He was a predator going to work, sorting out the strongest and the weakest of his victims in a glance.

Seven men in evening black met Steiner at the bottom

of the stairs. All of the men started talking at once, in three different languages. Each of them had a deal he wanted to present. Asia, Africa, Australia and North America were represented in the delegation.

Steiner was, Sam knew, fluent in those languages and a dozen others. Patiently and with diplomacy, Steiner shelved the topics for discussion, saying there would be plenty of time for business after the party. Sam barely heard the exchanges over the noise of the crowd and the roar of the speed metal rock band playing live in the next room.

"Sam, do you copy?" Riley prodded. There was an unusual edge to his voice.

"I've got him," Sam whispered. The miniature sending and receiving unit tucked in her ear picked up her voice easily and filtered out the extraneous noise. The device broadcast on a satellite phone frequency. The signal made the trip to the limousine Sam had arrived in, was encrypted there on hidden Agency hardware, and sent on to her mission controller.

Several of the partygoers used satellite phones to conduct business and keep in touch with their offices while at the castle. Steiner's security allowed for those signals to come and go and didn't jam them. That was a weak spot the intelligence division at the Agency had ferreted out to use for their own on-site sat-link communications.

The true trick in penetrating Steiner's stronghold had been in wangling an invitation to the party. Even the paparazzi hadn't been able to break into the castle. Steiner's estate security was top-notch. However, the man did like publicity that he could control. Sam had chosen that as her route into the castle party.

"Bret?" Riley asked.

"Affirmative." Bret Horn, Sam's partner on the mission, stood a few feet away. Blond and good-looking, Horn had immediately drawn the attention of several females attending the party. He masked his response with the glass of beer he held while pretending to listen to the two dark-haired women vying for his attention.

"Sam, we've identified the target's room and the computer he uses for his drops," Riley said. Until Bret had marked Steiner with the ultraviolet spray, they hadn't been able to ascertain that. "I'll direct you there when you're ready."

"Understood," Sam said. Immediately, adrenaline spiked through her body, invigorating her. But she kept herself under tight rein. She liked being in control of herself. Some of her friends insisted she was a control freak, never quite able to let herself go.

Sam didn't agree with that assessment completely, but she understood how others could see her that way. Control was a big part of her life and her career. So many other things in her childhood—her abandonment and who her parents had been—remained mysteries and out of her reach. She'd had to focus on the here and now, not think about parents who had walked away from her or surrogate families that had provided for her but made certain they never got close to the strange child who was something of a genius.

Growing up, Sam had only been a visitor in those homes. Not family. She hadn't had that until she'd reached the Athena Academy for the Advancement of Women. Her friendship with the Cassandras, as she and the others in her orientation group had called themselves, had been deeper than anything she'd ever known, then or since leaving the academy. She didn't trust the world to offer her anything like that again. She'd trained herself to be complete. Maybe she wasn't always happy, but she was independent.

"At the first sign of trouble," Riley stated quietly, "I want the two of you out of there."

Irritated, Sam said, "Maybe we could concentrate on a successful mission before we throw in the towel."

"I *am* concentrating on this mission's success," Riley stated sharply. "Getting you out of there alive is the greatest success." He paused. "*Both* of you."

Sam felt guilty at once because she knew Riley wasn't happy with getting sidelined from the action by his recent injury and didn't care for the role of mission controller. He wasn't cut out to be an observer. He was a player. Sending others into danger was hard for him.

Riley had gotten shot on his last mission nearly a month ago. That mission had brought them closer to Steiner, finally giving them enough information to realize what the man was doing. That was also why Riley had been put into place as mission controller.

Sam had served as part of the extraction team that had brought Riley out of downtown Munich, Germany, after his cover had been blown and he'd been wounded. Though he insisted he was now at one hundred percent and ready for fieldwork, Medical hadn't yet released him.

"I'm just reminding you of the mission parameters." Riley's voice took on an edge. "We're not all or nothing on this take. We'll have another chance. The target is a big fish, but he's not going to pull a fade on us. He's got too much to lose."

Sam knew that wasn't entirely true. Konrad Steiner had operated for years without being discovered. The action that had resulted in Riley's wounding had put the man close to ground for weeks. With all his money in Swiss and Cayman Islands banks, Steiner could slip away in an instant and become someone else.

"You don't have an extraction team there, Sam," Riley reminded. "And you're not exactly the most seasoned agent we could have sent."

Sam resisted the urge to argue the point. She was good at what she did; that was why she was there.

If Riley knew he'd angered her, he didn't act like it. He continued in the same commanding tone that grated on her nerves. "Tread lightly," he ordered. "This is my show. My call."

Sam grew more irritated. She could be a team player when she needed to be, but she preferred calling her own shots. Because of her size and the way she kept to herself, most people underestimated her. They often thought she was too small, too shy. She didn't like the fact that Riley seemed to be one of those people.

During her six years with the CIA, Sam had been on several missions. Generally those missions had depended on her linguistic abilities, translating conversations and documents, rather than hands-on work that could get her killed. Only a few missions had actually required her to operate in the field and at such close proximity to a dangerous target.

Steiner made his way through the crowd. He was known as an investor and a deal maker. His interests included developing music groups like the one playing in the next room, pharmaceuticals, transportation and genetic research. If a profit could be turned at an endeavor, Steiner seemed to find a way to become part of the enterprise. Everyone was eager to meet him.

Even me.

Sam knew that at least some of the others would not be so eager to make Steiner's acquaintance if those people knew how many people the man had compromised over the past fifteen years. That was how Steiner had made so many business acquisitions.

According to the files she'd read, Steiner's actions had resulted in seventeen suicides, twenty-three murders and eight disappearances. Nine corporations had succumbed to hostile takeovers or been broken up after going bankrupt because of his actions.

And that was only what the CIA intelligence services were successful in confirming. Estimations about the true number of those activities were likely to triple.

"Heads up," Riley said over the transmitter. "Sam, you've caught Steiner's eye."

Sam sipped her drink and watched as Steiner worked his way through the crowd toward her. Her heart sped up a little. The response wasn't out of anxiety, but rather her body getting ready for the unexpected encounter.

"Making contact with Steiner at this juncture isn't good," Riley said.

"I know," Sam replied. "Running away at this point isn't exactly acceptable behavior."

"Maybe if you had dressed more conservatively," Riley growled.

"If I'd dressed conservatively I'd have been more noticeable than I am now," Sam replied. Every woman there with a figure flaunted it, and there apparently were no women without figures there that night. "And I might not have made it through the metal detectors."

All of the women at the party wore revealing and tight evening dresses and gowns. Sam honestly felt that she blended quite well with the crowd in an ice-blue, off-the-shoulder number. But her dress shouldn't have caught the man's attention.

So what had put Konrad Steiner onto her scent?

Steiner came to a stop in front of Sam and extended his hand. She offered hers in return and suffered through the obligatory hand kissing, which made her skin crawl.

"Ah, Miss Werper, so good to meet you." Steiner oozed charm. He spoke English with a trace of an accent.

Sam was willing to bet Steiner knew about the accent and kept it on purpose. The man was polished and smooth, and the fact that he knew her, even though they had never been introduced proved that he did his homework.

"I have looked forward to meeting you, Herr Steiner," Sam responded.

"Call me Konrad. I insist."

Sam smiled at him. Her senses coiled within her. Steiner's three personal bodyguards remained a discreet distance away.

"All right, Konrad," Sam said, smiling again. "Then I insist that you call me Franziska."

"This is Odile." Steiner gestured to the young redhead at his side.

Sam told the young woman it was good to meet her, and Odile responded in kind. Both of them knew that neither of them cared.

"I'm told you are a reporter," Steiner said.

"A writer, actually," Sam corrected. "I write articles for different publications on a freelance basis." That fit the cover she was using, and the note of pride embellished it.

"I'm told you are quite good."

"Yes." The Agency kept her cover name in the press through ghostwriters.

"I was told you wanted to do a piece on the movie industry I have interests in."

"I would also like to do an interview with you, if possible." Sam gestured at the castle. "Having seen this place, I'd like to do a piece on your home, as well."

Steiner shook his head and smiled sadly. "I'm sorry. Someone should have told you that I don't give interviews."

"Someone did tell me that," Sam replied, meeting his gaze. "Someone should have told you that I don't take no for an answer. I'm here after all, aren't I?"

Steiner laughed. "Touché, Franziska." He nodded to her. "Perhaps later I'll allow you an opportunity to change my mind."

"I look forward to the challenge." Sam ignored the scathing glance Odile gave her.

"Enjoy the party." Steiner nodded politely and kept moving through his guests.

"Okay, Sam," Riley urged. "Let's go. The sooner you get out of there, the better I'll feel."

Sam made brief eye contact with Bret, then threaded through the crowd. The staircase and the upper rooms were open to guests for business meetings as well as private recreation in any form they could have wanted.

As she passed, Sam collected glances from men and

from a few women. She reached the top of the stairs without incident.

"Hold up," Riley ordered.

At the top of the stairs, Sam felt adrenaline rush through her body. The tension in Riley's voice was unmistakable. She took a position beside the stairs and glanced down over the crowd as if checking the view.

"What?" she whispered.

"I thought I recognized someone there."

Sam scanned the faces as best as she could from the angle. "You probably did. A lot of those faces have been on magazine covers and CNN."

Below, rock stars chatted with business moguls while actors mixed with sports figures.

"Not those faces," Riley growled. "Someone from our line of work. Who do you know at MI-6?"

MI-6 was Great Britain's external espionage agency, a counterpart of the CIA. Sam scanned the crowd more closely. None of the faces she knew were in view.

"Naming names right now might not be a good idea," she said. "Their presence here doesn't have to mean anything. They've got just as much interest in our target as we do."

Silence dragged over the connection.

"I'm going for it," Sam said. "Hesitation isn't going to net us anything."

Riley growled unintelligibly for a moment, then added, "Go."

Quickly Sam turned and headed down the hallway. Her pulse beat at her temples. She kept her stride full and determined, listening to the soft tick of the mental clock inside her head, counting down and eradicating her safety zone. She was in no-man's-land. There was no turning back now. She was off the hook and operating on the fly. Success and failure rode on the roll of the dice.

If she was caught, she had no doubt that she'd be executed immediately.

Chapter 2

Riley McLane paced the raised section of the small, compact control room floor in the Langley, Virginia, CIA HQ. More than anything, he wanted to be inside Konrad Steiner's castle-away-from-home. In Riley's opinion, Sam simply wasn't experienced enough to know what she was getting into.

She's a linguist, damn it, he thought. *Not a trained field operative.*

High-definition plasma monitors lined the wall in front of him. Six operatives sat at workstations that held monitors on smaller scales. Some of those monitors matched the views presented on the wall across the room. All of them came from the button-cams on-site and the sat-link.

The button-cams were miniaturized video sending units no bigger than a shirt button. Adhesive backs allowed their use almost anywhere. The confusion of the party atmosphere, as well as the electronic toys brought by the partygoers and those supplied by Steiner, had provided Sam and Bret with plenty of cover to activate the video surveillance equipment without discovery.

Riley wore jeans, a charcoal-gray turtleneck and hiking boots. A Smith & Wesson .40-caliber pistol rode in a pancake holster over his right hip instead of in its accustomed shoulder rig. The change was a concession to the tenderness of his left shoulder where he'd been shot. He stood two inches over six feet and had an athletic build from years in the gym and on the go. His dark hair set off his hazel eyes.

The phone on Riley's workstation lit up. He crossed the room in three long strides and scooped the headset up. "McLane."

"Why did I just authorize a high-level hack into British espionage circles?" CIA Director Stone Mitchell's voice was calm and uninflected. He'd put his time in over the years, rising from fieldwork to his current administrative position.

Riley turned toward the wall of monitors and stared at the images. Onscreen, Sam followed the verbal directions one of the techs gave her to Steiner's private rooms.

The view was from above, looking down onto and into the castle. The thermographic imaging revealed the building's structure in blues and violets, peering through the roof and floors. Special computer programming rendered the information into a three-dimensional display and gave measured distances at the press of a key. The people were translated into orange and red figures based on their body temperatures. Sam and Bret wore unique transponders that showed up on the satellite's thermographic imagers.

"Because I spotted a guy I think is with MI-6. I wanted to confirm that." Riley stared at the fox-faced man who had caught his attention. Jackson had plucked the man's features out of the crowd at Riley's insistence, then run him through the database.

"MI-6 is interested in our target, too," the deputy director pointed out. "Seeing them there is no surprise."

"To our knowledge, MI-6 hasn't penetrated Steiner's ID. This isn't one of Six's Intel agents, either. He's one of their hands-on black-bag guys who specialize in kidnapping and assassination. The problem is, this guy doesn't seem to be as interested in Steiner as he is in Sam—Special Agent St. John."

In the picture above the nearly full-faced shot of the man Riley had tentatively identified, the man watched Sam, frozen in midstride up the staircase. He hadn't been focused on Steiner.

Seeing Sam in the ice-blue evening gown had drawn Riley's attention, too. Agent St. John was an arresting woman. Despite her active outdoor lifestyle, her coloring remained fair, with just a hint of a tan warming her smooth skin. Her shock of shoulder-length, white-blond hair was pulled back in some kind of intricate knot that showed off her neck and shoulders.

"I don't like coincidences, sir." Riley gazed at the still image of Sam on the stairway. "The presence of an MI-6 black ops team at our site is a variable I want more information on."

Mitchell sighed. "I concur."

Jackson spun around in his chair. A big smile split his dark face. He was young and still excited by the cyber-snooping he did at the Agency. "Got it." He tapped the small screen beside him. "You're looking at Henry Watterson. Got another hit, too." He tapped keys and brought up another image on his personal screen.

A heavier and older man with a square jaw and cold, dead eyes filled the screen. The face was new to Riley.

"MI-6 operative Ian Callan," Jackson said. "He specializes in abduction and control of people MI-6 wants to interview."

Riley turned his attention back to the still image of the party scene. Callan's attention was on Sam, too. A cold, uncomfortable itch spread between Riley's shoulder blades.

"We've confirmed two men, sir," Riley told the deputy director. "Maybe you can go through channels and see why those men are there."

"I'll see what I can do," Mitchell promised.

Riley thanked his superior, broke the connection and watched the thermographic image of Sam stop at the door to Steiner's private quarters in the castle. Riley stood straight and watched, hoping that the woman stayed out of harm's way. His injured shoulder throbbed painfully, reminding him how quickly death could come for someone in his profession.

Sam removed a thin electronic device from the seam of her tiny purse. The fist-size clutch hadn't drawn a second look from security because it had hardly been large enough to hold a compact. Instead, the purse held the device she was using now as well as a sat-phone and another surprise.

An electronic lock sealed Steiner's door.

Opening her purse, Sam took out a small screwdriver and removed the two screws holding the lock's cover in place. She kept watch over her shoulder for wandering partyers and roving security people.

Steiner's voice boomed downstairs in the ballroom as he welcomed his guests over the public address system. He repeated his greeting in six different languages.

With the electronic lock's cover out of the way, Sam looked at the wire bundle inside the device. She moved her hand over the mechanism, allowing the ring camera she wore to transmit the image in color. "Blue and white wires?"

"Affirmative." Riley's voice was tense.

"Something up?" Sam asked, responding to the tension in his voice.

"No. Keep your mind focused. That lock can be tricky even with the decoder you're carrying."

She knew at once that Riley was concealing something, but at the same time she knew he wouldn't hide anything from her that was dangerous.

She attached the alligator clips from the device to the appropriate wires, twisting them slightly so the sharp teeth bit through the protective plastic coating. Then she tapped the lock decoder's power button to activate the search sequence.

The digital readout blurred, flipping through numbers. As each security number was revealed and locked into place, the decoder's red indicator light flickered. In four seconds the machine had broken a nine-digit number, stored it in memory and pulsed the sequence necessary to open it. The light went from red to green in an eye blink.

The lock clicked open with a metallic *ping*.

"I'm in," Sam declared.

"Go. The room's unoccupied."

Sam knew that the satellite relay could peer into the castle and view the room's interior through the stone ceiling. Still, she felt some trepidation at moving into the dark room. From Riley's description of the room, it was more living space than bedroom, a big spacious place.

"Okay," Riley said quietly, "let's get it done." He called out directions.

Trailing a hand along the chilly stone wall, Sam made her way to the section of the wall Riley identified. Following his instructions, she pressed a hand against a stone that the satellite surveillance had spotted earlier. Nothing about the stone made it stand out from the stones around it. If Bret hadn't tagged Steiner with the ultraviolet mist and the man hadn't accessed his hidden computer to make the deal Riley had set up as bait, the CIA would never have found the hidden vault.

Once the vault's location was known, the thermographic imager had enhanced the locking mechanism, revealing its construction. The system of counterweights was old-fashioned but wasn't dependent on constant power or potentially harmful to the computer beyond.

Sam pressed the blocks in the configuration Riley called out and felt the false front open. The castle walls were thick enough to hold the two-foot-deep space that contained the prize she sought. She traced her fingers over the cutting-edge notebook computer inside, found the releases and lifted the lid. At her touch, the screen lit up, bathing her in a blue glow that hurt her eyes for just a second.

When her vision cleared, she stared at the desktop image showing Steiner standing in front of the castle with the rugged, snowcapped Bavarian Mountains in the background. Evidently Steiner was more than a little proud of his new castle.

"Check the connections," Riley told her.

Irritated that he'd told her something he should have known she knew to do, Sam felt around the back of the computer and found the USB cord that undoubtedly led to the other computer systems in the castle's basement. The system also had a hardwired DSL connection that downloaded Steiner's work to an off-site backup dump. He kept nothing but a high-end operating system archived on the notebook computer's hard drive. The device served as a door to and from the business he conducted.

"Connected," Sam said. "I'm uploading the virus now." She pulled her purse into the glow given off by the computer monitor and slid a finger inside the lining. She took out a business-card-size CD that had been hidden as part of her purse's backing, then fitted the rectangular CD onto the notebook computer's CD-ROM tray.

Once the tray slid quietly back into place, she stroked the keyboard. "Loading."

The screen remained on the desktop view. The way the virus was set up, even an automated screen-capturing program wouldn't reveal that the computer had been tampered with. And the installation wouldn't show up as a new program.

Once the virus was activated, it would instantly spread throughout Steiner's network and carve back doors into the programming that would allow CIA hackers into the system at will. The virus was also designed to copy itself into Steiner's address book and e-mail itself to his contacts. The intelligence division thought that within three to four days Steiner's system and those of his contacts would be rife with the virus. All his secrets would belong to the Agency.

Static cracked in Sam's earpiece, then she felt like she'd gone deaf.

"Riley," she whispered.

There was no answer. Sam tried again in a louder voice with the same result. She tried to ignore the prickly feeling that raced across the back of her neck that something had gone terribly wrong.

"Sam!" Riley called. He pulled the headset's mouthpiece to the corner of his mouth to make certain it was close enough. He stared at the thermographic image on the main screen, watching as the three figures closed on Steiner's private room. There was no doubt where they were headed. "Sam!"

Thick, black silence filled his ears. None of the techs in the room made a sound.

Riley swore and turned to Melendez. "I've lost audio."

"Yes, sir," Melendez answered. She busied herself with her keyboard. "We're getting jammed at that end."

"By who?" Riley surveyed the screens. "If Steiner was responsible, he'd jam the video links as well." The video and audio transmitted over different frequencies.

Melendez shook her head. "I don't know. I'm trying to break through."

"Jackson," Riley said, stepping forward and watching the three red-and-yellow images moving toward Steiner's rooms. There was no hesitation, no possibility that they weren't headed there. "Who are they?"

"Don't know." Jackson stared at his own screen, maximizing the image, then reducing it. "I can tell you it isn't Steiner. There's no sign of the ultraviolet mist."

Riley felt some of the tension in his chest melt away. Thank God for that, then.

Jackson's voice took on a note of disbelief. "I can also tell you that one of the figures at the door isn't human."

Sam counted down silently. With no installation marker showing her the program's progress available and no contact with Riley Conner, she had to mark time herself.

At 1032, two seconds past the install time, she ejected the CD-ROM tray, took out the CD and closed the machine, then locked the secret door.

Trailing her hand along the wall again, she made her way back to the door by memory. Her heart pounded and her mouth had gone dry. Losing contact with Riley could have been a glitch in the system. Communications systems weren't perfect.

She kept calm as she reached the door. Hesitating just for a moment, wishing she still had the connection to Riley so he or the support team could tell her if the hallway was clear, she opened the door.

A naked man loomed in the doorway. He stood over six feet tall and had a shaggy mane of shoulder-length hair that was dyed the same amber color as the mountain lion on a leash at his side. The man was trim and muscular like the big cat. Bronze skin glowed warmly. He wore an emerald-studded collar that matched the one worn by his feline companion.

After a shocked moment, Sam recognized him as a professional model whose career Konrad Steiner had taken charge of only a few days ago. The male model had racked up a lot of attention by streaking various sporting events with Web site addresses written on his nude body. Two countries had listed him as an undesirable alien and forbidden his travel there.

The mountain lion was a new accessory.

"Who are you?" a harsh, feminine voice demanded in German.

Then Sam realized that a woman accompanied the model. His size and his nudity had seized Sam's full attention at first. He dwarfed the woman at his side.

The woman was Ingrid Eichmann, one of Steiner's top lieutenants. She was tall and beautiful, well into her forties but able to pass for a woman half her age. Her dark hair was cut in a short shag.

"Who are you?" Ingrid repeated. She reached to the back of the business skirt she wore and brought out a small black Walther .25 semiautomatic pistol, delicate but deadly.

Riley's voice erupted back into Sam's head in a spray of white noise and static. "Go! Get out of there!"

Ingrid raised the pistol to point at the center of Sam's face. The model jumped backward and covered his head in his arms. The mountain lion flattened its ears and snarled a little, and Sam knew that the animal must have been sedated.

Dodging back and to the side, Sam barely avoided the

bullet that caromed off the wall and shattered glass on the other side of the room. She slammed the door and heard the pistol's sharp report echo out in the hallway. Turning toward the darkness that filled the room, she knew that she was trapped.

Drawn by the action taking shape on the monitors in front of him, Riley stepped to the edge of the raised dais in the CIA control room. He made himself stand still when every nerve inside him screamed to move.

"Sam," he called as calmly as he could.

"I'm here." Her voice was icy, contained and calm. "I need a way out."

Riley studied the red-and-yellow silhouette on the sat-link monitor and wished that they'd had the time to install a button-cam in Steiner's suite of rooms. Not that it would have helped, though. The room was totally dark.

"Straight ahead of you," Riley said. "There's a window behind the drapes. Probably why you can't see it. Security bars over the window. They have a locking mechanism."

A moment later Sam said, "The lock's stuck. I'm going to blow the window."

"Do it," Riley agreed. "The door is holding for the moment."

"The two MI-6 agents are in motion, Agent McLane," Jackson called from his workstation. "They're going for Steiner's room."

Puzzled, Riley pulled his attention from Sam and glanced at the thermographic screen showing the castle ballroom. Two computer-inserted ID tags floated over the red-and-yellow silhouettes that were the British agents.

They fired their weapons. Ingrid Eichmann and the man with her broke and ran. The mountain lion followed them. The British agents advanced toward the door where Steiner's security teams converged.

Logic dictated that the agents wouldn't try to break into Steiner's rooms. If they were able, they'd spirit Steiner away. They knew he wasn't inside. Sam should be safe.

Unless Steiner isn't their target.

The thought chilled Riley. But it fit in a surreal way, and it explained Watterson and Callan's interest in Sam. And their interest in Steiner's private rooms.

"Jackson, sweep the outside grounds," Riley ordered. "I want anyone who comes toward that side of the castle identified." He knew the British team wasn't working alone. They'd have a backup team in place.

Outside the castle, the sat-link used night-vision mode, enhancing the existing moonlight so most of the night was stripped away. The rear of Steiner's castle perched on a tall precipice. Hundreds of years ago when Germany had still been a loose confederation of thirty-five monarchies and four free cities, whoever had built the castle had taken advantage of the topography. An army couldn't come at the castle from that direction.

Hopefully a lone CIA agent who was quick on her feet could make an escape, though.

"Agent McLane," another young tech called out. "I've got gunfire in the hallway."

Glancing at the hallway, Riley saw that shots were being exchanged in the hallway in front of Steiner's room. The MI-6 agents operated mercilessly, firing into the castle security teams. Four more men joined Watterson and Callan as Riley watched.

What the hell is going on?

Riley refocused on the screen showing Sam. She ducked down to the floor just as Watterson and Callan reached the door. Three bodies of security guards lay in the hallway. Warm blood pooled in cooling purples around the bodies.

Watterson stepped close to another downed man struggling to lift his weapon. Flame spat from the British Intelligence agent's pistol and the guard relaxed in death.

Callan slapped a short square against the front door and stepped back quickly.

"Sam," Riley called. "MI-6 agents are at the door."

"Are we coordinating with them on this?" Sam asked.

"No." Riley folded his arms across his chest and ignored the pain in his shoulder. "Stay away from them. I don't know if they're after Steiner's computer…or you."

Her response, if there was one, was lost in a sudden explosive detonation.

Chapter 3

Even tucked into a ball, clutching a pillow from the bed wrapped around her head, Sam reeled with the explosion that came from the window. The two-element chemical explosive had been disguised in the tiny bottle of hair spritz she carried in her clutch.

Twisting the cap tightly down and pressing the plunger broke the plastic membrane separating the two chemicals. She'd felt them reacting in a heated rush as she'd tucked the bottle into the window frame. Ten seconds after that, the contents of the bottle blew.

Slightly woozy from the massive concussive force generated by the explosive, Sam stood and dropped the pillow at her feet. She thought she heard Riley calling to her over the transceiver but wasn't certain because she'd been temporarily deafened by the incredible noise inside the room.

A brief investigation of the window revealed the blast had stripped the security bars loose. The ends glowed red-hot. Chipped stone and broken glass had sprayed across the floor.

Grabbing the bars, Sam shoved outward and felt the metal grate against the stone as the security unit tore loose. She still couldn't hear anything more than a low-pitched roar. The bars clanged distantly against the hard stone ground.

"I'm free," she said, hoping the transceiver hadn't suffered damage in the ear-splitting blast. She wanted Riley listening to her at the other end of the connection because she didn't want to feel alone.

Part of her resisted that want. Except for her six years among the Cassandras at the Athena Academy for the Advancement of Women, her whole life had been spent in some degree of seclusion. She hadn't gotten close to any of the foster families that had helped raise her. Working for the CIA had appealed to her because she could be part of something that mattered, a place where she could matter, without being overly intimate with it. In fact, anonymity was a plus.

Peering out the window, Sam saw the ground a little more than twenty feet below. A sharp drop lay less than three feet out from the castle wall. In the weak moonlight, her eyes still somewhat dazzled by the explosive, Sam couldn't tell how far the drop was.

Another explosion came as a dulled thump behind her. She turned and stared at the warped door. Light from the hallway blazed through the smoky ruin clouding into the room.

Subtlety obviously isn't a priority, Sam thought.

The door shivered from impacts. Evidently whoever had set the explosive was now trying to finish breaking in. Steiner's door had been bomb resistant—to a degree.

Lowering herself through the window, Sam held on to the window frame by her fingertips, her front plastered against the rough stone side of the castle. Her gown ripped. Glancing down, she tried to estimate how far away the ground was.

Fourteen feet, she told herself with some trepidation. At least.

The height wasn't much. She'd dropped farther than that while running *la parkour.* The French urban footrace over building tops, fences, cars, and anything else that got in a runner's way was something she excelled at.

But a drop onto uneven and treacherous ground in the dark without proper footgear was dangerous. If she broke, sprained or even just twisted an ankle, she'd slow down considerably and could be caught or killed in heartbeats. Neither outcome was enticing.

Tense male voices came from inside the room. They spoke English and sounded far away in her still-ringing ears.

"Where is she?"

Cones of illumination moved inside the room, letting Sam know the men carried flashlights.

"The window."

Sam released her hold and dropped. She remained limp, rolling with the impact instead of trying to resist it. Sharp pain ripped through her left heel as the spike of the shoe snapped off. She slid dangerously close to the drop-off, but managed to shove her palms out to bring herself to a stop. Her head and shoulders hung over the edge. Pebbles skated past her and fell. Gravel and stone scraped her palms.

"Sam," Riley called over the transceiver. His voice barely sounded above a whisper even though she knew he was speaking loudly or maybe even yelling. "Get up."

"I am," Sam snarled. Gingerly, mindful of her balance, she sat up, and kicked off her useless high-heeled shoes. One of them scooted over the drop-off and disappeared. Ringing sounded in her ears as she forced herself to her feet. Her bruised and scraped palms burned from the effort. She bent down and snatched up the clutch purse, then stuffed it into the dress's built-in bra.

"There!" someone shouted above her.

Sam didn't look up. Looking up could guarantee a bullet to the face or a loss of her night vision if she saw a muzzle flash or her pursuers caught her full-on with a flashlight beam.

"The parking lot's down the mountain," Riley called.

"I know." Sam felt irritable about the situation she was in, as though she had somehow failed. That was the only thing keeping her fear in check.

She grabbed her gown and ripped it from around her hips, freeing her legs for longer strides. Despite the summer season, the night air up in the mountains felt cold. She ran, dressed in the tattered remains of the gown and her underwear. When survival was on the line, modesty came in a distant second.

Calluses from years of running kept her feet somewhat protected, but she still felt sharp rocks and rough stone edges. Flashlight beams cut through the night around her.

"Have you still got a knife?" Riley asked.

"Yes." Sam carried a small folding knife disguised as fingernail clippers in her clutch. Her breath rasped in her lungs, but her movements became more fluid as the adrenaline hit her system and her muscles warmed up. The internal rhythm she'd developed over years of physical exercise took over. Her arms and legs pumped, driving her body like a high-performance machine.

"Ever hot-wire a car?"

"Yes."

"Under less-than-ideal circumstances?"

Sam didn't bother to answer. When was hot-wiring a car ideal?

The flashlight beams licked the cold stone of the mountain around her. One of them fell across her from behind, and her shadow stretched long and lean ahead of her.

"There are four armed guards in the parking area," Riley said.

"Where's Bret?" Sam broke free of the castle and ran along the stony ground behind the tall wall enclosing the main grounds. The ground there held more soil and didn't bruise her feet quite as badly. Grass actually grew in several spots.

"Getting away."

Flashlight beams continued to splash the countryside after Sam. She risked a glance behind her. One man was just rising from dropping out the window. Another one hit the ground in the next second.

"Who are these guys?" Sam asked.

"Save your breath for running."

"Who?" she demanded.

Riley didn't sound happy about being distracted or disobeyed. "British Intelligence."

"Why is British Intelligence chasing me when Steiner is such a prize?"

"I don't know."

Shots split the night behind Sam. Bullets struck sparks from the castle's outer-perimeter wall and stones farther down the incline. Several of them passed within inches of her while the two men behind her ordered her to stop.

"There are probably six cars down there that you can hot-wire," Riley said. "All of them old enough that they lack the antitheft devices of newer models."

Sam reached the bottom of the incline where the mountain leveled out toward the graveled parking area. Guards carrying flashlights took cover among the cars, SUVs and limousines.

One of the guards swung his flashlight up in her direction. Sam slitted her eyes against the glare to preserve some of her night vision, saw the massive semiautomatic pistol in the guard's hand and kept running.

"What are you doing?" Riley asked. "He sees you! Get down!"

Instead, Sam kept running. Hiding was an instinctive male reaction. She was female. A half-dressed female running out of the darkness was something a lot of men dreamed about. Especially bored security guards.

"Help!" Sam cried in a pathetic and frightened voice in German. "Those men!" She pointed behind her as she ran. "Help me!"

"Fräulein." The guard spoke German, as well. "Who is

chasing you?" He stood partially shielded by the massive bulk of an H2 SUV.

"I don't know," Sam replied, acting as though she were out of breath. She ran at the man, never breaking stride.

"Stop!" The command rang out behind Sam. A flurry of pistol shots punctuated the order. One of the bullets shattered the H2's passenger rearview mirror only inches from the guard's head.

The man abandoned all pretense of playing the dashing hero to the damsel in distress and got down to the selfish business of saving himself. He ducked behind the H2's bulk, then fired two shots toward the MI-6 agents.

"Help me!" Sam cried as she closed on the guard. She kept her hands up and away from her body, showing that she carried no weapon.

"Come here," the man said. His voice cracked with nervousness. "I will protect you."

Without leaving the safety of the H2, the guard reached for Sam. She caught his wrist in both her hands, set herself, and ruthlessly twisted the man's hand over, controlling the thumb and feeling it break in her grip.

Before the man could cry out in pain, Sam kicked the guard hard in the groin. The man's knees buckled. He couldn't get his breath. Still controlling the broken thumb, Sam kicked the man twice in the face. His head bounced from the H2's reinforced body with hollow thuds.

Even as the guard dropped unconscious, Sam plucked the big pistol from the man's hand. She identified the weapon at once as a Heckler & Koch Mark 23 chambered in .45ACP. The weapon was fierce, designed for knockdown power on the battlefield for special forces. With two shots fired, Sam knew the brutally compact pistol held eight more in the magazine.

"Get moving," Riley ordered.

Sam let the unconscious guard drop and resisted the impulse to look for more ammunition. Getting out of the confusing situation she was currently in relied more on mobility than firepower.

"What am I looking for?" she asked as she fled through the maze of parked cars. Her feet ached but she ignored the pain.

"Mercedes 450 SL," Riley replied. "Thirty-year-old-model. Midnight blue. It'll look black tonight. Three rows up and six cars down on your left."

Sam altered her course.

"C'mon," Riley said. "They're gaining."

They have shoes, Sam thought angrily. But she saved her breath for running.

She found the Mercedes seconds later, exactly where Riley had said it would be. The vehicle looked sleek and powerful. Although it was almost thirty years old, the two-seater model had classic lines that she recognized at once.

Without breaking stride, Sam pointed the pistol at the car and squeezed off two rounds. The bullets shattered the driver's side window, revealing at once that the glass wasn't bulletproof. The rounds dug deeply into the passenger seat and door.

"What the hell are you doing?" Riley asked.

"Opening the window. Faster this way."

"You just ID'ed your location." Riley sounded pissed and worried all at the same time.

Sam didn't have time to argue the point over an immediate entrance into the car versus picking the lock or hoping that the vehicle had been left open. She reached through the broken window and pulled up the door lock. A shadow drifted into her periphery on her right.

"On your right," Riley warned.

Sam wheeled, pulling the pistol up and pointing instinctively. She had one frozen flicker of time as she put the pistol's iron sights over the center of the guard's chest. She'd never shot at a human being before. She hesitated.

The guard fired. Heated air skated Sam's left cheek, letting her know how close the bullet had come to taking her head off.

"Damn it, Sam, fire! He'll kill—"

Sam squeezed the pistol's trigger three times, aiming at the man's beltline and riding the recoil up. He's not an innocent, she reminded herself. Steiner doesn't hire innocents.

The bullets knocked the guard backward, spinning him from a limousine before depositing him in a heap on the cracked rock covering the parking area.

Instant horror lanced through Sam. She didn't let herself dwell on what she had done. There was no doubt that the man would have killed her if he'd had the chance. She walled emotion away, thinking it was possible the man had even been wearing a bulletproof vest and had only had the wind knocked out of him, and turned her attention back to the Mercedes.

She opened the door, slid inside and dropped the pistol on the passenger seat. Reaching under the dash, she located the wiring harness bundle along the steering column and yanked it out. Taking the tiny knife from her purse, she cut through the starter wire and bypassed the ignition. She kept her head up, letting her peripheral vision scan her immediate vicinity.

Sparks flashed the instant the wires touched. The engine hesitated once, then rumbled to vibrant, powerful life just as one of the two men who had pursued Sam from Steiner's window arrived. He glanced around hurriedly, then spotted her inside the Mercedes. The man ran between rows of cars and suddenly stood before Sam with his pistol in both hands.

"Get out of the car, Agent St. John," the man ordered in English.

Like hell I will, Sam thought. In the same instant she realized the man knew her name. How does he know me?

Sam lifted the pistol and fired through the windshield. A silvery halo formed in the spiderwebbed glass where the bullets cored through the safety glass.

The British agent ducked for cover behind a nearby car. The glass had deflected her first shot, perhaps even her second.

When the pistol blew back empty, she dropped the H&K into the passenger seat. The weapon had her fingerprints on it; she wasn't getting rid of it till she wiped it clean. Holding the clutch down, she moved the gearshift into Reverse.

Draping an arm across the back seat, Sam gunned the engine and released the clutch. The rear tires spun as they fought for traction, then caught and yanked her backward so fiercely she almost banged her head on the steering wheel.

The seat was set for someone much taller. She had to

stretch to pin the accelerator to the floor. Reaching under the seat, she made the adjustment. The faint, clinging scent of a man's cologne stained the car's interior, mixing with the stink of cigars. She stopped the car, then shoved the gearshift into first, let out the clutch, and shot forward. The line of cars ended at the long, twisting road leading up to Steiner's castle.

"A vehicle is headed your way," Riley said.

"Who?"

"Damn it! At this point, it doesn't really matter who."

"MI-6 agents aren't the bad guys here," Sam argued. "Steiner's people are. I don't want to hurt one of them if I don't have to." Sam paused. "I won't."

Riley hesitated only a second. "We don't know. The car started moving about the same time the MI-6 agents started mobilizing to track you down."

"I'm their target?" Sam couldn't believe it.

"Yes. Now *move!*"

Sam sped out into the aisle just as a pair of headlights came around the long line of parked vehicles. The other driver swung his vehicle around and skidded sideways, blocking her.

In the next instant, the man shoved his hand through the window. She caught a glimpse of the pistol in his hand before the first muzzleflash blossomed. He fired rapidly as Sam stepped hard on the brake pedal. The shots went low, slamming into the Mercedes's grill and the gravel to Sam's left.

Moving effortlessly, the adrenaline slamming through her system masking whatever fear she might be feeling, Sam shoved the gearshift into Reverse. She turned and looked back over the seat as she accelerated. Gravel popped and crunched under the Mercedes's tires.

Headlights flared behind her as a second car shot forward to fill the gap between the rows of vehicles.

Knowing that speed was the only chance she had, Sam kept the accelerator on the floor and steered for the gap between the new arrival and the SUV parked at the end of the row. The rear of the Mercedes negotiated the narrow gap, then the other car banged into the passenger side. Sparks sprayed from the impact and the front bumper hung up with a jerk just for a moment before pulling free. Cracks ran across the windshield.

Airbags swelled up into the driver and passenger's faces in the other car. The driver might have had time to continue the pursuit if not impeded by the safety measure, but even deflating the airbag and freeing the steering wheel was going to take a few seconds.

Sam continued in reverse for another fifty yards, then tapped the brakes, cut the wheel sharply, and brought the Mercedes around in a tire-eating bootlegger U-turn. She'd mastered the Agency's defensive, offensive and pursuit mode driving classes during training, then put in extra time at the tracks.

When the Mercedes's nose slewed around, Sam gazed down the long mountain road that led up to Steiner's castle. With the ancillary parking area outside the castle's main walls, no security remained between her and freedom. She pushed into first gear, then floored the accelerator.

Wind rushed through the hole in the windshield. A quick glance at the rearview mirror showed figures converging on the wrecked car she'd left in her wake.

"Riley," Sam called over the transceiver.

"I'm here." Riley's voice cracked and spat. The distance was already pushing the limitations of the frequency booster in the limousine still in the parking area.

"They were after me."

"I know."

"Why?"

"I'm working on it, Sam. Maybe I'll have answers by the time you reach the safehouse."

"Going there might not be a good idea."

Riley's voice sounded testy. "Do you have a better place?"

Actually, Sam did. But she didn't want to announce that. Every mission she worked, she always kept a bolt-hole. Maybe she hadn't been out in the field on such a dangerous assignment before, but she'd been out there.

"No," she said, because she knew he was awaiting a response.

"Fine. Get in touch with me there. And try to stay safe. I don't want—"

Whatever Riley didn't want got lost when the connection finally failed.

Chapter 4

Dressed in stolen clothing she'd plucked off a laundry line strung between two buildings in an alley near where she'd ditched the Mercedes after wiping it clear of fingerprints, Sam stayed in the shadows of the Munich streets. Her satellite phone nestled in one of the pockets of the oversize ankle-length black duster she wore.

Local time was 11:14 p.m. Few pedestrians were out on the street. Munich was a city that had a lot to offer even after regular business hours were over.

Neon stained the dark streets, advertising the bars and clubs that were scattered along the thoroughfare. Pedestrians strolled the sidewalks and crossed the streets as they pursued the nightlife. Passing cars whickered across the pavement, and fragments of songs, American top forty as well as Euro pop, reached Sam's ears.

She wore boy's jeans, a T-shirt and a sweater under the duster. A black crocheted beanie disguised her platinum-blond locks. Black, fingerless skater's gloves covered her hands. At first glance, she knew most people would think she was a male teen, due to the clothing and her petite size. She'd smudged her face with grime to darken the highlights.

Raucous industrial metal rock and roll blared from the door of the basement club located in the Karlsplatz, which was the beginning of Old Munich. Only a short walk away, the Deutsches Theater towered among the buildings, possessing a grandeur all its own.

The location for the exfiltration was good, Sam thought as she looked over the young crowd enjoying the nightlife. She and Riley had arranged the meet over the sat-phone.

Tourists, convention-goers and young people gathered in Munich's downtown area, all of them looking for an evening's entertainment. Uniformed Munich policemen mixed with the crowd, generally at ease and having fun with the partyers.

Taxis mingled with the street traffic. Limousines plowed through the hustle and bustle, as well, which meant that Bret Horn's arrival would go largely unnoticed.

Sam stood in the shadows and surveyed the street. She kept reminding herself that the satellite phone was encrypted and couldn't easily be broken into.

The sat-phone vibrated inside her hand inside her coat pocket.

Shifting, Sam kept the device in the shadows because she knew possession of the sat-phone would mark her as a target for the pickpockets working the convention crowds. She held it to the side of her face and said, "Here."

"The limo has just turned onto Galeriestrasse," Riley said. "You should have a visual in a moment."

Sam peered out at the street. She breathed in and out, slow and regular. Before she took her next breath, she spotted the limousine. The big vehicle approached on her side of the street.

"I see it," she told Riley.

"Bret," Riley said.

"Go," Horn replied.

"Stop the car," Riley ordered. "Sam has confirmed a visual."

"You got it."

Sam envied Bret and Riley the calm and easy way they handled the situation. Fear scrambled around inside her, but she held on to the emotion tightly. Even when she'd been bounced from foster home to foster home, she'd never let anyone know how afraid she was.

"Are you okay, Sam?" Riley asked.

"I'm fine," she replied coldly. She also knew she'd answered too abruptly. Riley would know that she was anything but fine.

"We've got visual," Riley said.

Sam guessed that he deliberately didn't mention the anxiety he must have noticed in her voice. She was glad for that.

"The crowd there is a good cover," Riley said. "But it works against us, too. I didn't know the event was going to be this busy."

"It's a new industrial metal band kicking off a European tour," Sam said, trying to sound casual. "MTV is here."

"Where are you?"

"In the alley between the office buildings." Sam peered around, trying desperately to see if any of the faces she'd picked up at the safehouse had mysteriously appeared there. When she'd checked it out a little earlier, she'd seen people she didn't recognize posted inconspicuously nearby. Taking no chances, she'd assumed that whoever was after her knew where it was and had it staked out, waiting for her to show.

"We're losing the spy-sat capabilities," Riley said. "I can't make you out. I'm not going to be much help from this end."

"It's okay," Horn said. "Just come on, Sam. I've got you." His voice was calm and confident.

Easing away from the building, Sam stepped out into the crowd. She lost sight of the limousine intermittently as she made her way through the revelers dancing out in the street. From the snatches of conversations she heard, Sam learned that the basement concert area was filled to capacity and the Munich police were enforcing the safety laws. Roadies manned the speaker equipment that brought the sound of the concert out into the street.

"I see you," Horn said. "Keep coming."

The agent's declaration caught Sam by surprise. There was no way she could be seen through the crowd. "Bret, you can't see me. I don't see you." She peered through the massed bodies, feeling her heart pump a little faster.

"Yeah," Horn said. "I see you. Blond hair. Combat boots. Man, you really fit in with this crowd."

Panic clawed at Sam. "Bret, that's not me. You can't see me. I've got my head covered. You won't see me until I'm right up on you."

"Oh, hell," Bret said. "It's not you."

Sam made her way to a lamppost in the middle of the crowd. A couple teens were hanging onto the post, shouting the words to the song blasting through the outdoor speakers. Cameras flashed around them, snapping pictures. A street vendor sold beer by the cup nearby.

"Riley, I've got a prostitute at the limo's window," Horn said.

"Get rid of her."

Quickly Sam stepped up onto the base of the lamppost and stared out over the crowd. She spotted the limousine, then saw the young blonde in the short skirt, jacket and combat boots leaning heavily on the vehicle's rear window.

Horn's window rolled down to half-mast. Lamplight fell across his face, bringing his features out of the shadows.

The young woman refused to take no for an answer. She was a hustler working the tourist crowd. Her English was broken, but her intent—her terms and her price—were clear. She was also embarrassingly forward about what she was willing to do and what others had said about her abilities.

"Bret," Riley said.

Before Horn could respond, three men stepped out of the crowd. They were all dressed in street clothes, jeans, T-shirts and loose jackets so they fit in with the industrial metal fans. Walking deliberately, one arm tucked in close at their sides, they approached the woman and the limousine.

Hypnotized, Sam stood on the lamppost base. "Bret, three guys are bearing down on your position. Riley—"

"I see them," Riley said. "Bret, get the hell out of there. This is a busted play. These people are on to us."

Sam strained to hear the conversation in the limousine through the sat-phone as Bret informed the driver of what was taking place. Unfortunately the crowd that had spilled into the street kept the limousine driver from speeding away. Before he could get clear, the three men converged on the car.

One of the men grabbed the prostitute by the hair and yanked her down to her knees. Her sharp scream of pain pealed through the sat-phone, then reached Sam's ears again across the distance. He turned her face so her features were revealed in the light.

Another man made the mistake of thrusting his weapon into the back of the limousine. Horn caught the gunman's arm, broke it and took the pistol. As the man gave an agonized shout and sagged against the car, Horn pointed the weapon back at the men.

"Put the gun down, mate," someone said in English. "You just go on an' put that gun down easy like, or I'm gonna splatter this little lady's brains all over the street."

The man holding the woman shoved his pistol against the side of her head.

"That ain't her," someone else said. The English accent wasn't quite as pronounced. "Did you hear me? This bloody well ain't the one we're looking for."

"That's okay. This one here'll do for starters." The man raised his voice. "I'm gonna give you the count of three, Yank, then I'm gonna kill this bitch. The blood can be on your hands. *One.*"

The woman screamed again.

The limousine driver kept trying to edge out of the crowd and into the center of the street. Incredibly, no one seemed to notice the men with drawn pistols threatening the screaming hooker. The men trailed the luxury vehicle, and the one manhandling the woman dragged her along with him with the pistol against her temple.

"You better think quick, Yank. And do the right thing. *Two.*"

"Riley," Hart called.

Before Riley had a chance to reply, Sam shouted, "They've got guns! Help! They've got guns!" Atop the lamppost base, she pointed at the limousine mired in the crowd. "Robbery! Help!"

The partyers around her took up the warning at once. Immediately people started fighting to get away from the limousine, breaking out in an ever-widening circle like a ripple spreading across a pond. Hoarse screams and shouts drew the attention of nearby policemen. The policemen fought against the pull of the crowd, working their way toward the luxury car.

The prostitute chose that moment to rake her fingernails across her captor's face. The man cursed loudly as he stepped back and brought his arm to his head. His pistol roared, further inciting the crowd. The bullet missed the woman and knocked sparks from the street.

Sam watched helplessly.

In disbelief Riley watched the plan he'd put into motion fall completely to pieces. The image on the center screen showed the action in thermographic detail. Dialogue tags covered the identified players in the confrontation. "Agent St. John" stood in the middle of a maelstrom of activity.

Inside the limousine, Horn fired his captured pistol. The muzzle flash became a temporary mushroom burst of sudden yellow light that quickly faded. The man who had mishandled the woman dropped backward as if poleaxed.

"Agent McLane," Melendez called. "There are Munich police on the scene handling crowd control at the concert. They've already called for backup."

"Thank you, Melendez." Riley scanned the screen, watching as the remaining men took cover. "Bret, did you copy?"

"Affirmative," Horn said. "I don't see Sam."

"She called out the warning," Riley said. He glanced at the lamppost where he'd followed the red-and-yellow figure Jackson had tagged as Sam St. John.

"Agent St. John" still stood there.

Riley cursed. Sam had shown great initiative in calling the crowd's attention down on the kidnapping attempt, but now she was standing around like a rookie.

"Sam," he called, "go to Bret. Let the police take you both into custody. We'll work with them to get you both out."

"I'm not sure that's a good idea. I may be safer on my own."

Figures with drawn weapons converged on the limousine. Bret dropped his captured weapon outside the window and held his hands up. The two men who had closed on the limousine were also taken into custody. The man Hart had shot lay sprawled on the street.

"You'd be safer with the police," Riley said.

"I thought I was safe with you, too," Sam shot back.

"What the hell do you mean by that?"

"You know exactly what I mean. This meeting was a setup. By you. Or by someone who has penetrated your communications. Either way, I'm out of it. When we talk again, it's going to be on equal footing."

The connection popped in Riley's headset as he watched "Agent St. John" jog back into the concert crowd watching the Munich police take control of the situation. "Sam. *Sam.*"

There was no answer. Even the rolling thunder of the concert music in the background of the connection had faded.

Riley glanced at Melendez.

The tech shook her head. "She's gone."

Damn it, Sam. You can't just walk away like this. Where the hell do you think you're going? Riley made himself breathe.

Sam moved through the crowd, going quickly. None of the figures tagged "Munich Police" pursued her.

Then Riley noticed one figure that was moving in tandem with Sam. The heat signature was unmarked, an unknown. But the intention to intercept Sam was plain.

"Melendez," Riley said. "Get Sam back on the satphone. *Now.*"

Melendez tapped her keyboard.

Riley listened to the phone ring and ring in his headset. He watched the figure closing in on Sam. She wasn't answering. And in the next instant it was too late.

Whoever the new arrival was, he was on top of Sam.

Sam spotted the man coming out of the crowd at the last moment. He was an inch or two over six feet, in his late twenties or early thirties. His dark hair stuck out and a day-old growth of beard stained his jaw.

He reached for her without a word, grabbing the loose material of her jacket's right arm. "Agent St. John," he said softly, just loud enough to be heard over the confusion of the crowd. He held a pistol in his right hand and casually brought it up.

Sam resisted the instinctive urge to run away. The man outweighed her by at least seventy or eighty pounds and was nearly a foot taller. Instead, she whirled inside his left arm, stepping inside his personal space, and grabbed his gun arm. She knew at once that she couldn't overpower him, and the man knew it, too.

A smile spread across the man's face. "No way, small-fry. But it could be fun."

Sam didn't need to control his gun arm, though, she just needed to know where it was. Gripping his jacket with her right hand, she brought her knee up into his groin three times in quick succession. Sliding her left hand down to his gun hand, she stripped the pistol from his grip. Unfortunately he fought her, and the weapon slipped away in the darkness and skittered across the alley floor.

The man cursed, his words venomous. Shooting out a doubled fist, he almost caught Sam flatfooted. She saw the blow coming and moved at the last second, avoiding most of the impact along the side of her face. Her senses reeled. She knew she'd be bruised for days. Her right eye watered.

Despite the blow, Sam moved automatically. For years, every chance she'd made for herself, she'd studied martial arts. She had a natural affinity for several styles. No matter what foster home she'd ended up in, or what shelter, she'd found a way to take classes. Sometimes she'd traded janitorial services for training. At the Athena Academy she'd studied every form that had been offered, gradually working up to a teaching position before she'd left.

The man punched at her head again, still growling curses. He swayed a little unsteadily on his feet.

Moving her arms swiftly, Sam avoided the avalanche of powerful blows. She slapped some of them away, catching the man's wrists in passing and using his own strength against him. Other blows she interrupted by smashing a forearm against his as he barely started his swing.

He tried to stamp her feet with his heavy boots. On the second attempt she turned, set herself and drove the outside of her right foot down his support leg. Her boot caught him at the knee and traveled all the way to his ankle. She knew from experience that she'd torn hide and deeply bruised him.

Spinning swiftly to her right, she came around with a backhand blow that caught the side of the man's face and snapped his head around. When he turned to face her again, blood leaked out over his lips.

The man lunged for her. Sam ducked beneath his arms, grabbed his jacket in both hands and fell backward, catching his midsection on her feet and rolling backward. Deliberately, she brought the man over and down, banging his head against the cobblestones of the alley.

She rolled over on top of him, coming up astraddle him. Pain and a little confusion filled his eyes as he glared up at her. Then she grabbed him by the hair and slammed his head against the cobblestones. His eyes rolled back up into his head.

Glancing up, short of breath because of her exertions and the panic ripping at her, Sam saw that a small group had turned their attentions toward her. She pushed herself up from the unconscious man, ran her hands through his jacket and pants and took his wallet and money. She had some cash on her, but most of what she'd been doing for the CIA involved credit cards the Agency managed.

For the moment she was on her own.

Even as cries went out for the police, she turned and bolted down the alley. With MI-6 and the Munich police hot on her trail, there was only one place she could go for help.

And she wouldn't be turning to Riley McLane for assistance until she got a handle on things. One thing Sam knew, the whole meeting had been a setup. She couldn't believe she'd trusted the man.

Barely containing the anger that stirred within him, Riley stepped through the opening elevator doors and strode down the long corridor toward CIA Director Stone Mitchell's office. In Munich it was almost 10:00 p.m., but in Langley, Virginia, it wasn't quite yet five.

Several assistants and agents working in the offices along the way looked up at Riley as he passed them. He ignored them.

Before he reached the door to Mitchell's office, the director's stern voice rang out. "Come in, Agent McLane."

Riley glowered at the button-cam hidden over the door. He opened the door and stepped inside.

Mitchell sat at his desk. He was a compact man of medium height in his early fifties. A dedicated regimen kept him lean and fit. He wore glasses, which made him look bookish to an extent, but a person who knew what to look for discovered the cold stare of a killer in the flat brown eyes. His dark hair was cropped short, matching the thin mustache that flavored his narrow-lipped mouth in a permanent frown. His blue suit was carefully pressed, his tie carefully knotted. He skin was dark enough that he could pass for Mexican, Italian or Indio.

The office fit the director. It was also spare and lean, an efficient place to work, not warm or inviting. The only concession to any kind of personal life outside the sterile walls were the pictures of his wife and two college-age daughters and a handful of Mitchell coaching his girls in softball.

"You want to tell me what the hell is going on, Stone?" Riley demanded.

Calm and self-assured, Mitchell pointed to one of the two chairs in front of his desk. "Take a seat."

"Sam—Agent St. John—almost got captured by those cold-blooded bastards MI-6 sicced onto her. Someone penetrated our communications security."

"I know. Have a seat."

Riley paced the floor. "I don't feel like sitting."

"Are you in communication with Agent St. John at present?" Mitchell asked.

"Agent St. John has cut off communication to me through her sat-phone."

"That is unfortunate."

"Not that I blame her. If I was in her shoes, I'd have done the same damn thing."

"She has to trust you. She's trapped in a foreign country. No way out. Wanted by the police. Hunted by mercenaries working for MI-6. You're all she has."

"C'mon, Stone," Riley said. "A play gets busted this badly, this quickly, over what is supposed to be an encrypted communications network, you know what she's gotta be thinking."

The CIA director made no reply.

"It's the same thing that you or I would think. It's the same thing that brought me to your damn door in such a hurry after St. John pulled her fade."

Mitchell nodded slowly. "That someone here at the Agency sold her out."

"Yeah," Riley growled. "But I know it wasn't me." He leaned forward in his chair, piercing the director with his gaze. "So I'm here, Stone, and I want to know why you sold out Samantha St. John to the Brits."

More than an hour after her escape from the trap at Karlsplatz, Sam walked through the door of a cybercafé near the Franz Josef Strauss Airport. Neon tubing advertised the existence of the business tucked in between office buildings. Video cameras, carefully situated in the room so they couldn't view the computer monitors covering the high tables around the room, panned the door.

The knowledge that someone somewhere was getting her image made Sam nervous. Brief pieces of news footage she'd seen in an apartment she'd broken into for a change of clothes let her know that Munich police had taken several people into custody. No mention was made of who they were, and no mention was made of her by name, although the news anchor reported that some of the rioters had escaped.

After negotiating the computer and Internet rate, keeping the conversation in German and mimicking the local accent, Sam put herself behind one of the machines in the corner. Despite her anxiety and the urgency she felt, she ordered a tomato sandwich and a latte. Although there'd been food at Steiner's castle, she hadn't eaten much. Now she found she was famished.

One of the things she had learned about being in a succession of foster homes while growing up, of never knowing what kind of reception she was going to receive there or what the accommodations would be, was to eat whenever she was hungry. Served on a toasted bagel, the tomato sandwich was filled with a thick tomato slice, cream cheese, chopped onions and watercress.

She ate quickly, managing the keyboard with one hand. She used one of the e-mail addresses she'd set up for use while out in the field when she didn't want the Agency to track her every move. A blind e-mail was easy enough to set up, but couldn't be used more than once without possibly blowing the integrity of the security.

The trick was to contact someone who knew who she was despite the unfamiliar e-mail address. The second trick was to contact someone who would be in a position to help her.

With the chaotic background she'd lived through, and the succession of foster homes, Sam's resources outside the CIA were limited. The single happy time in her childhood that had fostered feelings of permanent relationships was her time at the Athena Academy.

Located in Arizona, outside the Glendale/Phoenix area, the Athena Academy for the Advancement of Women had come into being about two decades ago. Situated in the foothills of the White Tank Mountains, the five-hundred-acre educational facility offered an array of subjects for elite female students between the ages of ten through eighteen.

One of Arizona's senators at the time, Marion Gracelyn, became the Athena Academy's prime promoter. Calling on favors and using her knowledge of government operations, Senator Gracelyn laid out the plans for the school, then found the people and the money to make it come to fruition. Christine Evans, a retired army captain, was chosen as the school's principal.

The goals of the school were multifold. Creating opportunities for women in all branches of the military, espionage agencies, national law enforcement bodies such as the FBI and the United States Marshals Office, as well as political office was the first goal.

Students who attended the Athena Academy were special: scholastically and physically superior, the kind of women who could succeed at anything they gave their hearts to. When the school first opened, only one hundred students attended. At present, the student body was limited to two hundred.

Sam St. John had gotten into the school at age nine, a full year earlier than the youngest students were usually admitted. At home, Sam had hacked into a secure computer site that handled sensitive espionage matters for the United States Government. After her astounding feat had been discovered, and her foster parents at the time had admitted that they wouldn't be willing to take any further responsibility for her, a full scholarship had been awarded to Sam. She'd gone to live at the academy, thinking that it was just another way station on her way to adulthood and a time when she could take care of herself.

But in that first year at the Athena Academy, Sam had been assigned to an orientation group with girls who had become known as the Cassandras. Groups were assigned at the beginning of each year as thirty new students were brought into the school and divided into five groups of six members, each group delegated to a senior mentor. The groups of first-years were pitted against each other in several friendly competitions. Tory, Josie, Darcy, Kayla, and Alex had seemed about as different from one another as they could be, but Rainy—Lorraine Miller, at the time—had been made their mentor.

In spite of her best intentions to simply survive the school, get an education and get out, Sam had ended up making friends who she was sure would remain in her life forever. No matter how hectic things became, they still got together on special occasions.

Kayla Ryan had gone on to become a police officer. Alexandra Forsythe had become a forensic scientist with the FBI. Josie Lockworth was an air force captain. Victoria, or Tory, Patton became a reporter and now worked for a national news agency. Darcy Allen had worked in Hollywood as a costume designer and makeup artist before marrying a famous movie producer. Rainy Miller Carrington was now an attorney.

And they'd sworn at the end of that first year that they would always be there for each other. They'd called their vow the Cassandra Promise.

Unfortunately, Sam felt that none of her closest friends

could currently help her. But the Cassandras weren't the only friends Sam had made through Athena.

Given her present situation, only one person came to Sam's mind. If the woman wasn't there, Sam had no choice but to either proceed without information or hunker down and try to wait out the storm that had overtaken her.

Allison Gracelyn, daughter of Senator Marion Gracelyn, had graduated the Athena Academy with Rainy. Like Rainy, Allison had maintained close ties with the school. Currently, Allison worked as a computer programmer and mathematician at the National Security Agency, the most top-secret spy organization in the United States. However, she also served as a board consultant and overseer at Athena.

When Sam had applied for the CIA, Allison had stepped forward and written a letter of recommendation on Sam's behalf. The act had surprised Sam, because she hadn't been close to Allison. Not that she was terribly close to anyone outside of the Cassandras. But Allison was a good friend of Rainy's. Sam had guessed that Rainy had triggered the letter from Allison.

Since that time, Allison had kept in touch with Sam and had provided some guidance while Sam worked with the Agency. On a few occasions Allison had asked Sam to translate some of the HUMINT and SIGNIT intelligence the NSA's spy satellites and agents had gathered.

HUMINT was human intelligence, conversations and confessions garnered or overheard by NSA agents in the field. SIGNIT was signal intelligence, stolen away by listening devices and computers. Although she'd been able to help with the translations on most occasions, Sam still didn't know for certain what significance those brief bits of information had. Allison had been appreciative of the help and had written more letters to the CIA directors that had helped Sam's career.

That doesn't mean I can e-mail Allison and expect help, Sam reminded herself.

In point of fact, there was a good chance Allison could trace Sam through the Internet Service Provider and give her location to MI-6, in return for an espionage favor, or to the CIA. Sam had no doubt that Riley McLane was desperately hunting her.

Lightning flashed outside the cybercafé, startling Sam. Then the dark heavens opened up and rain drummed the street.

She turned her full attention to the computer. She went online and tapped into one of the Web sites where she stored her computer tools and programs, then downloaded them to the computer she was on.

All of the tools were cutting edge, programs that she had either written herself or modified. Some of them were designed to break into sites. Others allowed her to trace people through the Internet. And some, like the ones she downloaded now, allowed her to mask the ISP she was logged on at.

Her configuration set, she typed, ONLINE?, hesitated a moment, then sent the message.

Chapter 5

The computer pinged to let Sam know the message had been successfully sent.

She took a sip of her latte and waited. She was just about to give up when an Instant Message box opened on the screen.

I'M HERE.

IT'S MIRAGE. Whenever Sam contacted Allison, she always used e-mail that pertained to mythological beings and places.

WHAT CAN I DO FOR YOU, MIRAGE?

Sam quickly logged on to the IM box and opened the dialogue. She typed rapidly. *I THINK I'M IN TROUBLE.*

WHAT KIND OF TROUBLE?

I DON'T KNOW YET.

SO TELL ME.

Sam hesitated but couldn't keep her fingers from typing, *CAN I TRUST YOU?* She hated asking the question and immediately felt embarrassed. But that was one of the questions she'd always wanted to ask the different sets of foster parents she'd met over the years. And it was usually the one question she never asked but always got the answer to at some point.

YOU ALREADY HAVE, Allison replied.

After a brief hesitation, Sam typed, *NOT TRUSTED COMPLETELY. I'VE MASKED THE ISP I'M USING. IF YOU TRY TO FIND OUT ANYTHING MORE ABOUT MY LOCATION, I'LL KNOW YOU'RE LOOKING AND I'LL BE GONE.*

DON'T BLAME YOU. SCARY OUT THERE.

WHAT DO YOU KNOW?

NOT MUCH.

THE BRITISH SHADOWS ARE CHASING ME.

I KNEW THAT.

WHY?

Allison's answer came back at once. I HAVEN'T FOUND OUT YET. IT'S A SENSITIVE MATTER. NO ONE'S TALKING ABOUT IT. I DON'T WANT TO PUSH TOO HARD. THE SITUATION ISN'T IN ANY OF THE FIELDS I'M RESPONSIBLE FOR. I ONLY FOUND OUT A FEW MINUTES AGO.

Sam thought about that. *HOW DID YOU FIND OUT?*

CIA DIRECTOR MITCHELL CALLED ME. SAID YOU MIGHT BE IN CONTACT. THAT MADE ME CURIOUS.

WHAT DID YOU TELL HIM?

THAT I'D LET HIM KNOW IF YOU GOT IN TOUCH WITH ME.

An iron fist wrapped around Sam's stomach. For a moment she thought she was going to throw up. She glanced over her shoulder, half expecting MI-6 agents to come busting through the door. Instead, she caught the two young men gazing at her, then saw them quickly try to cover that fact up.

The computer pinged, letting her know Allison had already sent another message.

I LIED.

The fist clenching Sam's middle relaxed. But only a little. She hated trusting anyone outside her own skin. Nobody had ever looked out for her the way she'd looked out for herself.

Well, almost nobody. The Cassandras had come close. Rainy had been like the big sister Sam had never had. And Darcy had become almost like a mother.

WHY ARE THEY AFTER YOU? Allison asked.

I HAVEN'T STOPPED LONG ENOUGH TO ASK.

The cursor blinked for a moment, then Allison asked, HOW MUCH INVOLVEMENT HAVE YOU HAD WITH THEM?

PRACTICALLY NONE. SPOT ASSIGNMENTS. NOTHING HANDS-ON WITHOUT OTHER AGENTS BEING PRESENT.

WHAT DO YOU NEED FROM ME?

Sam thought about that only for a moment. *I NEED TO KNOW WHERE THE HEAT'S COMING FROM.*

WHAT ARE YOU GOING TO DO?

STAY HUNKERED DOWN UNTIL I FIGURE OUT MY NEXT MOVE.

THAT MEANS YOU'RE NOT GOING TO BE HERE

FOR THE FUNERAL. THAT'S GOING TO BE HARD ON THE OTHERS. THEY WERE HOPING YOU WOULD ALL BE TOGETHER TO SAY GOODBYE.

A creeping chill filled Sam. She made herself read the words again. Nothing there made sense. Breaking the thrall that held her, she typed, *WHAT FUNERAL?*

YOU DON'T KNOW?

Sam waited. The list of people that Allison knew Sam would be upset over was short. And all of those people meant the world to her.

RAINY.

The single word froze Sam's heart. Her hands turned numb. She couldn't type. Images of Rainy—Lorraine Miller Carrington to anyone who didn't know her—danced through Sam's head.

Rainy had thick chestnut-colored hair and bright blue eyes. She was quick out on the mats in a martial arts dojo, a whirlwind of determination. Rainy had served as an instructor at the Athena Academy. She'd thought she had taught Sam some new moves. Sam had just never let her friend see how good she really was.

More than anything, the night when Rainy had "injured" her ankle while on a survival camping trip, Rainy had somehow managed to defeat Sam's ingrained emotional defenses. Rainy had been the group leader of the Cassandras. They'd been an odd group, none of them getting along well with the others. They'd done poorly at every competition in their first trimester at Athena. None of them had worked well with the others at first, and it showed in their poor performance in group activities.

Sam had been the youngest member. At that time, she'd

carried a lot of anger inside her and unleashed it on anyone who tried to get close to her. Rainy had changed all
that when she'd pretended to be injured out there in the
mountains. During that night, while caring for Rainy, all
of them—Tory, Josie, Darcy, Kayla, Alex and Sam—had
somehow pulled together to take care of Rainy and each
other. And the Cassandras had become the strongest of all
the groups that year.

No. Not Rainy. Rainy can't be dead. Nothing can happen to Rainy.

Sam felt the hot flash of tears burn at the backs of her
eyes. She walled those feelings off, drawing on the skills
she'd learned while getting bounced from foster home to
foster home.

Nothing could touch her. She wouldn't let it.

I'M SO SORRY, Allison typed. OH, GOD, I'M SO
SORRY. YOU SHOULDN'T HAVE TO FIND OUT
LIKE THIS.

Sam stared at the screen, then blocked out the hurtful
words. She typed *WHAT HAPPENED?*

"Miss, would you like a pillow?"

Torn from her thoughts, Sam glanced up at the flight attendant. He was young and slim, elegant looking in his uni-
form.

"No," Sam replied. She heard the strain in her voice. Fatigue had settled in like a heavy quilt once the jet had
taken off. She hadn't spoken since the jet had lifted from
Innsbruck, Austria.

After finishing her conversation with Allison Gracelyn, Sam had abandoned Munich at once. She'd rented a

car in one of her cover names and driven down to St. Anton, Austria. Once there, she'd spent the night in one of the ski resorts under yet another name. After she'd lost herself among the skiing crowd and made certain she hadn't been followed, she'd rented a car and driven to Innsbruck to take the first plane headed west that offered jumps to Tucson, Arizona, where Rainy was going to be buried. She was going to have to say goodbye to her friend forever.

Tomorrow. How am I going to do that, Rainy? How am I supposed to go on and never see you again?

It wasn't fair. This hurt too much. Sam had gotten really good at telling foster families goodbye. She'd made certain after the first few that she never got to know the families that followed.

Sam glanced at her watch. Tomorrow was only hours away. She was somewhere over the Atlantic seaboard of the United States. With the layovers she had scheduled in Atlanta, Georgia, and St. Louis, Missouri, getting to the funeral on time was going to be close.

"A magazine, then?" the flight attendant suggested, as if uncomfortable leaving her there staring into the darkness outside the window. "Or headphones for the television or radio?"

From the corner of her eye, Sam noticed that the rest of the travelers on the late-night flight were asleep or reading or watching the recycled sit-com on the small television monitors that flipped down from the cabin roof.

"Headphones, please." Sam paid for the disposable headphones, plugged them into the appropriate slot on the seat, and didn't switch the sound on. With the headphones in place, her inability to sleep and preoccupation with the painful memories and incessant questions that kept slamming around in her mind were effectively disguised.

Satisfied, the attendant offered a beverage of her choice, accepted her polite refusal of the same and went away.

Fatigue leeched at Sam's reserves, but she couldn't rest. Even if she hadn't been running from the combined forces of the CIA and MI-6, she wouldn't have been able to sleep.

Rainy was dead.

And with her friend gone, something of Sam St. John felt dead and MIA, as well.

Sam still hadn't cried. She refused to allow herself. Crying had never done her any good while she was shuttling from family to family, usually wearing out her welcome and sometimes alienating the families because she wouldn't socialize with them.

None of them had accepted her. They couldn't. Sam had been too intelligent. Too independent. Too *different.*

And she wasn't vulnerable. She'd worked hard to keep herself from being vulnerable. No one was allowed to hurt her.

Now, with the pain of Rainy's death heavy on her heart, Sam felt angry with her friend, as well. Rainy had no right to die. Especially not by something as stupid as falling asleep behind the wheel of her car and crashing.

Not after you made me love you, Sam thought. Her throat tightened painfully. It's just not fair. Damn you, Rainy.

That thought immediately felt selfish. Rainy was married. Her husband, Marshall, was a great guy and completely in love with Rainy. How must he be feeling?

Barely able to hold back the tears, Sam stared at her reflection in the jet's window. Backlit by a reading light behind her, Sam's reflection looked gray and paper thin in the clean glass. Her image there was insubstantial; nothing could touch it; nothing could stick to it or hurt it.

Sam wished she could be more like that reflection. There was a time in her life, she knew, that she was like that image. There had been three kids in her fourth foster family. All of those kids had been older than she was. None of them had liked her. Because of her white-blond hair, pale complexion and the quiet way she had when she was six years old, those kids had called her Ghost Girl. They had made fun of her.

At that time, Sam had been too young to take any real command of her life. So she'd chosen to exist simply because she didn't know how to stop existing. Then she'd discovered computers and had her first few lessons in martial arts. She'd found a way to connect to her own life. Computers offered a world of logic, of checks and balances. In a way, martial arts offered the same foundation. She had learned to be good at both those things.

She studied her reflection in the window. She was pretty. She knew that. Made up properly, she might even own up to being beautiful. Boys who had gotten to know her while she was attending Athena Academy called her the Ice Princess. They'd thought she was egotistical, a snob. None of them had guessed that the demeanor she exhibited was purely there as a defense mechanism.

But it had been so long since she had hurt like this that she was afraid she wouldn't make it back from the loss to be whole again.

No, she admonished herself, you've never hurt like this. Oh God, Rainy, what am I going to do now that you're not there?

Her reflection held no answers for her. Her pain didn't even show in the image of her face. She breathed out, keeping herself centered. During the last day and a half, Allison hadn't been able to penetrate the security regarding the search for CIA Special Agent Samantha St. John.

Her government, at least in spy circles, had declared her a fugitive for reasons that she didn't know.

She pushed the confusion out of her mind. One problem at a time, she chided herself. She intended to go to the funeral first, then work out the details of finding out what had gone wrong in Munich.

The funeral left her exposed, though. If anyone at the Agency managed to put Rainy's death into the picture, they might know that she wouldn't stay away. The way Sam had it figured she only had to worry about one agent.

And Riley McLane had already betrayed her once.

"Did you know St. John was taken into custody by the FBI?"

Looking up from the personnel reports he was perusing, Riley looked at Howie Dunn sitting across the desk from him. They both worked out of the Agency bullpens in investigative services.

"The Feebs?" Riley asked, his interest sparking at once. Samantha St. John was turning out to be an interesting study. Never mind that the slim-hipped build and get-back stare that she maintained had already whetted his interest.

But an FBI arrest? Riley would never have guessed that. Sam was full of surprises. Especially the part about being a traitor.

"What did the Feebs arrest her for?" he asked.

Howie grinned and shook his head. "She hacked into a Web site filled with government secrets." The other agent was a big, blocky guy in his mid-twenties who looked like he'd be more at home at a university frat house than working profiling and background checks for the CIA. He had his jacket hung on the back of his chair and his shirtsleeves rolled up to mid-forearm.

"And she was cleared for service with the Agency in spite of that?" Riley couldn't believe it.

Howie grinned as mirthless as a shark. "St. John was eight at the time of the incident. Until she became listed as an international threat yesterday, her juvenile records were sealed."

"Eight?" Riley reached for the computer monitor Howie was looking at and spun it around. He scanned the court documents in quick succession, flipping through the pages with the mouse.

"Just a kid. She borrowed the computer in her foster parents' house and hacked into the system."

"Why?"

"According to the child advocate representing her, St. John was just curious."

"Why did she have a child advocate?" Normally, an attorney specializing in child advocacy—protecting a minor's rights when the interests diverged from the parents'—only showed up in civil matters.

"She was living with foster parents. The parents' attorney convinced them to separate their interests from St. John's because they were afraid they were going to be sued by the government."

"That wouldn't have happened," Riley growled.

"Those people were scared to death. While St. John was on the computer, poking through records no one was supposed to have access to, the FBI hit the house with a full-on raid. Black suits. Riot gear. Tear gas. They kicked the doors down at two o'clock in the morning and handcuffed the whole family. The foster parents were in way over their heads. And they'd had St. John with them less than a year. They didn't know anything about her."

"Sounds like they were looking out for their own hides. Not for that of a little girl. Hell, she was a kid."

Howie flipped through statements taken by the parents' attorney. "They said they liked her, but she was distant."

Frustrated and feeling guilty, Riley pushed up out of the chair. He'd been sitting for over two hours straight and hadn't noticed how long it had been until he'd seen the time on Howie's computer screen. While the other agent had searched through electronic documents, Riley had gone through text files. He liked working with his hands when his thoughts were jumbled.

And Sam St. John definitely had them jumbled. He hadn't slept since she'd disappeared in Munich twenty-eight hours ago. With the mission going on, he'd been up for over seventy-six hours. He knew he wasn't at his best, but he couldn't stay away from the investigation.

By rights, Mitchell could have pulled him from the hunt for Sam, but the director had chosen to let Riley work on a secondary effort. The primary team on the hunt was searching through the movements Sam had made during the forty-eight hours up to the Steiner op.

"St. John was a child prodigy," Howie said. "A real computer savant. That's why she's so good with languages, too. That could intimidate the hell out of a normal parent."

"What happened to Sam…St. John as a result of the court case?"

If Howie noticed the slip, he didn't mention it. From what Riley had seen of the agent, he was a solid, stand-up guy.

"Sam was placed on probation—"

"At *eight*?" Riley was stunned. "We're talking about a kid here."

"Yeah." Howie nodded. "But we're also talking about a high-security agency she broke into. And that was eighteen years ago. Phone phreaks and hackers were recognized as a threat then. Cybersecurity and firewalls were in their infancy stages. There was little protection against hackers and other subversive elements raiding the Internet. Her parents were ordered to keep her away from computers and the Internet unless she was supervised."

Riley went back to the notes he'd made on a legal pad. "She entered the Athena Academy at nine. The files I've read on that place say that a kid normally isn't allowed to enter till the age of ten."

Howie checked the files. "Entrance to the Athena Academy was one of the conditions the judge stipulated for St. John's probation."

Riley flipped through pages till he found what he was looking for. "The student body at the Athena Academy is limited to two hundred students."

"That's a hell of a lot smaller than my graduating class."

"Two hundred kids scattered across six grade levels," Riley emphasized. "Figure less than thirty kids per level. What do you bet the chances are that other graduates knew Sam St. John?"

"I'd say the odds are pretty good."

"So would I. Let's make some calls and see what we can find out."

Bright morning sunlight streamed down over the cemetery in Tucson, Arizona. A quiet, dry wind moved across the parched land and seemed to shy away from the landscaped areas.

Clothed in a prim black dress, Sam sat in her rented car and watched over the cemetery with a pair of binoculars. The service would be a good four hundred yards away, through a line of imported trees. She would easily escape detection by anyone at the funeral.

Sam left the window down, but the breeze wasn't cool and the car's interior was reaching sweltering conditions. If she'd left the air conditioner running, though, a large pool of condensation on the ground could draw someone's attention.

So far, she hadn't gotten in touch with Alex, Darcy, Tory, Kayla or Josie. She hadn't dared to.

In part, she was afraid that someone from the Agency might be watching. But the biggest reason she didn't talk to her friends was because she didn't know what to say.

At ten-thirty, the funeral procession came into view along the two-lane highway that twisted through the foothills like a broken-backed snake. The cemetery was located on one of the highest areas surrounding the city.

Fear quavered through Sam when she spotted the two police motorcycles leading the long line of cars. A midnight-blue hearse followed next, trailed by two family cars. The line of vehicles seemed to go on forever.

Grave diggers lounged beneath a tree not far from the green-canopied grave site. They smoked cigarettes and talked, watching the arrival.

Sam tried to will herself numb as she watched the pallbearers take the casket from the back of the hearse. She forced herself to remember Rainy as she had been, not as she must be inside that horrible box.

A car accident. Rainy had fallen asleep at the steering wheel and driven off the road.

Even after Allison Gracelyn had told her about Rainy's death, Sam hadn't believed it. An accident couldn't have happened to Rainy, who was so careful and meticulous.

When Sam saw Alex, Kayla, Tory and Darcy step to the row of family seats, she wanted to go join them. But just as she started to get out of the car, her emotions burst inside her. Hot tears ran down her face. She remained seated in the car. No one was going to see her when she wasn't in full command of herself and her feelings. She wouldn't allow it.

The mourners gathered at the canopy-covered grave site. The preacher began speaking, and his voice rolled over the cemetery.

Resolutely, knowing that she couldn't stay away without telling Rainy goodbye in person, Sam opened the car door and got out. She strode down the hill toward the graveside service.

She had covered only a short distance when a group of

men standing at another grave site turned toward her. They moved deliberately, converging on her quickly and efficiently, cutting off her approach to Rainy's grave site.

Desperately Sam turned back toward the rental car. If she could reach the vehicle, she had a chance. She could—

Four more men surrounded the rental car. They'd come up behind her. They'd had her under surveillance, Sam realized. They'd waited for her to quit the car to catch her out in the open.

And she had missed them. She felt incredibly stupid. Someone had found her ties to the Athena Academy and tracked them back to Rainy.

"St. John," one of the men called.

Sam turned toward the speaker. He was dressed in a black suit and wraparound black sunglasses.

"Don't run, St. John," Riley McLane warned. "If you do, we're going to chase you. And if we chase you, I can guarantee that your friend isn't going to get the kind of burial you'd like to see her have."

"What are the charges?" Sam demanded. "What is it you think I've done?"

"We aren't going into it here. Give it up, St. John. It'll be easier on you."

Frustrated, Sam stood her ground. She clenched her fists, unconsciously dropping into a T-stance.

The agents flanking Riley slowed their approach. Riley kept coming.

"I didn't come here to walk away empty-handed, St. John," Riley said. "Stand down. You choose which way you want it, but you're coming with me."

Sam wanted to run. She even wanted to fight. Maybe

she would lose against so many opponents, but the effort would at least allow her to work through some of the hurt and confusion she felt. She didn't know why Rainy had had to die, and she didn't know why MI-6 had begun pursuing her or why the CIA now seemed intent on taking up the chase.

But she couldn't do that to Rainy or her family. Or to their friends. She looked at the grave site as the preacher continued his message. They all deserved to say goodbye to their friend in peace. She had no doubt that Riley would carry out his threat to take her into custody by force even during the funeral if he had to.

"All right," she said to Riley.

"Hands behind your back, St. John," Riley said gruffly. "You know the drill." The metal links of the handcuffs gleamed in his fingers.

Sam placed her hands behind her back and surrendered herself. She pushed her feelings away. Nothing was going to touch her. She wouldn't allow the fear or frustration inside her. She forced the pain away, ripped the confusion apart and concentrated on being empty.

Chapter 6

Despite the fact that Riley had a dozen trained agents around him, men who had worked takedowns before in war zones and battlegrounds around the world, he didn't feel completely confident they would take Samantha St. John without a fight. He knew they'd take her; he had more than enough men to do that and she had no place to run. But he hoped she didn't force them to hurt her. Giving up wasn't something he believed was in her nature. She was a fighter, a warrior to the last.

He'd faced her on the racquetball court. Other times, he'd seen her practicing martial arts with agents and instructors. She hadn't won all the time, but she'd never given up, never simply accepted defeat.

Sam didn't accept it now. She only permitted it. He saw that as he closed on her. Standing straight and tall despite her petite stature, every inch of her screaming defiance, Sam accepted the fact that she could do nothing to effect her escape.

Dammit, Sam, what the hell is going on with you? Why did you do what you did?

Riley stepped behind her. It would have been easier if she had run, if she had shown her guilt. Riley would have felt better if he'd had the chance to get his own adrenaline levels pumped. Adrenaline took away all moral thinking and left only the animal need to survive, to win. He could have lived with that.

The way things sat now, he felt guilty. As the oldest of four brothers in his family, guilt was part of his nature, tied closely to responsibility. He didn't undertake a mission to fail, and he never gave less than everything he had. He never had.

But putting the cuffs on Sam St. John, even after he'd seen the evidence of guilt Mitchell had offered, didn't give him any sense of satisfaction. More than that, the action didn't feel like the right thing to do.

Standing behind her, Riley was acutely aware of the size difference between them. He stood nearly a foot taller and weighed nearly twice what she did. He'd been conscious of that difference in size on the racquetball court, but there it hadn't been so apparent. Sam had played big.

She felt vulnerable now. Not helpless, because he felt certain if she'd chosen to fight, it would have been a hell of a thing. But she definitely felt vulnerable.

The black dress hugged her slim hips, emphasizing the womanly curves. Black hose covered taut legs. She wore a red wig, and the disguise might have fooled a lot of people, but Riley had known her instantly. Her size marked her, and the controlled way she moved, fluid and graceful, identified her to him immediately. He loved watching her move, whether on the racquetball courts or the exercise mats. He'd never seen another woman in any part of the world that he'd been in who moved quite like Sam St. John.

He took one of her hands in his, feeling the ridge of calluses along the side of her hand and on her fingers. A lot of women would have been embarrassed by the lack of softness, but these were hands of a woman not afraid to get her hands dirty. Riley's mother was like that. She sometimes still climbed aboard one of the farm's tractors and put in a day tilling fields, bucking hay or shucking corn.

Riley respected women like that. He'd grown up around them.

He closed one cuff around her wrist. In a whisper he said, "Let me know if they're too tight."

Sam said nothing. Her black-lensed gaze remained locked on the funeral service. Her arms stayed limp, giving no indication of resistance.

"C'mon, St. John." Travers, a young agent who always liked playing the hard guy, grabbed Sam's arm and started to pull.

Sam hesitated just a moment. Riley knew that Travers was leaving himself open to attack. Travers was too cocky, too sure of himself. But the young agent was also good at dealing physical punishment. Travers would use on attack as an excuse to respond. Sam could have turned in a heartbeat and kicked him to the ground before he'd known the attack was coming. Riley knew she'd had to stop herself from doing exactly that, and he knew that Sam was having control issues as much as he was.

"Let her go," Riley growled.

Travers looked up at him.

"We're staying through the service." Riley stepped forward and pulled Travers's hand from Sam's arm.

"You're taking a chance." Travers's voice was thin and hard. "She might not be here just for the funeral. She could be meeting someone."

Howie Dunn stepped up without a word, invading Travers's space and making the other agent step back. Howie kept his hands crossed in front of him and didn't say a word, but there was no way to ignore his presence.

Although Howie normally stayed in the records office, Riley had requested Howie to accompany him. They'd continued working on St. John's file during the flight out to Tucson, in case St. John hadn't shown.

"We're staying through the service," Riley repeated.

"If anything goes wrong, it's going to be on your head," Travers warned. "And this is going in my report."

"When you write that up, let me know if you have any trouble with the big words," Howie said, taking another step forward and forcing Travers back again. He turned and stood behind St. John, dwarfing her like some protective giant.

Riley stood at Sam's right. Between Howie and himself, Riley knew they created a wall between the young woman and the rest of the CIA team. No one besides Travers seemed to have a problem with staying.

Sam stood quietly for a moment. She spoke without turning to address him. "Thank you."

"You're welcome," Riley said. He noticed the glint of a tear sliding down her cheek. He resisted the immediate impulse to wipe it away. If Sam could have found a way, he knew she'd have broken his arm for even trying.

The preacher talked for a while longer. Then, after the final prayer, the group broke up and began talking. Only a few of them looked up at the quiet gathering of CIA agents and prisoner only a short distance away.

Riley lifted his arm and spoke into the pencil mike on the inside of his wrist. "Bring up the truck."

"On my way."

Taking the inside of Sam's right elbow, Riley turned and walked her back to the narrow courtesy road through the cemetery. None of the graveside attendees came after them. A black Chevy Suburban with dark-tinted windows rolled down other roads and came to a stop in a swirl of dust that quickly eddied back to the ground.

Riley opened the door and helped Sam into the vehicle's rear seat. A shield of bulletproof glass protected the driver and the man in the other front seat from the rear seat's occupants.

Sam sat at the other end of the seat. The single tear had dried on her face, but Riley could still see the trail that it had left.

Standing in the open doorway, Riley asked, "Want to talk about this, St. John?"

"About what, Special Agent McLane?" Her voice sounded hard and flat.

"About why we're here."

"Maybe you want to tell me."

Riley felt some of the tension in his stomach release.

She wasn't broken. That mattered. He felt good about that. Even with the odds stacked against her the way they were, she wasn't giving in. Riley respected that, even if he didn't respect what she'd done.

"Why did you do it?" Riley asked.

"I don't know what you're talking about."

Frustrated, Riley shook his head. "You had a career ahead of you, St. John. A good career. If you'd wanted it."

Sam kept her eyes forward. "Are you turning me over to MI-6?"

Riley waited a moment, letting her think about that possibility.

"If you're not going to answer, then let's get moving," Sam said. "I'll find out when we get there. I can wait."

Riley cursed to himself. It would have been better if she'd been afraid. She is afraid, he realized, thinking about the young kid she'd been who had never known a true mother and father. Or even a true home. She'd been bounced to a dozen different places by the time she was seven.

"I might not be able to help you once we get there," Riley warned.

"Then help me now." Sam turned her black-lensed gaze on him.

Riley looked at her for a moment. The two agents in the front of the Suburban could hear the conversation. They were also taping. That was standard operating procedure. A law enforcement vehicle was considered public property and privacy laws did not protect conversations held within them.

"I can't," he said. "Damn, but you're hardheaded."

"And that bothers you more than thinking I'm some

kind of criminal? Or a national threat?" Her voice was cold and distant.

Exasperated, not trusting his own emotions and not truly understanding them either, Riley turned to Howie. "Hold the truck here a little while longer. I'll be right back."

A thousand questions shot through Sam's mind as she sat in the air-conditioned Suburban. What had turned Riley against her? Whatever was going on with British Intelligence must be severe.

Was the Agency really going to turn her over to MI-6? She didn't know if the CIA would do that. Or even if they could. She had rights as an American citizen.

However, she also knew that the world had changed after September 11. Nations had a tendency to look after their own needs first instead of the rights of individuals. The weight of the handcuffs around her wrists reminded her of that.

She was conscious of the Suburban driver's attention on her in the rearview mirror. The passenger sat with his hand wrapped around the barrel of the .12-gauge shotgun tucked between the seats.

From the corner of her eye, Sam watched Riley cross the cemetery to the grave site. Panic welled up inside her and almost burst loose. Riley couldn't talk to Alex or Darcy or any of the others. That wasn't right. Whatever business Riley had with her, it wasn't supposed to touch the Cassandras. Her friends had been through enough in losing Rainy.

She watched Riley, wondering why he had chosen to confront the people at the grave site. Surely his instructions hadn't included interviewing the people she had known back in school.

The big agent who had interceded on her behalf shifted outside the Suburban as he took a call over his cell phone. He blocked Sam's view of the grave site. She had to bite her lip to keep from telling him to move.

Minutes passed. The two agents in front talked about the coming football season.

Then the big agent moved again. Riley walked toward the Suburban.

Unable to totally assess the situation through her peripheral vision, Sam looked past Riley. The attendees drifted apart, going their own ways in small groups.

Riley opened the door. His sunglasses covered his eyes and helped mask his expression.

"Turn around, St. John," he ordered. "It's a long ride to the airport."

Without a word, Sam turned and presented her handcuffs to him.

Riley opened one of the cuffs and allowed her to bring her hands around in front of her. Then he took a length of chain from the Suburban's driver and secured the cuffs to the D-ring mounted on the vehicle's floor.

Sam felt the heaviness of the chains around her wrists. At least in her current position she could sit comfortably.

"I got you something," Riley said, sounding a little unsure of himself.

Surprised, Sam looked at him.

"I know the Carrington woman was a friend of yours," Riley said. "I know coming here had to have been hard."

"Why did you go down there?" Sam demanded. "Who did you talk to?"

"I got you this." Riley held out a single white rose.

Sam made no move to take the rose.

"I didn't know if you would want it or not," Riley said, looking more than a little uncomfortable. "My mother always kept a flower from the funerals of people she loved. From both my grandfathers and one of my grandmothers. From her sister's."

Sam sat silent and still.

"I didn't know if you were like that, St. John," Riley apologized. "But if you wanted something to remember your friend by, I wanted you to have something."

Hypnotized by the rose and all that it represented, that it meant she would never again see Rainy, Sam found she couldn't move. The grief pressed down on her, paralyzing her with pain that she refused to show.

"Sorry," Riley said. "I presumed too much." He started to walk away.

"Wait." Sam's voice came out strained and cracked at the end.

Riley looked at her. He didn't speak.

Struggling to control the sudden grief that assailed her, Sam reached out for the rose. Riley laid it in her cupped hands. The flower felt soft and fragile against her fingers and palms.

A look of surprise touched Riley's handsome face for a moment, then he twitched his full lips and the expression was gone.

"What does your mother do with the flowers?" Sam asked. She turned her gaze from Riley. She didn't want to have to deal with him looking at her.

"She dries them out," Riley said softly. "She presses them between the pages of her family Bible and saves them in a memory book." He paused. "Sometimes she says doing that is foolish, that it's more trouble than it's worth, and that it gives her one more thing to worry about and grieve over when it's gone. Then she says that sometimes the things that are the most trouble are actually worth the most."

When he closed the door, Sam watched him walk away without turning her head. She was alone in the rear of the Suburban. A moment later the big vehicle got underway. Sam kept her eyes open, taking in the final sight of Rainy's coffin perched on the metal device that would lower it into the ground.

When she could no longer see that, she closed her eyes and retreated into the small corner of her mind that she had created for herself all those years ago when she was a little girl. Some of the counselors had claimed she was helpless when she did that, but Sam had learned that she was invulnerable there.

Chapter 7

For nine days Sam was kept in one of the holding cells in a building in Langley. Her contact with people was non-existent, because she didn't even get to see them. Three times a day, someone—maybe not even the same some-one—brought her meals to the cell and slid the tray through the opening at the bottom of the heavy steel door.

Often, Sam wondered why she had been locked up. Especially since she had no human contact. What did they think she had done? Why didn't they talk to her? Those questions were in her head every day, but she had no answers. Nor did it seem those answers were going to come any time soon.

Sam ate the meals, all under the watchful eyes of who-ever manned the protected video cameras that kept surveillance inside the cell. When she was finished with her

meals, and she made certain she finished because she'd retreated to her childhood survival system and even saved
back wedges of apples and cheese and crackers for snacks
later when she got hungry, she passed the tray back through
the slot. She never once tried to see whoever brought the
food or took the tray later. Whoever watched her would
have seen that as weakness on her part.

The cell was a little larger than solitary confinement in
prison. After days of pacing, she was certain it measured
twelve feet wide by fourteen feet long and had about an
eight-foot ceiling. Chains held a single bed screwed into
the wall suspended off the floor. Cubbies for her clothing
occupied the space beneath the bed.

The toilet and shower, outfitted with opaque windows,
offered her a little privacy. She took care of showers and
her private needs in the dark after lights-out. Possibly the
surveillance teams had access to night-vision systems on
the cameras, but she didn't see any sign of it. She also told
herself that the night crews probably weren't as alert as the
day crews.

However, the possibility existed that Riley might sit in
on the surveillance sessions.

Sam didn't know how she felt about that. She tried hard
not to *feel* anything. But it was impossible not to feel
trapped. The room had no windows and only the one door.

Or maybe Riley wasn't there at all. By now he was
probably released from Medical and returned to duty. She
was just another takedown he'd arranged, another success
that had gone into his dossier.

Given the solitude, she worked on coming to grips with
Rainy's death. Letting go of her friend was the hardest

thing she'd ever had to do. She'd never lost anyone close to her. She'd never let anyone close to her outside of the Cassandras.

The white rose that Riley had gotten for her sat in one of the cubbies beneath the bed as a grim reminder of Rainy's loss. She wondered what her friends thought about her continued absence. Maybe they thought she was on a mission; they knew she was in the CIA. Without a phone or a means of contact with the outside world, she had no way of knowing.

All she had was the rose.

During the plane trip to Washington, D.C., she'd had to ask Riley how to preserve the flower. He'd told her that his mother had always hung the flowers upside down for a few days if she didn't immediately press them into the family Bible.

Sam didn't have a Bible. She didn't have a book of any kind. She'd hung the rose upside down from one of the cubbies until it was dry.

After that, there had been nothing to do. With all of the dead hours in the day and the night, Sam's mind played with possibilities. If she hadn't been self-taught in discipline and waiting, the building anxiety could have been agony.

Instead, she chose to take the time to consider her future moves. With her CIA career obviously in flames for some reason, she didn't know what she would do once she was released. If she was released.

She had money saved up. Money meant freedom. As soon as she had started working as a teen, she'd saved money, putting back everything she could. That habit had continued in the Agency.

She could live for a few months. Then, depending on what the circumstances were when the CIA eventually let her go, she could always return to New York and use her linguistic skills for corporations. The work had been offered before while she was in college, but she hadn't been interested. She wasn't now, but having a plan was a step toward freedom and out of the cage where the Agency held her.

Once she had made tentative plans, the hours of the passing days grew longer. Where she had once thought CIA interviewers would be in at any moment, she now began to think they weren't coming at all. The new Homeland Security regulations that had been passed after 9/11 effectively stripped a person suspected of terrorism or espionage of any rights. As long as they thought she was guilty of whatever the hell they thought her guilty of, they could hold her forever.

The certainty that she'd been forgotten grew a little more every day. Whatever the Agency had brought her in for might have gotten put on a back burner, and her with it. She'd read about Chinese illegals who had gotten arrested in New York and were currently being confined years later because the United States Government didn't know what to do with them.

The Triad, the Chinese Mafia, had sworn to kill the people being detained if they went back to that country, making it impossible for the United States to return them to their native land. On the other hand, the American Government couldn't allow someone to forcibly enter the country and become a citizen.

Those people, Sam knew, existed apart.

And that was how she existed—minute by minute, hour by hour and, lately, day by day. Apart.

She wore a sleeveless gray top and unflattering dark-gray sweatpants. They'd taken her shoes and not given her anything to wear. Being barefoot in a controlled climate wasn't much of a hardship.

As she did every day, she exercised, going through her martial arts forms one after the other effortlessly. Staying fit while incarcerated was a problem, but she knew she couldn't afford to lose her edge. In the beginning she went slow, loosening and warming her muscles. Then she started pushing, stressing her training and her endurance. Her arms and legs moved automatically.

She didn't think about anything but the movements and the motion. In her mind, she was no longer in the cell. She was in Master Chong's dojo, where she'd first started learning, paying for her schooling by sweeping the floors and doing laundry after class.

She'd only been seven years old, slipping away again because supervision in the home where she'd stayed had been a joke. If she'd wanted to, if she'd had a place to go, she could have been gone in a heartbeat.

After she had gone through all of the forms, had her heart rate up so that blood exploded through her and the exercise had turned anaerobic, she changed to tai chi. A lot of the movements were the same as her forms and called on the same level of discipline, but they relaxed her and gave her a chance to breathe normally.

And, like always, time disappeared.

"How long has she been at this?"

"Hours."

"Man, you're kidding me."

"No. She's incredible. Never seen anybody like her."

"How long has she been locked up?"

"Eleven days."

"And she's done this every day?"

"Every day."

"What's she in for?"

"Nobody's saying."

"So you haven't even caught a whisper?"

Standing in the doorway to the security observation post cued in to Samantha St. John's holding cell, Riley McLane curbed the immediate anger he felt at the two young agents pulling the night security detail. Still, his voice was sharp when he spoke.

"If you were supposed to know what she was in for, you'd have been briefed."

Both agents jerked around, whipping their heads back to look at Riley.

"Special Agent McLane." Tom Lackland, the senior of the two agents, looked embarrassed and relieved. "I didn't hear you come in."

"Good thing I'm one of the good guys," Riley said lightly.

"Yeah."

On the screen, Sam stepped up her exercise routine again. She whirled and kicked, feinted and punched. Her motions were compact and deadly.

"When is lights-out?" Riley asked.

Lackland consulted his watch. "Seven minutes. Eleven o'clock."

Riley nodded. "Why don't the two of you take a break? I'll watch the monitors for a while."

"All right." Lackland and his partner left the room.

Leaning against the side wall, Riley watched Sam go through her forms. He wondered what it would be like to face her in combat. Even with the size difference he had over her, it would be a close match. She was much better at martial arts than he was. Every move was smooth, fluid. Her focus was complete.

Watching the single-minded purpose she maintained, Riley envied her ability to stay calm. Eleven days had passed since she'd had a conversation with anyone. He'd put her in the cell and walked away. She had never tried to talk to any of the people that brought her meals. She was good at waiting. Riley didn't think he could have lasted this long.

Stone Mitchell felt certain that the process might take a little longer, but the director was confident that Sam would break in the end. Riley didn't think that was the case at all. He'd pushed at Mitchell to let him interview her.

With the turn of events that had happened that afternoon, Riley knew the director wasn't going to be able to hold out much longer. Despite St. John's personal agenda, she had good friends. Those friends also had a certain amount of political pull.

Riley wondered if those women would stand by Sam so adamantly if they knew what she was accused of doing.

Sam went through a series of cool-down exercises.

Riley looked at the smooth lines of Sam's small breasts, made visible by the way the soaked sleeveless shirt clung to her. The loose, baggy sweat pants couldn't hide the swell of her hips or the long legs for her build.

At precisely 11:00 p.m., the room went dark.

Riley blinked at the darkness. He closed the door to the security room, shut down the computer monitors, and switched out the room's lights, dampening the light in the room, as well. He stood in the darkness for a moment, listening to his heartbeat in his ears and feeling the power of it in his chest.

He stared at the dark monitor and thought he could make out movement. He actually couldn't, but he knew what was going on. Somewhere in that darkness, Sam St. John was stripping off for her nightly shower.

Unable to stop himself, Riley tapped Lackland's keyboard, shifting the camera feed over to the backup systems while he used the manual controls. The monitor blinked, then fuzzed for a moment and presented a green-tinted picture. Another moment passed and picture cleared.

The night-vision-capable cameras planted in the room revealed Sam St. John as she pulled the sweat-soaked top over her head, unveiling her dark bra and gleaming flesh.

Riley's breath caught in the back of his throat at the sight. His arousal was immediate and painful.

Nine days ago he had discovered that Sam waited until after lights-out to take her shower before going to bed. He'd walked in on the two agents watching the surveillance camera and listened to the derogatory comments they'd made at Sam's expense. Riley had shut the night-vision capabilities down and stood watch for the next hour.

The next day Riley had transferred the men from the detail and brought in Tom Lackland and a female agent who had been reassigned that evening. With the female agent in the room, Lackland hadn't used the night-vision capability. There had been no need, and the female agent would have protested and probably reported him.

Knowing that two male agents were in charge of surveillance that night, Riley had decided to step in to maintain Sam's privacy.

Not exactly what you're doing here, is it? Irritated with his inability to control his impulse, Riley reached for the control.

At that moment Sam skinned out of the sweatpants. In the artificial-light enhancement, Riley couldn't see what color her panties were. They probably matched the black or navy or dark green of her bra. Riley knew those colors were possible because he'd checked the list of clothing Sam was issued. He hadn't intended to; he'd just thought about that while looking over her list of personal items inside the cell.

His gaze traveled up the expanse of legs and over Sam's slim, rounded bottom. Other cameras in the room provided different views, but he keyed in the one from the rear. His mouth went dry and his pulse beat at his temples.

Sam stepped out of the sweatpants and placed them in the dirty clothes hamper along with the sleeveless shirt. With a sinuous movement that was sexy as hell by nature rather than design, she reached behind her back with both hands and unfastened her bra, stripping the material away.

Riley's gaze followed the swell of her breasts. He breathed in, as though he could catch her scent through the monitor if he tried hard enough. He barely stopped himself from tapping the keyboard and shifting the cameras to look at her from the front.

Then she hooked her thumbs in her panties and hiked

the wisp of cloth down over her rounded buttocks. In spite of her slim build, she had generous hips. As active as she was, as small as she was, Riley hadn't expected that.

A growl sounded in the surveillance room. Riley realized with a start that the sound came from him.

On the screen, Sam tossed her underthings into the dirty clothes hamper and stepped into the shower. The opaque plastic prevented the night vision from penetrating the shower walls, but her shadow still showed through. She turned the water on and stood beneath the spray for a while, luxuriating in the feel of the water cascading over her body.

The night vision was sensitive enough to pick up the rising steam that clouded Sam's body and occasionally hid her completely from Riley's view. The view tortured him. He wanted to turn away, but he couldn't. All those times he'd watched Sam on the racquetball court, all those times he had seen her on the mats sparring with opponents, he had wondered what she would look like nude.

Now…he almost knew.

A few minutes later Sam turned the water off. The clouds of vapor thinned and disappeared. He closed his eyes as she stepped from the cubicle, intending to give her privacy. But he opened them seconds later, unable to stop himself. He exhaled as he realized Sam had picked up the towel she'd placed on the floor and wrapped it around herself.

After she was dry, Sam dressed in bra, panties, sweatpants and a tunic top. The clothing was virtually sexless, but Riley couldn't get the sight of her out of his head.

In the dark, Sam trailed her fingers down the wall and

found her way to the bed. She lay down on her side, facing the wall and tucked into a ball.

Riley knew that some observers who didn't know Sam St. John's history might think she'd curled up into a fetal position. Riley knew that she had just assumed the best defensive position she could against someone who might attack her while she slept. Her back and shoulders could take more punishment than her face or front. He had no doubt that she'd wake at the slightest touch, the slightest sound.

Sam's foster years hadn't been pleasant. And Riley knew the reports he'd read only revealed part of what she had been through.

He watched her sleep. After settling in, she was still. He envied her that. He hadn't had a good night's sleep since he'd brought her in.

Finding her hadn't seemed like he was doing his job; it had felt more like a betrayal.

Riley switched the night vision off. Reluctant to leave, he triggered the audio pickups in the room. He increased the volume till he could hear Sam's breathing, slow and steady.

She slept.

For a moment Riley listened to her, made himself realize that she was all right. And he told himself Sam's situation was going to change tomorrow. That realization didn't make him feel much better. The change still wasn't going to set her free.

He hated the conflict that raged within him. Sam didn't deserve to be free. He'd seen the digital recordings that Mitchell had gotten from British intelligence.

There was no way she wasn't guilty.

* * *

On the twelfth day, the cell door opened without warning.

Sam stood in the center of the floor in a relaxed martial arts L-stance, right foot back and perpendicular to the left foot forward. Her arms hung at her sides, but she could lift them instantly to defend herself if she had to. She stared at the swinging door and imagined that the air outside the room felt and tasted a lot different from what was trapped in the cell with her, but she knew that wasn't true.

When Riley McLane stepped into the room, Sam experienced mixed feelings. Anger came first, which she expected, but hope and attraction came as well. She forced the hope away. She'd learned a long time ago that hoping for something was nearly useless. The only thing that truly mattered was the ability to make something happen.

The attraction was confusing. She'd always noticed an undercurrent of it when she was around him, but now the sensation was like a live thing. She didn't know what to do about it and couldn't help standing there feeling very much like a deer in headlights.

During the past twelve days, it seemed as though not a moment had passed that she hadn't thought of Riley McLane. Of course, those thoughts were mixed. Sometimes she missed him and other times she wanted to kick his teeth in for taking advantage of Rainy's funeral to capture her.

Confronted with him now, she didn't know how to respond.

"St. John," Riley said in a deadpan voice. He carried an armload of clothes that included a teal blouse and wheat-colored slacks. There was even a pack of hose. "You'll need to get dressed." He offered the clothes.

Sam stood her ground. "No one told me when check-out was."

Riley grimaced. "Don't be a smart-ass." He wadded up the clothes and fired them off his chest like a basketball pass.

The clothes separated in midflight. Sam had to scramble to keep them from hitting the ground. For a moment, she considered letting them scatter, but the opportunity to get dressed in slacks and a blouse instead of sweats was too enticing.

You're getting weak, she chided herself. But she consoled herself with the fact that if she could recognize her weakness, she wasn't really weak. Getting dressed in those clothes was something she deserved, but she didn't have to have it.

"Where are we going?" Sam asked.

"You'll find out soon enough," Riley told her. "Get dressed."

"Now we're on a timetable?" Sam took her time and sorted through the clothing. When she got to the bra and panties that had come from Victoria's Secret, one of her guilty pleasures and one that Rainy had empathized with yet teased her about, she knew Riley had been to her home. Knowing Riley and the men with him were watching embarrassed her. She kept her head down, cheeks flaming in spite of her attempt at iron control, and didn't make eye contact.

The bra and panties weren't hers, though. These still had the price tags on them.

And that's a weakness of yours, Riley McLane. You didn't have the guts to go through my panty drawer. Sam was mildly surprised. During the time she'd known Riley, she'd felt certain he was the kind of agent that could do anything.

"We're on a timetable," Riley said.

"And I'll want a shower and some privacy." Sam glared up at him.

"We don't have time for a shower."

"We," Sam stated coldly, "aren't taking a shower."

One of the two agents standing at the open door snickered.

Riley looked vastly irritated, but his cheekbones showed a little color. Sam knew she'd struck a nerve. "We need to go now."

"Then I can go barefoot and in sweats."

"St. John, now isn't the time to be difficult."

"Oh? Is there going to be a time later? See, I didn't get the itinerary. I've just been locked away for the last twelve days and left without human contact. Not exactly conducive to gaining a positive response from a subject."

"Nobody thought we needed a positive response." Riley returned her glare. "A lot of people still don't think we need one."

Sam let that hang for a moment, then—because she couldn't help herself even though she knew not to ask—she asked, "What about you, McLane? Do you want a positive response?"

Too late, Sam realized that the question could have dual meanings. The two agents minding the door grinned at each other.

Riley looked more irritated than ever. "Take a shower. Get dressed. You've got ten minutes." Without another word, he turned and left the room, closing the cell door behind him.

After he'd gone, Sam was surprised to find out how alone she felt. A lump rose to the back of her throat. She didn't want to admit how scared she was, but she was. And she did. She didn't like doing it, but she'd always tried to be honest with herself.

Quickly she laid out the clothes on the bed. When she got to the business-cut jacket, she discovered a package in the pocket. A plastic bag inside the pocket contained deodorant, perfume and a few makeup items. After twelve days of being without those things, Sam felt as if she'd discovered a treasure trove.

The small perfume bottle shouldn't have entered the room at all. The bottle could be broken and the shards used for a weapon or to slice her wrists. A small disposable razor lay at the bottom of the bag.

Sam weighed the bottle and the razor in her hand. Only grim determination and a lot of time would have made the disposable razor a threat. But the bottle was a different matter.

Was Riley that certain of her? That she wouldn't use the shards as a weapon? Or that she wouldn't try to commit suicide out of guilt for whatever it was she was supposed to have done? Or because of the futility she had to be feeling about being locked up and not being able to get free?

Or was he just giving her a way out?

The possibility crept into Sam's mind without warning. She felt chilled to the bone.

Never in all the years that she'd spent in one foster home after another had she felt like ending her life. She'd always dreamed that there would be a way out. She had known that eventually she would grow up and she could be on her own.

But what about now? she asked herself. Her hand trembled slightly, and she instantly got frustrated with herself. For all she knew, she was paroled, on her way to freedom. Of course, Riley McLane hadn't acted that way. Or maybe he was just upset because he believed she was guilty of whatever it was she hadn't done.

She made herself stop speculating. She didn't have any answers. She had questions, but they weren't the right ones she needed to ask.

Despite the fact that Riley had wanted her to hurry, she stayed in the shower long enough to put the razor to good use. When she finished, she truly felt clean for the first time in days.

Someone banged on the door as she started getting dressed. Each piece, from the underwear to the hose to the slacks and blouse, felt like battle armor sliding into place. Her confidence grew.

"We're late," Riley growled through the door.

"Another minute," Sam called, starting on the makeup by touch since she didn't have a mirror. Riley had even provided a brush. When she finished, she walked to the door.

"—father always told me a woman would be late to her own funeral," a man was saying. He fell silent as Sam stepped through the door.

Riley stood out in the hall. Dark, wraparound sunglasses masked his eyes.

The other two agents stared at Sam.

"Wow," one of them said in a low voice.

Sam almost blushed. She didn't make eye contact with either of the two men. Instead she waited without saying a word.

"Let's go." Riley gestured to the other end of the hall. "Director Mitchell's office. You know the way."

Sam started walking.

"Wait, Agent McLane." The agent who spoke produced a pair of handcuffs. "We need to cuff her."

A shudder passed through Sam despite her resolve not to show a reaction. The long trip back by plane with her hands manacled in her lap and covered by a jacket had been claustrophobic. Going to the bathroom, even with a female agent along, had been embarrassing. The worst part had been the way kids had stared at her.

"No cuffs," Riley replied.

"Standard operating procedure—"

Riley wheeled on the speaker, freezing the man in mid-stride with the handcuffs swinging before him. "Isn't something we're worried about today, Gautier. Got that?"

Gautier hesitated for a moment and looked thoroughly pissed. "Got it. But if she gets away—"

"No," Riley said. "No getting away. And, Sam, if you try, if I have to shoot you to stop you, I will. Understood?"

"Understood," Sam said. As she looked at the stony glare he gave her, she knew that he meant what he said. She also thought she saw a flicker of sadness in his dark eyes. But when she turned away, she felt his hard gaze on her, tracking like a sniper's cross hairs.

Chapter 8

"Have a seat, St. John."

"No, sir," Sam replied, forcing herself to remain calm. The fact that Director Stone Mitchell hadn't addressed her as "agent" spoke volumes. "I'll stand."

"Suit yourself." Mitchell didn't sound like he cared. He flicked his gaze to Riley. "No handcuffs?"

"My decision," Riley said.

Mitchell waited expectantly for an explanation.

Riley didn't give one. He stood between Sam and the door, to one side of the director so that he could intercept her if she chose to try to attack Mitchell.

"Not a good decision, Agent McLane," Mitchell said.

"She's here." McLane hesitated. "Sir."

Opening a folder on the desk, Mitchell said, "How's your shoulder?"

"Better," Riley answered. "I'll probably be released any day by Medical."

"Probably so." The comment coming from Mitchell sounded like a threat. The director glanced up at Sam. "You've been quiet for twelve days. You haven't asked to see anyone. You haven't asked to talk to anyone."

"Would it have done any good?"

Mitchell's flat expression didn't change. "No."

Sam knew the man was baiting her, offering hope only so he could yank it away. She'd seen him work an interview before.

"We won't let you talk to anyone until we are ready," Mitchell said.

"You're ready now," Sam observed. "And you want me to talk to you. Otherwise I wouldn't be here." She was conscious of Riley watching her, standing silent guard with his hands resting lightly crossed in front of him. "My decision is whether or not I want to talk to you."

"I thought maybe you would want to talk to me," Mitchell suggested. "I could be in a position to help you. Provided you help me."

Sam stayed quiet, smothering a sharp retort. One thing she had learned in all the unfriendly foster homes she'd been in was to stay quiet when she was talking to someone who had power over her and was looking to use it. That was Mitchell now.

Mitchell feigned boredom. Sam didn't buy the act. He was a man who made every moment count. He wouldn't have had her brought to his office for no reason. Not even to kick her while she was down.

"I find myself in a desperate situation," Mitchell admitted. "I've never personally dealt with a traitor before."

Still, Sam told herself, sipping air through her nostrils. Stay still. He's just talking, trying to rattle you.

But *traitor?*

"For the record," Sam said in an icy voice, "I'm not a traitor. Furthermore, for the record, I resent any and all implications and references you have made and you may continue to make about my integrity." She knew someone was taping the interview.

Mitchell's demeanor took on more of an edge. "Who are you protecting?"

"No one."

"Who turned you against this country?"

"I've not turned against this country."

"You've been conducting criminal activities that endanger this country."

Anger seethed inside Sam. "No, sir, I have not."

Mitchell glared at her. "You're lying."

Sam barely held back a hot response.

"Do you know how I know you're lying?" Mitchell challenged.

Confusion swirled within Sam for a moment. Mitchell wasn't a man who bluffed.

"I'm not lying," Sam said.

Mitchell stared at her.

"Sir," Riley said, "maybe—"

"Agent McLane," Mitchell interrupted sharply without looking at Riley, "if you utter another word, I'll have you escorted out of this room."

For a moment Sam thought that Riley was going to

continue his protest. She had no doubt that Mitchell would make good on his threat. Thinking of being in the office facing Mitchell alone, or even with other agents around—being without Riley—wasn't a pleasant thought. She hoped that Riley knew when to shut up.

Riley breathed in deeply through his nose, but didn't say anything.

"Would you like to see the evidence I have?" Mitchell asked.

"Yes, sir," Sam replied. You bet your ass I would.

Without hesitation, Mitchell pressed a button underneath his desk. Across the room, a projector rolled smoothly down from the ceiling like one of the monitors on a passenger jet. The screen pulsed for a moment, then cleared and went to high-definition digital image.

"This is a copy of one of the disks I received from MI-6," Mitchell said.

Sam studied the images. The footage seemed to have been shot in the Middle East. Men, women and children in loose white clothing and some Western clothes converged on an open-air bazaar. Cages containing chickens, crates filled with vegetables and stands of cloth and Western DVDs and Japanese electronics created a maze of merchandizing.

"Do you recognize this place?" Mitchell asked.

Sam studied the footage, waiting for some clue. She was always careful and considered when she was forced into an answer.

Mitchell tapped the keyboard. The video stopped clear and clean, leaving a picture with crystal clarity. "Well?"

"I don't know," Sam answered in a neutral voice. "It

looks like the Middle East. Iran. Iraq. Saudia Arabia. But there are some pockets in Eastern Europe that—"

"It's Suwan," Mitchell said.

Sam took a deep breath. Suwan was the capital of Berzhaan, a small country in the Middle East north of Iran. The United States maintained a presence there to support the current government headed by Prime Minister Omar Razidae.

"You know Suwan," Mitchell said.

"Yes, sir." There was no denying that.

"You've been there."

"Yes, sir." Sam returned Mitchell's gaze. "On assignments. Assignments that you ordered me on." During those missions, she had translated documents agents had stolen from various "businessmen" dealing with the Berzhaan Government as well as the two factions vying for control of the country. Berzhaan had a large amount of undeveloped oil reserves that could turn it into a wealthy nation overnight. But allowing in the wrong foreign power or the wrong foreign corporations could turn it into a puppet state of politics or economics.

"I know," Mitchell said. "However, I hadn't counted on those assignments helping your other, more clandestine, acts."

"I don't know what you're talking about."

"Are you sure about that?"

"Yes."

Mitchell tapped the keyboard again. "Then tell me what you see."

The digital record started again. The camera work was deft and certain. The observer followed a swarthy man in casual Western clothing down the crowded streets. No audio accompanied the video, but Sam could imagine the hubbub of voices that surrounded the slow and steady pursuit through the crowded streets and alleys.

The man met another man in front of a small curio shop.

Mitchell paused the video again. He tapped more buttons and zoomed in on the newcomer's face. "Do you recognize this man?"

The man was heavy-set. His face was broad and soft, marking a life of excesses. He wore a mustache and beard trimmed close to the skin. A scar, pink in its newness, cut through the beard on his left cheek. He wore loose white robes and a burnoose.

"Abdul Hassan." Sam knew the man instantly. She'd been with a team that had tracked him for a few days.

"Correct. And you know what he does?"

"He's an arms dealer. I was with a team that tracked him for a time. He slipped away from us."

"I know," Mitchell stated dryly. "Hassan has been connected with the Q'Rajn for four years. Even before the United States decided to support Prime Minister Razidae and his staff against the Kemeni rebels."

Sam knew that as well. The Kemeni rebels worked to oust the present government and even curried favor with the United States. The Kemenis had taken care not to attack American Consulate staff, business interests or tourists. The Q'Rajn terrorists actively targeted both the current government officials as well as Americans.

"Over those years," Mitchell continued, "Hassan has proven able to slip through the best efforts of the Berzhaan military and the people we've managed to field there. We've had reason to believe that someone hacked into the Agency's files regarding operations in Berzhaan." He pursed his lips. "We've never been able to prove or disprove that." He paused. "Until now."

From the corner of her eye, Sam saw the corners of Riley's mouth turn downward. He was obviously displeased. An impending feeling of doom filled Sam. She'd learned to pay attention to feelings like that while she'd been bounced from house to house. The other shoe was about to drop.

Mitchell set the video into motion again.

Silently, though questions filled her, Sam watched the video. Hassan and the man the observer had been following disappeared into the curio shop. The video cut, picking up from inside the shop as Hassan and his companion entered through the door.

"MI-6 knew where Hassan was going that day," Mitchell said. "They had a man on the inside."

Hassan and the man passed through the shop and walked out into the alley.

Another viewpoint change took place, and this time the man capturing the video was in one of the buildings overlooking the alley behind the shop. Hassan and his companion stood and waited.

"The British team had been dogging their quarry's movements for over a week," Mitchell said. "They'd gotten a tip that Hassan was setting up an arms deal. They wanted to catch him with his hand in the cookie jar."

The camera angle shifted slightly, picking up the dirty white Toyota van that pulled into the alley. Two figures sat in the front seats behind the dirty glass. A moment later the van rocked to a stop in front of Hassan and his companion.

"Watch closely," Mitchell advised. "I don't want you to miss this." He watched Sam instead of the screen.

Sam tried to ignore the CIA director's attention. Her throat felt dry with dread.

"Things move quickly here," Mitchell said. "MI-6 was well set up for their observation. They'd been tipped off early enough to get their agents into play. However, they didn't know the Kemenis had sat in on the game, too. Not until it was too late."

Onscreen, violence broke out. Bullets struck the van, shattering the windshield and striking the driver. The van lurched forward and rammed into the side of the building. Mortar and stone broke free and cascaded to the ground. Other bullets ripped holes along the van's side. Hassan and his companion doubled back into the curio shop. The MI-6 observer leaned out from the window of the building.

"Pay careful attention," Mitchell said.

The rear of the van opened and three people bolted out into the open. Two men and one woman, all carrying assault rifles, took up quick defensive positions around the van.

"Here." Mitchell tapped the keyboard. The camera view locked on the woman. Her face was in profile, her mouth slightly parted in surprise. She wore jeans, a white cotton blouse and a green nylon windbreaker that had to have been hot considering the temperature. She was raising the AK-47 Russian assault rifle she held to her shoulder. "Do you recognize her?"

Sam stared at the woman. There was something familiar about her. The woman was lean and graceful, much
smaller than her companions. Her skin was pale. The eye
that was visible was ice-blue. A burnoose covered the top
of her head, but a few blond hairs leaked around the side.

"Do you recognize her?" Mitchell asked.

"No," Sam said. The picture wasn't clear enough to
make a positive identification.

"Keep watching." Mitchell tapped keys again.

The digitalized video moved at a reduced speed, putting everything in slow motion. Sam would have sworn
that she could see bullets cutting through the air before
striking the van, the wall and the alley floor.

On the screen, the woman pushed up and turned toward
the camera. The empty magazine dropped free of the assault rifle as the woman tugged another one free from a
shoulder bandolier beneath her robe. The folds of her robe
jumped as bullets tore through the material. She moved so
slowly that Sam felt certain the enemy fire was going to
cut her down at any moment.

Just as the woman's face turned toward the MI-6 camera so that Sam could view the woman's face fully, one of
her companions got hit several times. The man jerked
back, responding to the bullets that ripped into his flesh,
standing as he forced himself up in what was going to be
a last-ditch effort to get away. His body blocked the MI-6
operative's view of the woman's face.

"Do you know who it is?" Mitchell asked.

"No," Sam said quietly. *Don't you mean, who she was?*
Sam felt certain that the woman couldn't possibly have
lived through the attack.

Amazingly, the woman was still in motion. Bullets peppered the back of the van where she'd just been. She turned in slow motion, following the speed of Mitchell's presentation. When she stepped out from behind her stricken companion, she was in profile again, presenting the other side of her face. Again Sam had the strange feeling that she knew the woman.

Two Kemeni rebels raced from the other end of the alley. The woman fired deliberate three-round bursts at her attackers as she ran. Both Kemenis went down, tumbling like dervishes in slow motion.

In the next instant, the camera view shifted, dropping and plunging toward the street. The camera tumbled end over end, only occasionally catching the woman as she advanced along the van's side.

"The cameraman was hit and killed," Mitchell said in a quiet, conversational voice. "But the agent who followed Hassan and the unidentified man into the shop was in position by this time."

The view shifted, swinging around quickly to pick up the woman as she ran toward the front of the van. The other MI-6 agent's plunge from the other building caught part of the frame. Sam felt sick to her stomach as the man's body slammed against the alley floor. He fell, sprawled and didn't move. Blood showed on the robes and burnoose he wore. He'd been hit several times.

Onscreen, the woman caught hold of the door and yanked it open. The driver leaned across the steering wheel. From where the second MI-6 observer was, the view afforded showed the inside of the van. Calmly the woman reached inside, grabbed the dead man by the collar, and yanked him out. Bullets that searched for her caught the dead man, jerking his body with the impacts. As the man tumbled to the ground, struck again and again by bullets, the woman stepped up into the cab. Her arm masked her face as she started the van and backed it up.

More Kemeni rebels raced toward her. Rips appeared along the van's front and cracks spiderwebbed the windshield.

The woman drew a pistol and fired smoothly as she continued backing the van free of the wall. Her bullets chopped into the two men and spun them away. A rebel ran for the rear of the van.

Sam felt sure she was about to see the woman gunned down by the surprise assailant.

Incredibly, the woman braked the van and turned around in the seat as the rebel gained the open doors of the van. From the camera's vantage point, Sam saw the woman turn around and point the pistol at the rebel hauling himself into the rear of the van. In the next instant, the rebel toppled back from the van with a bullet between his eyes.

The rearview mirrors, Sam thought, impressed at the woman's skill. That was how she had seen her attacker coming.

One of the woman's companions broke from cover and ran to the van. She waited till he reached her, then gunned the engine and rocketed through the alley. Just once, she looked through the driver's side window to lift her pistol and fire again.

Mitchell froze the image. His timing was impeccable, offering silent proof that he'd grown used to stopping the video in that spot.

"Do you know who she is now?" Mitchell asked.

Not believing what she was seeing, Sam stared into the woman's face. The blond hair, the blue eyes and the features matched hers exactly.

"No." Sam barely forced the word through her clenched teeth. Although she didn't know what was going on, she was certain that she was being set up.

Silently Mitchell worked the keyboard. The image of the blond-haired woman separated from the rest of the violence and filled the left side of the screen. The right side of the screen was dark for only an instant, then another picture surfaced from a murky haze to fill it.

Sam recognized her own CIA ID file picture on the right side of the screen. Although the woman's head was turned at a slightly different angle than her own, Sam knew the resemblance was unmistakable.

"That's not me," Sam insisted.

Mitchell didn't argue. He tapped more keys. The woman on the left turned as the digital reimaging program seized hold and turned her face to the same angle as the ID. In the next moment the two images shuddered, then slid into each other, overlapping so they were two layers deep.

The mystery woman's face slipped over Sam's ID picture like a hand inside a glove.

"That's not me." Sam's voice was weaker than it had been. She knew the woman in the footage wasn't her, but she had no explanation for what she witnessed. "This isn't possible. There's been some mistake. Someone is setting me up. The video is a fake."

"The video isn't faked," Mitchell said. He leaned forward and rested his chin on his index fingers. "I've had experts going over every second of this footage for the last fourteen days. Since the Munich assignment. The video is legitimate."

"It can't be."

Mitchell let out a long sigh. "It is. How long have you been working with the Q'Rajn?"

"I haven't," Sam answered. "And I won't."

"Things would go easier on you if you confessed."

"How would they go easier?"

"You could cut a deal. This thing is bigger than you. There are people who want to know who else is involved. We've got several operations involving Berzhaan that may be compromised. The Agency wants to know how exposed those agents and those operations are." He paused. "*I* want to know."

Tight-lipped and scared, Sam said nothing. She knew there was nothing she could say in her defense.

"St. John," Mitchell prompted.

"That's not me," Sam whispered, staring at the haunting pair of faces on the monitor. "When was this shot?"

"This footage, according to MI-6," Mitchell said, "was shot four months ago. In May."

"I wasn't in Suwan in May," Sam said. "I wasn't even in Berzhaan."

"No," Mitchell agreed. He pulled one of the folders from his desk and opened it. Sam's picture was neatly clipped on the left side of the folder. "But you were in Prague. You could have been in Suwan long enough to manage this arms deal."

Sam remembered Prague. The assignment she'd been

on involved a Chinese director working for Hollywood who worked for the Triads, the Chinese Mafia, and was coordinating arms buys for the rising Romanian criminal underground. With the economic boom Prague was experiencing by becoming a favorite hangout for the jet-set and Hollywood moviemakers, a boom in criminal industry had naturally followed.

Sam had interpreted several documents captured and stolen from the Romanian contingent. Her work, and that of the agents involved in the mission, had resulted in getting a clearer picture of the transportation of money and arms. As a result the fragile trust between the Chinese Triads and the Romanians had almost been dismantled.

"You had a lot of downtime in Prague," Mitchell commented. "You served in an advisory capacity. The agents there left you on your own a lot of the time."

That wasn't exactly how it had been. Sam had been the newest addition to the team. The group had included only one other woman, and she was a field agent, not an expert sidelined to pushing papers. The group had spent a lot of their downtime with each other when they weren't at post. And they had shut Sam out, relying on e-mail transmissions at times. Sometimes days had passed without human contact.

"I. Never. Left." Sam's made her voice cold and hard.

Mitchell regarded her blankly. "Unfortunately, you can't prove that any more than I can."

"There were e-mail transmissions," Sam pointed out.

Mitchell riffed a stack of paper included in the folder. "I have them."

"I never missed a transmission. I was never not there for the team."

"No," Mitchell commented. "No, you weren't. But the e-mail transmissions don't show where you were at the time you made your response. The Agency allowed that open window for you by assigning you a satellite phone and giving you access to a rolling IP address."

Sam couldn't say anything. The rolling Internet Protocol address was SOP in the field, and standard operating procedure existed to protect operatives. Having an agent log on at the same IP address opened the whole mission up to attack if the address was traced.

"I didn't leave Prague," Sam replied.

"Can you prove that?"

Sam met the director's gaze boldly, but felt trapped and helpless. She didn't speak. She *couldn't* speak.

Mitchell leaned back in his chair and kept his eyes locked on the double image on the monitor. "Neither can I."

Fear filled Sam. She controlled it only by using the same skills she'd learned long ago when she was helpless.

"We're both trapped by this, St. John," Mitchell said in a dull voice. "I can't prove that you're guilty, and you can't prove that you're innocent."

"I haven't asked for an attorney," Sam said in a quiet voice, "but I'm asking for one now."

"Duly noted, St. John, but it won't do you any good. Under the Homeland Security Act, the Agency can keep you sequestered here till Hell freezes over."

The sharp bite of tears burned the backs of Sam's eyes. God, she hated feeling helpless. She'd had to feel that way so much of her life.

"Even if the Agency were inclined to set you free or

even use you as bait," Mitchell said, "even if *I* were so inclined, no one can do that. MI-6 lost several agents over
there the last few months. They attribute those losses to information leakage that could only have been gotten from
the CIA." He nodded at the monitor. "They think they
have an answer. If you were set free, it would be like leading a lamb to the slaughter. Their agents are looking for
their pound of flesh. They would find you eventually, and
they won't settle for containing you."

Sam made herself breathe. Her heart thudded like a
lead balloon.

"However," Mitchell continued as he shuffled papers on
his desk, "it appears we have a new problem."

Sam focused on Mitchell. Anything that was a problem
for him might be leverage she could use.

"You know Josie Lockworth, a captain in the USAF,"
Mitchell said.

Josie. Mixed feelings warred within Sam. Rainy's loss
had come without warning. Josie was a pilot in the air force,
and lately she'd been testing her own experimental plane design. Had something happened to Josie? Sam made herself
go dead inside, choosing to feel no hope and no dread.

"We went to school together," Sam answered.

"It seems several of your classmates are curious about
why you didn't put in an appearance at the funeral of your
mutual friend. Josie, who wasn't there, either, has taken it
upon herself to track you down for the group."

Sam didn't respond. If Josie was trying to find her, it
meant Josie was all right.

"Did you know that her grandfather was once a CIA
director?"

Sam waited. She had known that, but she'd gotten into the Agency on her own merits. Although Josie had offered her grandfather's intercession, Sam hadn't wanted any help.

"Joseph Lockworth remains highly thought of," Mitchell stated. "He's still got the ear of several politicians."

Standing at ease in front of Mitchell's desk, Sam kept calm. She knew Mitchell was waiting for her to speak, to ask questions or to claim some kind of triumph.

"Captain Lockworth insists on speaking to you," Mitchell said. "She wants to make certain you know about your friend's death. And she wants to make certain you're all right."

Sam thought that was curious. Why would Josie think anything was wrong with her? It was one thing to wonder why Sam hadn't been at Rainy's funeral, but directly calling the CIA seemed like overkill.

"I've put the captain off as long as possible," Mitchell said. "She's asked her grandfather to intervene. I'm starting to get some pressure from the White House."

Slightly surprised, Sam thought about that. She'd known Joseph Lockworth maintained political connections, and he'd used them to help fund the Athena Academy, but she hadn't known he had enough clout to put pressure on a CIA director in Langley. The fact that Josie had asked her grandfather to do something like that was even more interesting.

"I've been told to grant the air force captain access to you," Mitchell said, clearly not happy about the situation. "But it's going to be limited, and it's going to be monitored."

All right, Sam thought, I can live with that. Josie was good at reading between the lines. All of the Cassandras were.

"I'm going to have an e-mail account established for you," Mitchell told her. "We'll clear the messages you send as well as the ones you receive." He looked at her. "The captain will be informed that you are locked into an important mission and can't call her. The e-mail contact will be limited."

"Josie will check whatever story you give her," Sam said. She knew her friend would do exactly that. "Your cover is going to need to be bulletproof."

"Why should she check?"

"Because she knows it would take a lot to keep me from being at Rainy's funeral."

Mitchell scowled. "We'll make the story bulletproof. But you're going to have to help." He paused, his face totally without emotion. "If Captain Lockworth discovers that you're being held against your will and tries to interfere in any way, this Agency will take appropriate steps. You'll be formally charged with treason. Do you understand?"

"Yes," Sam answered.

"You've got some good friends," Mitchell said, "but I don't know if they'll stand so steadfastly by you once they learn what you've done."

For the first time, Sam thought about that. Until that moment, she hadn't considered what the Cassandras might think of the accusations against her. She wasn't used to thinking about her world impacting the lives of others. She'd always managed a separate existence. Moving away from the academy had effectively pressed the reset button on her independent lifestyle. Except for occasional gatherings. Would they believe her? Or would they believe the charges?

Sam looked at the identical faces on the monitor. The evidence, however it was arranged, was damning.

"So when do I get e-mail access?" Sam stood inside the cell. She wrapped her arms around herself. Even Riley noticed that the room somehow felt colder than when she'd left it.

He stood on the other side of the doorway. He kept his expression neutral. Keeping himself distant from her and the problems she presented was harder. "You'll get it when Mitchell says you do." He stared at her and tried to forget that she looked so damn sexy. He also tried to forget that he'd been responsible for locking her away—again. Guilt was a weapon a spy *used,* not a consequence one suffered.

"Josie won't wait on an answer forever."

"Don't put pressure on me, St. John. I'm not the one calling the shots here."

A flicker of defiance ignited in Sam's ice-blue eyes. Then it passed. "Tell Mitchell that Josie won't wait."

"I think he's already got that impression." Anger roiled inside Riley. He hated leaving her in the cell. The guilt that assailed him twisted through his guts. "It's not my fault you're in here." And he said that more to put things in perspective for himself than to post any blame.

Sam obviously didn't take the assignation of guilt like that. She glared at him. "Do you think I'm a spy for another country? Or a terrorist?"

Riley looked at her for a moment. More than anything, he didn't want to believe the beautiful woman before him could possibly be a spy or served terrorist masters against the country that he loved and had sworn to defend.

Before he could speak, before he even knew what he was going to say, Sam said, "Because if you think that was me in that video footage, then you're an idiot." Without another word she turned away from him and walked toward the wall on the other side of the room.

Unable to stop himself, Riley snarled, "You want to give me another answer, St. John? Want to tell me how that woman just happens to have your face? Want to tell me why anyone would masquerade as a low-level, wannabe field agent to cause problems for the Agency?"

Silence stretched between them for a moment.

"Tell Mitchell," Sam said in a flat, dead voice. "Tell him that Josie Lockworth won't wait long before she attacks the situation another way. That's just how she is."

Riley stood for a moment, trying to think of something to say. In the end he could only close the door and walk away feeling empty and miserable for reasons that he couldn't explain even to himself.

Chapter 9

SO, IF YOU TELL ME WHAT YOU'RE DOING, YOU HAVE TO KILL ME, RIGHT?

Sam stared at the words on the computer monitor. She almost laughed in spite of her situation, and maybe she would have if she hadn't had two agents in the room with her and known that another team was analyzing everything that was sent either way over the Internet connection. Each message was read by the analysis team before being kicked through cyberspace.

THAT'S RIGHT, Sam typed, trying to keep the tone light. SORRY I COULDN'T COME TO THE FUNERAL. Keep the topic to Rainy's death. There's less chance of blowing your cover then.

I MISSED IT, TOO. Josie Lockworth responded. BUT THE OTHERS TOLD ME ABOUT IT. THEY ASKED IF

I'D HEARD FROM YOU. DARCY'S REALLY WOR-
RIED ABOUT YOU.

Back in school, Darcy had been like a mother to Sam,
caring for her and making certain Sam had everything she
needed. At first Sam hadn't wanted all the attention the
other girl had shown. She hadn't known how to react to it.
But once they'd all bonded and become the best of friends,
it had become second nature to her to seek comfort from
Darcy when she felt down. She'd missed the attention
when Darcy had moved away after graduation.

Darcy had shown a gift for theater and the dramatic arts.
After graduation at the Athena Academy, Darcy had gone
on to UCLA and had gotten a job in Hollywood as a
makeup artist. She'd married and had a son, but there had
been trouble that had caused her to split up with her husband. Sam knew that Rainy had helped Darcy leave her
husband, but that was all she knew. Darcy had dropped out
of sight. It was good to know she was back enough to
worry about Sam.

TELL DARCY I'M ALL RIGHT, Sam typed. She sat in
a hard straight-backed chair in front of the notebook computer on a rolling cart.

YOU SHOULD TELL HER YOURSELF. I HAVE
HER PHONE NUMBER.

I CAN'T MAKE PHONE CALLS FROM HERE.

CAN'T YOU GIVE ME A HINT WHERE "HERE" IS?

*I DON'T HAVE TIME TO TRACK YOU DOWN, AND
THEY TELL ME YOU HAVE TO BURY THE BODIES RE-
ALLY DEEP. BESIDES THAT, THE AIR FORCE WOULD
PROBABLY MISS YOU AND THERE WOULD BE ALL
KINDS OF FORMS TO FILL OUT.*

LOL. JUST TELL ME YOU'RE SOMEPLACE EX-OTIC, WHERE GUYS IN SWIMSUITS PLAY VOL-LEYBALL IN THE SAND ALL DAY AND ALL THE DRINKS COME WITH THOSE CUTE LITTLE PLAS-TIC UMBRELLAS.

YEAH, Sam typed. *IT'S REALLY INCREDIBLE HERE.* She was fifteen days into her incarceration now. The four walls remained the same. Although, when she paced the cell and the area measured out the same distance, she still had the definite feeling that the walls were closing in on her.

AFTER WHAT SEEMS LIKE ENDLESS DAYS OF LAB AND DESERT, ANYPLACE WOULD SEEM EX-OTIC TO ME.

LUCKY ME, Sam replied. *OF COURSE, I CAN'T MEET ANYONE, AND DOING ENDLESS AUDIO AND WRITTEN TRANSLATIONS CAN'T BE THAT MUCH DIFFERENT THAN STARING AT BLUEPRINTS ALL DAY. OR PLAYING IN A WIND TUNNEL WITH MODEL PLANES.*

SO THE SPY WORLD ISN'T ALL THAT EXCIT-ING?

NO.

BET YOU NEVER THOUGHT YOU'D GROW UP TO BE A REAL-LIFE SPY.

NOT ONCE. Or arrested for being a traitor to my country. Thinking about the threat Mitchell had made, about how the Cassandras would react once they found out about the charges of treason that could be filed against her, Sam realized that Josie most of all would more than likely turn against her. Sam had several pictures of Josie in her air force uniforms as she'd gone through ranks. More than that, Josie was currently working in the espionage field herself, though from a research and development angle.

I HAVE DARCY'S E-MAIL ADDRESS, Josie typed.

I'LL HAVE TO GET CLEARANCE TO USE IT. THIS OPERATION IS CLOSED UP TIGHT.

I UNDERSTAND. I'VE BEEN LIVING IN A LAB MYSELF. FOR FREAKING MONTHS!!!

THE PLANE? Josie was working with a robot spy plane that could be remote controlled from space-based satellites.

OF COURSE, THE PLANE.

Deciding that talking about top-secret projects was getting a little too close to home, Sam asked, *HOW ARE RAINY'S PARENTS?* Despite her choice to live in Arizona after college instead of returning to California where her family still lived, Rainy had remained close to her mom and dad.

THEY'RE TAKING IT HARD. SO IS MARSHALL.

Marshall Carrington was Rainy's husband. Sam had met him a few times and liked him.

I NEVER DID FIND OUT WHAT HAPPENED TO RAINY, Sam typed. *THE ONLY INFORMATION I'VE SEEN SAID THAT IT WAS A TRAFFIC ACCIDENT.*

THAT'S HOW IT WAS WRITTEN UP. SINGLE-CAR COLLISION. THE INVESTIGATORS BELIEVE RAINY FELL ASLEEP IN THE CAR AND WENT OFF THE ROAD.

Sam stared at the line of type. The words seemed so artless and ineffective. She didn't think anyone's death should have been summed up so succinctly, so bloodlessly. She hesitated before she started typing again.

THAT DOESN'T SOUND LIKE RAINY. SHE WAS AL-WAYS CAREFUL ABOUT EVERYTHING SHE DID. IF SHE WERE SLEEPY, SHE WOULD HAVE PULLED OFF THE ROAD AND STAYED SOMEWHERE. OR HAD MARSHALL COME GET HER.

I KNOW. NONE OF US CAN BELIEVE IT. ESPE-CIALLY SINCE RAINY INVOKED THE CASSANDRA PROMISE AND WAS ON HER WAY TO MEET US AT ATHENA WHEN SHE CRASHED. DIDN'T YOU GET A MESSAGE FROM HER? IT WAS EARLY AUGUST.

Sam swallowed. Rainy had called on the Cassandra Promise? That meant something serious had happened.

I DIDN'T GET THE MESSAGE. I'VE BEEN IN THE FIELD FOR A FEW MONTHS. WHAT DID SHE SAY?

WE NEVER FOUND OUT. SHE WAS GOING TO TELL US WHEN SHE GOT TO ATHENA. WE ALL THINK IT'S SIGNIFICANT THAT SHE DIED ON HER WAY THERE. The cursor blinked for a moment. ALEX SAT IN ON RAINY'S AUTOPSY, BUT SHE DIDN'T FEEL LIKE THE EXAM WAS ENOUGH. SHE GOT MARSHALL'S PERMISSION TO DO ANOTHER POST. KAYLA HELPED HER MOVE RAINY'S BODY TO ATHENS AND SHE EXAMINED RAINY HER-SELF. SHE FOUND SOMETHING REALLY STRANGE.

WHAT?

Alexandra Forsythe was a forensic investigator for the FBI. She'd become a recognized authority in her field. Kayla Ryan was a lieutenant in the Youngstown Police Department and served in the Athens satellite station. She and her daughter, Jazz, lived in Athens. As a single mother and a police lieutenant, Kayla wouldn't have wasted time on something she didn't believe in. Likewise, with her contacts through the police department, she would have had access to all the information regarding Rainy's death.

Together, Alex and Kayla must have turned the investigation upside down and inside out.

REMEMBER WHEN RAINY TOLD US ABOUT THE APPENDECTOMY SHE HAD WHEN SHE WAS TWELVE? Josie typed.

YES.

WELL, THE PRELIMINARY AUTOPSY SHOWED THAT RAINY STILL HAD HER APPENDIX.

The information sent a chill through Sam.

LATER THAT NIGHT, SOMEONE BROKE INTO THE MORGUE AND ALEX WALKED IN ON IT. SHE THOUGHT THE PERSON WAS TRYING TO DO SOMETHING TO RAINY'S BODY.

WHO WAS IT? WHAT WAS HE TRYING TO DO?

DON'T KNOW. HE GOT AWAY. BUT DURING ALEX'S POST IN ATHENS, SHE FOUND OLD SCARS ON RAINY'S OVARIES.

HER OVARIES?

YES.

WHY? Sam typed.

THIS IS WHERE IT STARTS GETTING FREAKY. WHILE KAYLA WAS SEARCHING THROUGH RAINY'S THINGS, KAYLA FOUND OUT RAINY HAD BEEN DOING RESEARCH ON EGG MINING. YOU'RE FAMILIAR WITH THAT?

FOR FERTILITY TREATMENT.

EXACTLY.

WHAT WAS RAINY'S INTEREST?

AT FIRST WE THOUGHT IT WAS BECAUSE SHE AND MARSHALL WERE HAVING TROUBLE GETTING PREGNANT AND WERE CONSIDERING IN-VITRO. BUT NOW WE THINK SHE'D SOMEHOW DISCOVERED THAT SHE HADN'T HAD AN APPENDECTOMY ALL THOSE YEARS AGO AND WAS ABOUT TO FIGURE OUT WHAT HAD REALLY HAPPENED. ALL OF US—KAYLA, ALEX, DARCY AND ME—THINK RAINY WAS MURDERED TO COVER UP THE TRUTH ABOUT WHAT SOMEONE DID TO HER. WE THINK HER EGGS WERE MINED.

Sam stared at the screen.

WHEN KAYLA INVESTIGATED ALEX'S CAR, SHE FOUND OUT THE SEAT BELT HAD FAILED.

The announcement struck a chord in Sam's mind. Accidents and failed seat belts reminded her of something she'd studied during her CIA training.

THERE WAS NO REASON FOR THE SEAT BELT TO FAIL, Josie typed. IT JUST DID.

Sam reached for the memory but couldn't quite find it.

KAYLA WANTED ME TO ASK YOU A FAVOR IF I GOT IN TOUCH WITH YOU, Josie typed.

ANYTHING, Sam typed.

SHE WANTED YOU TO CHECK THROUGH RAINY'S FILES. SEE IF ONE OF THE ENEMIES RAINY MADE AS AN ATTORNEY MIGHT HAVE HAD MOTIVE TO KILL HER.

I CAN LOOK AROUND. Sam would force Mitchell to allow her to do that. Or assign someone like Howie Dunn to do that.

LET ME KNOW WHAT YOU FIND OUT. WE WANT TO CHECK ALL POSSIBILITIES.

I WILL.

ANOTHER WEIRD THING HAPPENED, TOO. ALEX CAUGHT AN FBI AGENT SNOOPING AROUND AT ATHENA.

WHY WOULD THE FBI BE INTERESTED? Again, that tendril of almost-recognition danced in Sam's brain.

HE DIDN'T STICK AROUND TO TELL HER. ALEX WILL TRACK HIM DOWN.

The cursor paused again. Sam waited, absorbing the information. Had someone stolen Rainy's eggs when she was just a kid, and then killed her years later when she found out what they'd done?

Josie finally continued. AND HERE'S ANOTHER WEIRD THING. WHILE KAYLA WAS CHECKING RAINY'S MEDICAL FILES AT ATHENA, SHE BLACKED OUT.

WHAT CAUSED IT?

DON'T KNOW. SHE WAS EXAMINED AND FOUND HEALTHY. YOU KNOW KAYLA. HARDLY EVER SICK. SHE JUST…PASSED OUT. NO WARNING.

The near-memory tugged at Sam's attention again. Something was there, but she couldn't get hold of it. Mysterious blackouts and failed seat belts tied together somehow.

YOU'LL LET ME KNOW WHAT THEY FIND OUT?

OF COURSE. WANT TO HEAR SOME NEWS THAT WILL WANT TO MAKE YOU BARF?

NOT REALLY.

WELL, YOU'RE GOING TO ANYWAY. GUESS WHO SHOWED UP AT THE FUNERAL?

Sam remembered the vast number of people. The possibilities were staggering. DON'T KNOW.

SHANNON CONNER.

The memory twisted through Sam's mind. Shannon had been a student at the Athena Academy, too. She'd started the same year that the Cassandras had, and had been part of another orientation group led by Allison Gracelyn. In their junior year, Shannon had tried to frame Josie for theft and create a black mark against all of the Cassandras. Tory had proven that Shannon had staged the theft. As a result, Shannon had gotten kicked out of the academy, the first and only girl to ever be expelled from the school, as far as Sam knew.

Shannon had gone on to success, though. Oddly enough, she'd become a TV news reporter—as had Tory. Occasionally, Sam had seen Shannon on cable anchoring news for ABS, Tory's rival station. Tory was a reporter for UBS and covered world news, seeking out headline stories. The rivalry that had begun at the academy had continued out into the world of news. Shannon seemed to be constantly on Tory's trail, on the verge of getting stories that Tory scooped her on.

WHAT WAS SHANNON DOING THERE? Sam asked.

SOMEHOW SHANNON HEARD ABOUT THE EGG-MINING POSSIBILITY. WE STILL DON'T KNOW HOW. SHANNON SHOWED UP AT THE CHURCH RIGHT AFTER THE SERVICE AND STARTED ASKING ALL KINDS OF QUESTIONS ABOUT SCIENTIFIC EXPERIMENTS BEING DONE ON RAINY AND OTHER ATHENA STUDENTS.

YOU'RE KIDDING.

NO. ALEX TOLD HER OFF, BUT IT DID HIT THE NEWS.

The cursor blinked for a moment while Sam gathered her thoughts. She was having to deal with *way* too much in a short amount of time.

OOOOOOPPPS! Josie wrote. GOTTA SCOOT. GOT ANOTHER MEETING TO ATTEND THAT I'M ABOUT TO BE LATE FOR, AND I'M THE ONE HOSTING IT. GOOD TALKIN' TO YA. STAY IN TOUCH, SPYGIRL.

I WILL.

I'LL BE CHECKING IN ON YOU FROM TIME TO TIME.

DO THAT, Sam typed, and hoped that her friend would. The contact with the outside world, brief as it was, made her situation easier to bear. She logged off the computer.

Without a word, the two CIA agents bundled the computer, the chair and the cart up and departed.

Filled with nervous energy and frustration that she wasn't there with her friends, that she wasn't helping look into Rainy's death if they all felt something had warranted the attention, Sam started pacing. Once she caught herself doing that, she took a couple of quick breaths, then launched into her martial arts forms, hoping to find temporary peace there.

Riley McLane had been missing for the past three days, which bothered her, as well. Her nights rotated nightmares about finding Rainy in her wrecked car and unsettling dreams of naked racquetball games with Riley. The nightmares had disrupted her sleep with fears and pain and loss. But the nude dreams had left Sam frustrated in ways she'd never before experienced.

* * *

SOMETHING TRULY WEIRD IS GOING ON, SPYGIRL.

Trepidation oozed through Sam as she read Josie Lockworth's message.

WHAT DO YOU MEAN? Sam typed.

ALEX HAD A FAINTING EPISODE, TOO. LIKE KAYLA. ALEX, WHO'S HARDLY HAD A SICK DAY IN HER LIFE.

Sam stared at the screen. Nearly two weeks had passed since she'd first chatted with Josie over e-mail. She'd been locked up for a month. Personally, she knew she was a surprise to the CIA who were keeping her under observation. Only the resiliency she'd learned as a child served to keep her physically, mentally and emotionally away from the abyss of loneliness and despair.

None of the other Cassandras had been cleared for contact. Sam had the impression that Mitchell wasn't going to make that happen unless he was forced to. However, Mitchell had allowed Howie Dunn to search for possible enemies among Rainy's clients. There hadn't been any, and she had let Kayla know via Josie.

HOW DID THE BLACKOUT HAPPEN? Sam asked.

ALEX WAS DRIVING HOME FROM WORK. DRIVING. JUST LIKE RAINY.

Sam automatically fit the details to the scenario she had created about Rainy. *WHAT ABOUT THE SEAT BELT?*

IT HELD. SO IF SOMEONE WAS BEHIND ALEX'S BLACKOUT, THEY DIDN'T WANT IT TO LOOK TOO MUCH LIKE RAINY'S ACCIDENT.

ALEX IS OKAY?

YES, THANK GOD. SHE WAS REALLY LUCKY.

Sam's throat closed up, Someone was after her friends…and she couldn't help them.

ALEX FOUND OUT MORE ABOUT THE MYSTERIOUS FBI AGENT. I JUST FOUND OUT TODAY MYSELF AND WANTED TO LET YOU KNOW.

TELL ME.

HIS NAME IS JUSTIN COHEN. REMEMBER THE LEGEND AROUND ATHENA ABOUT THE DARK ANGEL?

Sam did. And back in school, Alex had actually seen him from a distance. The young man had broken in to the academy twice, the second time being while the Cassandras were there. He'd claimed the academy had killed his sister. Over the years, the Dark Angel had become something of a Robin Hood figure to the school, a legend the girls giggled over late at night.

JUSTIN COHEN IS THE DARK ANGEL. HIS SISTER DIED ABOUT NINE MONTHS AFTER RAINY'S "APPENDECTOMY." DOING THE MATH ON THIS ONE, SPYGIRL?

YEAH.

TURNS OUT THAT JUSTIN'S SISTER, KELLY, ACCEPTED FIFTY THOUSAND DOLLARS TO BECOME A SURROGATE MOTHER. UNFORTUNATELY, SOMETHING WENT WRONG WITH THE PREGNANCY AND SHE DIED.

WHAT ABOUT THE BABY?

HOSPITAL RECORDS SAY IT DIED AS WELL. DARCY IS CHECKING UP ON THE POSSIBILITY

OF OTHER SURROGATE MOTHERS. RAINY MIGHT HAVE A CHILD OUT THERE. IN A STRANGER'S HANDS.

That thought chilled Sam. *WHO DID THIS?* she asked.

WE DON'T KNOW YET. BUT HERE'S WHY JUSTIN BELIEVES ATHENA ACADEMY HAS SOMETHING TO DO WITH HIS SISTER'S DEATH. THE NURSE WHO TOOK CARE OF HER AT THE HOSPITAL WAS BETSY STONE. KAYLA'S GOING TO TALK TO HER.

Sam sat, stunned. Betsy Stone had been Athena's resident nurse since the academy began. Sam chatted with Josie a little while longer, batting around possibilities, that Betsy Stone or Athena Academy were in on whatever had happened to Rainy. All too soon, their chat time was up.

When she was alone again, Sam's thoughts turned dark. Someone had claimed the life of one of her friends and nearly taken the life of another. As long as the Cassandras saw fit to pursue the mystery, Sam felt certain that all of their lives were potentially forfeit.

And she was stuck in a damn cell on bogus charges that she couldn't disprove and couldn't begin to understand. She couldn't help them. Most of all she hated the helpless feeling that filled her.

However, the past two weeks hadn't gone unrewarded. She'd finally remembered the elusive memory involving failed seat belts and blackouts. Now all she had to do was get someone to listen to her.

Riley stopped in front of the security door to Sam's private holding cell and pushed his hand against the palm scanner mounted to the right. The screen pulsed and the reader read his palm print. Three seconds later after the ID had been confirmed by the automated system and the agent manning security on the video camera overlooking the hallway, the locks clicked open.

He started to enter, then felt uncomfortable just barging in. Sam was waiting for him. He knew that because he'd stopped off at the observation room after his arrival. And she had sent for him. Still, he couldn't help thinking that just walking in was an invasion of whatever privacy she had left.

He closed his fist and knocked. The thumps sounded hollow and lonesome out in the hallway. She'd been inside for five weeks, more or less in solitary confinement. He knew he couldn't have gone as long as she had and still remain as sane as she was. It was almost as if she thrived on the solitude.

"Come in." Sam's voice sounded surprisingly normal.

Taking a deep breath, Riley pushed the door open and followed it inside.

Sam stood across the room, leaving plenty of space between them. She wore sweatpants and a sleeveless shirt that muffled her natural curves somewhat.

"You knocked," Sam pointed out.

Riley nodded. "Seemed like the thing to do."

"Thank you for that."

"You're welcome." Out of habit Riley swept the room with his peripheral vision. He spotted the white rose beneath the bed. The flower looked fragile and delicate.

"Thanks for coming, too," she added. She wrapped her arms around herself, showing a hint of insecurity.

"I was told it was urgent. If Mitchell hadn't okayed the meet, I wouldn't have been able to come."

"I think he expects me to confess everything to you."

Disappointment flooded Riley. He didn't want to be the confessor figure. If Sam had really worked with terrorists smuggling arms, he didn't want to be the one to go on record as a witness, didn't want to hear it from her lips. But he would, and the room's surveillance systems would keep track of her every word.

"Don't worry, McLane," she said. "I'm not confessing to anything."

Riley felt immediately relieved, then got frustrated with himself. He didn't like the fact that she was able to see through him so easily.

"I'm not worried," he said.

"If you say so."

Her casual dismissal of his brief defense irritated him. "What did you want, St. John?" His tone came out harsher than he'd intended.

Sam dropped her arms to her sides and placed her right foot behind her left at a ninety-degree angle. The movement was unconscious, and Riley felt she hadn't even noticed her own movements. He felt bad about her response. He couldn't help wondering how many harsh voices she'd endured in those foster homes, and how many of them led to other forms of abuse.

"I didn't mean to interrupt whatever you had planned," Sam said.

"I didn't have anything planned."

An eyebrow arched over one ice-blue eye. Her look took on a sardonic cast. "Rumpled slacks, ditto on the shirt and tie and a sports coat. I don't think you were at home watching ESPN with the guys."

"I was out."

"And unless my eyesight is failing me, that's a lipstick smudge on your shirt collar."

Riley resisted the impulse to reach for his shirt. He had been out with someone he occasionally dated and slept with while in the Langley area. The woman was a fellow agent he'd developed a casual relationship with in the field and had tracked that back into the occasional hotel room. Neither of them took the relationship home or took the involvement as anything more than physical release.

"I was out," Riley said.

For a minute he thought she was going to press him on the issue.

Then she broke eye contact. "I didn't mean to intrude on your personal life."

"You didn't."

"Maybe the woman you were with felt like I did."

"It's a friendship, St. John." Agents who spent most of their time out in the field undercover or beating the bushes learned to have liaisons rather than love affairs, one-night stands instead of meaningful relationships. Riley had seen too many agent marriages crumble under the pressure of long-distance relationships and a job that was anything but nine to five. Of course, there were exceptions to the rule, but he'd never wanted to buck the odds, or found a woman worth taking the chance with.

"You have many friends like that?" Her tone was sharp.

Riley thought about how he should respond. The answer was no, but the woman he'd been with was truly a friend. They shared themselves when they could and when they needed to let someone in who understood the dark and dangerous world in which they lived. But it had to be someone who wouldn't take it personally when each of them chose to shut down and deal with personal crises and issues when those times came.

There had been other women over the years. Some had moved on. Two of them were dead, and one of them Riley had killed when she'd tried to murder him.

"Forget it." Sam raised her hands and brushed the question away. "What you do isn't any of my business."

Riley wanted to tell her that, no, it wasn't any of her business, but he was too surprised. Is that just a little jealousy, St. John? Is that what's going on here? The thought took him totally by surprise. Still, it was understandable because he hadn't been able to be as cold and strict as Mitchell during the few times they'd encountered each other.

"She's just a friend," Riley said, before he could stop himself.

"Okay. You have a friend. I got that." Those ice-blue eyes flashed angrily.

Riley felt even more uncomfortable and grew increasingly irritated with himself. Her reaction to the situation wasn't logical, but she had a reason not to be logical. She'd been locked up for five weeks with limited human contact and a hell of a stress load on her. He, on the other hand, had no excuse for the way he felt. He'd abandoned a warm and willing woman in a hotel she had paid for to come and stand before another woman who was probably the most trouble he'd ever seen. All so he could feel guilty and mad at himself.

"My friend has nothing to do with this, St. John," he growled.

"Good. Then I'm happy for you and your friend."

"Is that what you called me here for? To pick a fight?"

"I'm not picking a fight."

"You should try standing on this side of the conversation."

Sam looked at him. "Try being locked up for five weeks."

Riley held his hands up at his sides. "Okay. You win. You've got it worse than I do. I hope calling me here and reading me the riot act about the fact that I have a life and you don't helps you out."

"I don't need help."

"And I don't need the grief." Riley turned toward the door, cursing himself out for not simply staying away. When Mitchell had called about Sam's request, the director had advised him to stay away, but they both recognized the fact that Sam had more resources to survive in her situation than just about anyone they knew. That was saying a lot. So Riley had come and Mitchell had allowed it because Sam had them both over the barrel. Riley needed to exorcise some of his guilt, and Mitchell still needed answers regarding the terrorist activity in Berzhaan.

"Riley." Her voice was softer, more vulnerable. "Wait."

Standing still, one hand on the door, Riley said, "I can't help you, Sam. You're going to have to help yourself out of this mess. I don't have any answers."

"Please." Her voice broke.

"Mitchell's not going to listen to me," Riley said. "And I don't have anything to tell him."

"It's not about me."

He waited, not knowing what she was going to say.

"I think my friends might be in danger."

That caught Riley's attention and came far enough out of left field that he turned around. "What friends?"

Sam glanced pointedly at the lipstick mark on his collar. "Obviously not the same kind of friends that you have."

He looked at her, not knowing how to respond but unwilling to leave her. Damn, but she looked so vulnerable with her arms wrapped around herself. Just the same, he knew she'd try to kick his ass if he mentioned it.

She broke eye contact and let out a shuddering breath. "I'm sorry. That's not what I intended to say. I apologize. I'm just not very good at being helpless."

"It's okay. If I was in your shoes, I don't think I could handle five weeks of solitude."

Her eyes flashed again. "Being trapped in here isn't the problem, McLane. I can do this. Sooner or later I'll get out. No matter what Mitchell says or does, I know that's true. Believing anything else just won't work. I've been in lots of places worse than this."

For a split second Riley got an image of what Sam St. John had been like as a foster child. Quiet and willful, she'd learned to bide her time even when she was very small.

"The problem is I can't help them," she went on.

"Your friends?"

Sam nodded.

"Are they in trouble?"

"I think so."

"What makes you think that?"

"From the information Josie has been giving me."

"Josie?" Then the name clicked. "You mean Captain

Lockworth." Riley hadn't been part of that information loop.

"Yes."

"What kind of trouble?"

"I think they may be in danger."

"From what?"

"Not what," Sam corrected. "Whom."

Riley pointed to the bed. "Do you mind if I sit?"

"Go ahead."

Crossing the room, Riley sat on the edge of the bed. He tried not to remember that she slept there, all curled up tight in a ball against the wall in the corner. The bed was neatly made, with military precision corners. One of Sam's earliest foster parents had been an army drill sergeant. Evidently he'd taught her how to make beds.

"Whom do you think your friends are in danger from?" he asked.

Sam held his gaze for a moment, then looked away. "I don't know." Before Riley could say anything, she hurried on. "I also think Rainy was killed. I don't think she died in a traffic accident."

Surprised, Riley looked at Sam. "You're saying she was murdered?"

Sam took a deep breath. The answer came hard. "Yes. My friends think so, too."

"Why?"

"You'd have to have known Rainy," Sam said. "Dying in some kind of accident—" Emotion took her words.

Tears gleamed in her ice-blue eyes, and Riley knew it took a real effort of will not to let them fall.

When Sam continued, her throat was husky with pain.

"Rainy—Rainy just wouldn't have died in an accident. She was one of the most complete people I've known."

Riley spoke softly, wishing he could ease Sam's pain. "Accidents happen, Sam. Life has a habit of not turning out the way we think it should."

"Rainy's death wasn't an accident. Her seat belt failed."

That caught Riley's attention. "Failed?"

"Yes. And that isn't all."

Though Riley was certain that Sam didn't know what she was doing, she started to pace. He watched her, trying to figure out what her angle was, what she wanted from him. His attention kept wandering to the taut flesh that rippled beneath her sweatpants. Even the loose material couldn't disguise the coiling and bunching taking place.

In terse sentences, Sam briefed Riley on the information about Rainy and the blackouts that had befallen two of her other friends. Her report was nearly emotionless as she stayed centered.

When she stopped her report, he asked, "If we accept that your friend was murdered, your other friends' blackouts were caused by the same source—"

"Kayla and Alex," Sam said.

Riley looked at her.

"Their names," Sam said.

"Kayla's the police lieutenant?"

"Yes."

"And Alex is the forensics expert with the FBI?" Riley remembered the woman from the research he'd done with Howie Dunn.

Sam nodded.

"She sat in on the autopsy before the funeral?"

"That's what Josie said. The Cassandras—"

"Cassandras?"

An embarrassed look flashed on Sam's beautiful features. "A name we gave ourselves. The academy was big on breaking the new students into groups that worked together. We were the Cassandras."

Riley waited. She didn't continue, so he prompted her. "And Josie's working on a spy plane."

Sam shot him a quick, suspicious look. "I didn't tell you that."

But Riley knew from the disoriented flicker in her eyes that for just an instant she thought she might have. "You didn't tell me that, Sam. I did background checks on all the women you went to school with. I don't know the particulars of what Josie is doing, but I know what program she's attached to."

"That's privileged information."

"Yeah, but when you're dealing with someone who might be assisting terrorist activity against the United States, a lot of doors get opened damn quick." Too late, Riley realized the pain his words caused Sam. "I didn't mean anything by that, Sam. It was just a statement of fact. Once you were labeled a threat, I was given a blank check to prowl."

Taking a deep breath, getting rid of the emotion, Sam nodded. "Okay. Fine. We'll make that work for us."

"We?" Riley repeated. "Us?"

She looked at him in exasperation. "I need help. Haven't you been listening?"

"Sure I've been listening. But all you've trotted out is a lot of supposition."

"Supposition didn't get Rainy killed. Neither did a failed seat belt. There's an assassin out there." Sam drew a breath. "He's code-named the Cipher."

A chill touched Riley then. He'd heard of the Cipher. No intelligence agency knew much about the man. Or if he was a man for certain. He was a phantom, supposedly able to walk through solid walls and assassinate targets.

"No one even knows if the Cipher exists," Riley said.

"Then give me the chance to find out."

"How?"

"Let me have the files on every assassination that the Cipher's name has turned up in. Let me research him."

"I thought he was a myth. A bogeyman the intelligence community dreamed up to challenge new recruits."

"Do you remember what his signature is? The thing that all of his kills reportedly have in common?"

Riley shook his head.

"All of his victims fall asleep before they die in what is supposed to be an accident."

"How do you know this?"

"He's mentioned in the files on Berzhaan. I read about him—or her—while I was working the op in Suwan last year."

"You read this a year ago?"

"Yes."

"And you haven't forgotten it?"

"I forget very little of what I read or see or hear," Sam replied. "Gift for languages, remember? That's part of how it seems to work for me."

Riley was impressed. Mostly he operated by garbage in,

garbage out. If he attained knowledge but didn't use it at least every now and again, he lost it.

"Let's go with that for a moment, then," he said. "Let's assume there is some master assassin lurking out there in the deep shadows between nations. Why would he be interested in your friends?"

"Have you been keeping up with the news?"

"World events. Baseball scores."

"You researched the Athena Academy."

"Yes."

"Have you heard about the potential scandal going on there? About students being used for scientific experiments without their knowledge?"

That caught Riley's attention. "No."

"The story was reported by Shannon Conner."

"Who's she?"

"A reporter for the ABS network. She was also a student at Athena for a time."

"Is there any truth to the scientific experimentation accusation?"

"Not that I know of. But the academy does have a medical facility and a lot of lab space."

"If there's no scientific experimentation going on—"

"Listen to me." Sam's face took on a hard cast. "All the Cassandras made a vow—a promise to come, no questions asked, if any one of us called. It was only to be used in dire circumstances. Rainy made that call while I was in Munich in August. She died on the way to the meeting. I'm not buying for a minute that it was some tragic accident. I think she discovered something. And was killed for it."

"Sam—"

"Riley," Sam pleaded, "I just need you to get me access to those files. That's all."

Staring at her, Riley turned the situation around in his head, trying to find what it was Sam hoped to gain by convincing him of the reality of the hit-and-run assassin. Even if she proved the Cipher was after her friends, she wasn't going to get out of solitary confinement. She still had the terrorist charges to answer.

"Mitchell's not going to go for it," he said.

"Make him."

"I'll tell him to talk to you." Riley stood to leave.

"He won't listen to me."

"That's up to you." Riley started for the door.

In a quick blur of motion, Sam intercepted him. She put one firm, small hand against his chest. Her touch seared his skin. Her musk and traces of soap and shampoo, a hint of cologne, filled his nostrils. The urge to take her in his arms and crush her to him filled him.

And then she'd break your neck for trying anything, Riley chided himself. He had to steel himself. "What are you doing, St. John?"

Those ice-blue eyes peered into his soul. "Trying to convince you to help me help my friends."

"By bucking Mitchell?" Riley shook his head. "That's not going to—" Before he could say anything further, Sam snaked a hand behind his neck and pulled his face down toward hers. At first he almost resisted, thinking she was going to put him in some kind of martial arts hold.

Then he felt her hot lips colliding with his with bruising force. Control slipped through his fingers in the space of a single, ragged breath.

Chapter 10

Sam couldn't believe she was doing what she was doing. Or with whom. All those evenings she'd sometimes thought of Riley McLane after a racquetball game, or after a briefing or debriefing she'd attended that he'd been involved in, seemed to come alive in her mind as she kissed him. Worse than that, all those nights she'd dreamed of him in the nude came to the forefront of her mind.

Electricity passed through her body, filling her with a heated rush of liquid desire. At first he didn't kiss her back. Maybe he doesn't find you attractive, she told herself. And maybe if you didn't have your face glued to his and you were in better control of yourself, you'd worry about that.

But she wasn't worried. At least, she definitely wasn't worried enough. More than anything, she was amazed at how easily her body responded to his. She'd never done any heavy kissing before, never been involved with a male at all before. There hadn't been a need, and she'd never experienced more than a fleeting desire. She'd always judged the cost too high.

She didn't want to end up wrecked like some of the women she knew had. In their last year at Athena Academy Kayla had fallen for Mike Bridges, a young officer she'd met, and ended up raising a child on her own.

Sam had always had her hands full keeping herself together. There had always been lines that she wouldn't cross, chances that she wouldn't take. It had been one thing to pit herself against a physical exertion—she'd known her abilities, and she'd had to trust only in herself. But a relationship? No way. That had never felt safe. She would have had to place too much trust outside herself.

However, at the moment, she was surprised at how right everything felt, as though this was something she barely remembered but still had the knowledge to perform.

The lack of response from her partner shook her confidence, though. Embarrassed, she tried to think of a way to disentangle herself from Riley with at least a shred of self-respect and dignity. Stepping away from his lean, muscular body was going to be one of the hardest things she'd ever done.

Through sheer willpower, she forced herself back. Their lips parted for an instant. Then Riley swept over her with a cry that was part pain and part passion. He wrapped his arms around her, lifting her from the floor. A dozen martial arts moves flickered through her mind, all of them ways of breaking his hold on her, of escaping his grasp.

But that was the last thing she wanted to do at the moment.

His mouth pressed against hers. His lips melded to hers, blowing her mind and tearing apart her doubts. This moment was crystal clear; it was right and she seized it. His kiss was hot and couldn't be denied. Her lips parted involuntarily and she felt his tongue invade her mouth. She craved the taste of him, the strength and determination of him, and she blended it to her own. Before she knew what she was doing, she'd doubled her fists up in his jacket and pulled herself up his lean frame. Her legs lifted and wrapped around his hips, pulling him against her.

He held tight. She held him just as fiercely, as though if she let go she would fall a million miles.

Stumbling, he reached the wall beside the door. He put a hand behind her head, cupping her neck and turning her face more up to his. Braced against the wall, she released her hold with her arms and put her hands on the sides of his face. Whiskers felt like fine sandpaper to her touch, and the rough texture sent another wave of desire thrilling through her. Her breath came in ragged gasps, worse than it did when she put herself through her forms.

He moved against her, his hips grinding into hers. She felt his erection through his clothing and hers, hard and insistent, and knew what it was instantly even though she'd never had the pleasure before. And it was pleasure. She couldn't *believe* how much pleasure was involved in the contact. He rubbed against her, and she felt incredibly exposed. Wanted to be even more exposed.

His hands slid under her shirt. His callused palms caressed her back, spanned her shoulders, then slipped around to her breasts. He covered her breasts with his hands, and her erect nipples scraped against his flesh. An ache like nothing she'd ever experienced shot through her. Part of her, that small part of her mind that remained civilized, screamed at her that what she was doing was wrong.

Sam didn't care. Maybe what she was doing was wrong, but it felt right enough at the moment. Her hips bucked against his, increasing the pressure against both their bodies. She felt his response as he grew even harder.

"Sam," Riley croaked, breathing into her mouth, then inhaling and taking her breath away. His voice was hard and tight, totally male. He turned his head, breaking the kiss. His body surged against hers. "We can't do this."

She wanted to scream, *Why not?* But she couldn't be distracted that long. Her mouth sought his again. Maybe he whispered no, but his body screamed yes.

"Sam. No."

No? Even that only barely penetrated. Her mind seemed as if it had shut down, gone nuclear and suffered one hell of a meltdown.

"Don't."

Sam wanted to speak. She wanted to tell him that it was all right, that they couldn't stop, that she couldn't even possibly imagine wanting to stop.

He pulled back from her, but he couldn't step away with her legs wrapped around her hips. His hands left her breasts and she instantly missed the pressure and strength of him holding her. Her breasts felt heavier than they ever had in her life. She wanted him to touch her.

"Sam, I mean it. This can't happen." Riley's face held anger and disgust.

Looking at him, Sam couldn't believe it. What the hell was he thinking? *This can't happen? It is happening!* She instinctively gripped him, maintaining contact. Some of that was from her martial arts training, not wanting to get out into easy striking range now that she was up against him. Inside his reach, she could use his own size and strength against him. But she wanted to be against him for more than that reason.

"Sam." Riley put his hands on her again, but this time he gripped her shoulders and pushed her back from him. His face was suddenly serious. "Sam! Dammit! Stop!"

Surprised and hurt, and more than a little embarrassed now, Sam dropped her legs from around his hips. Her feet hit the floor, but she didn't think her knees would hold her up. Cool air against bare skin let her know that her top had crept up way past any point of decency. Mortified, she pulled the shirt down where it belonged. Her nipples stood out prominently against the material. Self-consciously, she crossed her arms to hide them.

Someone banged on the door outside.

"Special Agent McLane," a male voice called through the door. "Special Agent McLane. Are you all right?"

"I'm fine," McLane said. His eyes never left hers.

Sam stood straight and tall, defiant. Inside, she just wanted to hide. If she hadn't needed his help—if Alex and Kayla and the others—hadn't needed his help, she knew she would have demanded that he leave immediately. She hated the way she could still feel his touch and still long for it at the same time.

"Are you sure, Special Agent McLane?" the man asked through the door. "Because it looked like—"

"Pete," Riley growled, still gazing at Sam.

"Yeah," Pete responded.

"Go away."

There was a hesitation. "All right. But if you need anything—"

"I won't."

Sam returned Riley's gaze.

"What the hell do you think you were doing, St. John?" he demanded.

Now we're back to St. John, Sam thought angrily. She could still hear her name whispered in a warm, ragged breath in her ear. "I was trying to convince you to help me. To help me help my friends."

"What?" He shot her a look of disbelief.

"I thought maybe you might be more inclined to help me if—" Sam couldn't finish. Her face burned with embarrassment.

"You thought I'd be more inclined to help you if you seduced me?" Riley blew out his breath and paced.

Sam didn't know what to say, but she felt she had to say something. Usually she got along with silence just fine, but this silence between them was unbearable. "I didn't think things would get so out of control."

"What did you think *would* happen?"

"I thought you would help."

"Because you offered me sex?"

His words stung her. Calling what she'd offered, what she'd never offered before, *sex* made her sound cheap and childish. She wanted to turn away from him. She wanted him out of her prison.

"Damn it, St. John. I'm not that kind of guy."

She reached for her own anger out of defense and found it. "You couldn't have convinced me. Not with that lipstick smear on your collar."

"You'd break up a relationship to get what you want?"

She frowned at him. "If you'd had a relationship, I'd have known it."

"How? ESP?"

Sam didn't want to explain. Couldn't, really, she just… knew.

"Is that it, then, Riley?" she asked him. "Are you in a relationship? Did I step over some moral barrier? Because just a few minutes ago it didn't seem like it was just me caught up in what was going on."

Obviously struggling to get control of himself, Riley paced. "That was real. Too real. But I'm not for sale, St. John. Not to you. Not to anybody. I hold myself accountable for my actions."

"Are you insinuating that I don't?"

"I didn't say that."

"I want to help my friends," Sam said. "I can't do that from in here. You and Mitchell have walled me off from everything I could do. I can't just sit in here and pretend everything's all right when everything inside me is screaming that it isn't."

"So you decided if you jumped me, delivered a sexual payoff, I'd do whatever you wanted?"

Actually, Sam had fostered hopes.

"Do you know how calculated that sounds?" he asked.

It had been calculated. Sam acknowledged that. But the results, her heated involvement and response, had been totally unexpected.

Riley ran a hand through his hair. He cursed. A crooked,

mirthless smile fitted itself to his lower face but never reached his eyes. "God, St. John, you're some piece of work. Were you trying to throw my career away, too?"

The accusation stung Sam on several levels. She tried to answer but her voice got stuck in her throat and wouldn't come out.

Exhaling, Riley pointed at the walls. "They've got cameras viewing your room 24/7, St. John. That little attempt at seduction you just threw was recorded. We'll be lucky if it's not plastered all over the Internet tomorrow."

Sam groaned inside. She'd forgotten all about the damn cameras once the fireworks had ignited inside her. "I wasn't thinking—I *didn't* think—about the cameras."

"That was pretty damn stupid, wasn't it?"

"I just wanted to get…get your attention."

"Damn straight you got my attention, St. John. How do you like my attention now?"

Sam didn't. Not one little bit. She was frustrated; how could he go from desirable one second and turn into a complete jerk in the next? A change that drastic could give someone whiplash.

"I need help," she repeated. "I want to help my friends. I can't do that from in here."

"So you offer me sex?" Riley cursed, ran his hand through his hair again, and cursed some more. "You could have given me all the sex in the world and I still couldn't get you through that door without Mitchell's okay."

"Things…got out of hand," Sam said.

"Man, that's the understatement of the year."

Sam felt the harsh burn of tears at the back of her eyes. She clamped down on her feelings, pushing them again and creating space so they wouldn't touch her until she was ready.

"I need help for my friends," she insisted.

Riley shook his head in disbelief. "Because you think some mythical assassin is after them?"

"Yes."

"Have you told your friend the air force captain about the Cipher?"

"No."

"Why not?"

"Because it would cause problems."

"What problems?"

"They would want to know why I wasn't there to help them. They would want to know why I couldn't get more information for them. They would investigate, and they'd find out I'm not on a mission." Sam took a deep breath, feeling a little more in control of herself now. "Besides, Mitchell's cyberwatchdogs wouldn't let a message like that go through to Josie."

Riley took his tie off and shoved it into his jacket pocket. "No. They wouldn't."

Sam thought frantically. There had to be a way to turn the situation around. Seducing Riley had been a desperate move, but there was still another angle she could play.

"Tell Mitchell that the Cipher is my contact in Berzhaan," Sam said. A chill filled her as she made the statement. Once she'd spoken, she knew she couldn't take the false confession back. Mitchell would use that against her, and if he could, he'd hang her with it.

Riley looked at her. "Sam," he said in a quiet voice, "don't do this."

For a moment Sam reconsidered what she was doing. In the end, though, she knew there was nothing else she could do. She'd failed miserably at seducing Riley over to her side. Worse than that, she'd made a fool of herself. The camera's digital recording had captured every moment of it.

"It's done," she said. "Tell Mitchell."

"Sam, you don't know the Cipher."

"No," she agreed. "He contacted me through a blind drop. That's why I'll have to help the Agency find him. And to do that, I'll need access to his records."

She knew the ploy was one born of desperation, but "desperate" was her zip code at the moment. After she'd learned of the mysterious blackouts, tied in to the fact that some kind of medical procedure had been performed on Rainy all those years ago, and that Kayla, Alex and Darcy were now following up on one lead they could find, Sam knew that she couldn't sit idly by anymore.

Her friends didn't have the resources of the CIA, and only Sam was in a position to give them access to that information.

"This is stupid," Riley said.

More stupid than trying to seduce you? Sam wondered. But she didn't give voice to the question. She was afraid of the answer.

"Mitchell's not going to buy it."

"Tell him if he doesn't, he's going to be partly responsible for the problems that come up in Berzhaan," Sam said in a flat voice.

Riley glowered at her. "Damn you, Sam."

In control of her emotions once more, Sam looked at him. "I'd like you to leave, Agent McLane."

"You're digging yourself in too deep."

"I'd like you to leave now," she repeated.

Riley stood still. He looked frustrated and worried and confused.

Sam raised her voice. "Guard." She didn't know what else to call the agents who watched her. "I want Agent McLane out of here *now*."

"Sam—"

"Don't," she whispered with cold neutrality, "don't tell me that I'm stupid one more time, McLane, or they're going to pull me off you when they get here. I swear I'll put you right back in the hospital."

Footsteps sounded out in the hall. "McLane. McLane, you've got to get out of there."

Without a word Riley walked to the door.

Sam turned away, unable to watch him walk away from her. She thought she'd gotten over the pain that accompanied people walking away from her years ago. She was surprised and disappointed in herself to find that such a simple act could still hurt her.

She stood still until the door locked. She closed her eyes and felt the lonely emptiness of the cell. After a moment she made herself walk to the bed. Agents were going to be watching her. She didn't want them to see any more of what she was going through than they had already seen.

Quietly, just as she had when she'd been a little girl in all those strange and unfriendly houses, she drew into herself and walled the world away.

"What do you think, Agent McLane?"

Riley kept his eyes locked on the image of Sam sitting

quietly in her cell. From what he'd been told, she hadn't moved since last night.

"McLane," Stone Mitchell called from his desk.

"Sir," Riley said, "she's lying."

"About being involved with the Cipher?"

"Yes, sir." Reluctantly Riley faced the director.

Mitchell sat at his desk in a dark suit. His face was set, somber. In addition to seeing the digital footage of Sam's "confession," Riley knew Mitchell had also seen footage of her attempted seduction of him. They hadn't talked about that yet, but Riley was certain they would.

"Do you know that she's lying?" Mitchell asked.

"Yes." Riley answered without hesitation.

Mitchell thought about that for a moment, then re-phrased his question. "Can you *prove* that she's lying?"

"No, sir."

Mitchell leaned back in his chair. "Then we have a problem."

"Sir, with all due respect, you can't possibly believe Sam St. John has any kind of connection to the Cipher."

"Why not?"

Riley drew in a deep breath. "Because, despite that damned footage MI-6 sent over, Sam is a good agent. An agent you can trust."

"You were reluctant to add her to the Munich opera-tion."

"That wasn't a trust issue. She's green for that kind of op."

"From the evidence suggested by the firefight she was involved in while in Suwan, I'd venture to say that she's not as green as you believed. Or anyone believed. She took out the Kemenis without hesitation, and with skill that few agents would exhibit under similar circumstances. Not many of our people have been under fire like that."

"If you believe her, sir, you're making a mistake."

"And if I don't follow up on her confession, I'd be remiss in my duties."

"Yes, sir. I understand that, sir. But there's a greater problem here."

Mitchell looked at him.

"St. John believes the Cipher was responsible for the death of her friend."

Mitchell tapped the computer keyboard and glanced at the screen. "Lorraine Miller Carrington."

"Yes, sir."

"You don't think the Carrington woman was killed by the Cipher?"

"No, sir."

"Why?"

"St. John is grieving, sir. I took her away from that funeral, and from her friends. She never even had the chance to speak to them. You've seen St. John's background. She's never known family. The women she went to school with at the academy are the closest thing she's ever had to one."

"So, in your opinion, if her friend hadn't gotten killed in a car wreck, St. John wouldn't have confessed?"

"No, sir."

"That still doesn't mean she's not guilty."

"No, sir."

"In fact, based on the footage I've seen of St. John in action, I'd say she's very guilty. Maybe she's playing the sympathy card, angling for some kind of breakdown to use in her defense."

"I don't think so. I think she really believes—"

Mitchell tapped another key and the monitor flickered as new information filled the screen. "Would it surprise you to know that Police Lieutenant Kayla Ryan of the Youngstown, Arizona, PD has been requesting files regarding the Carrington woman's accident? *After* the funeral?"

"I don't think any of those women were prepared to lose one of their own."

"Would it surprise you to know that Alex Forsythe, a forensics expert for the FBI—and also a graduate of the Athena Academy—has been investigating the Carrington woman's death as well as medical practices at the academy?"

"Same answer," Riley replied. "When a team loses an agent in the field, the people who live through it go through similar things. It's survivor's guilt. Nothing more."

Mitchell folded his hands in front of him, and Riley knew he was in for hell.

"I'm glad you're so sure of yourself, Agent McLane," Mitchell said. "Because I'm not at all certain that it's not true."

"You think the Cipher killed the Carrington woman?"

"Let me walk you through a scenario." Mitchell sipped his coffee. "We have a young CIA agent—we'll call her St. John to keep things simple."

Riley bit back a retort.

"St. John is young and ambitious. She gets to be a CIA agent, but she's not advancing as quickly as she thinks she should. Or maybe the job isn't as financially rewarding as she thinks it should be. Or maybe her interests haven't been pro-American from the beginning."

"What are you talking about?"

"Maybe you didn't read St. John's background closely enough," Mitchell suggested. "Did you know that her first language was Russian?"

Riley stayed silent. How the hell had he missed that?

"Whatever the case," Mitchell continued, "St. John decided that she could get financially more secure or complete her real mission, however you want to play it out. So she hooked up with the Cipher to—"

"She only gave that confession because she thinks she's protecting her friends."

"Maybe she is protecting her friends. Have you even considered that? She could have betrayed the Cipher. Maybe killing one of her friends was his way of getting back at her. Or chasing her out into the open."

"You think the Carrington woman was murdered?"

"The seat belt failed," Mitchell said. "It happens. But how often does a driver fall asleep at the wheel *and* have a seat belt fail?"

"It could happen."

"Again, I've got St. John's confession that she's been working with the Cipher."

"She's lying."

"Which time, Agent McLane? When she told us that wasn't her in the MI-6 footage? Or when she told us it *was* her?"

Riley stared at the director. "You're going to try to railroad St. John on this, aren't you?"

"I didn't lay the tracks for this pileup. I'm just following what's there." Mitchell stared up at him without expression. "I'm going to do my job. I suggest you do the same. You've already stepped way over the line in this operation."

Chapter 11

"Knock, knock," Howie Dunn called from the other side of the security door to Sam's personal prison. As he had for the past four days, he sounded cheerful.

Sam stopped her morning tai chi exercises and turned toward the door. "Come in."

The electronic locks snapped in their housings. A moment later Howie stepped through the doorway with a bag of coffee and bagels in one hand, a notebook computer and a briefcase tucked under his arm. If he hadn't been so large, he would have looked overburdened. He wore a jacket over a dark-green turtleneck.

"Breakfast." Howie shook the bag gently. "Hope you haven't eaten the sawdust they usually try to pawn off on you."

"No," Sam said. "I was hoping you'd bring breakfast."

He took a look at her and shook his head. "Man, have you tried sleeping?"

Despite the seriousness of her situation and the very real danger she thought existed for her friends, Sam couldn't help being slightly cheered by the CIA agent's concern. Howie Dunn was one guy who wore his heart on his sleeve.

Rainy would have said, One of the keepers. Locked up as she was in the cell, Sam often found Rainy in her thoughts. She'd wished time and again that she could have talked to her friend. If anyone could have made sense of the emotions rolling loose inside her, it would have been Rainy.

"I tried sleeping," Sam said. She rolled her head and tried to loosen stiff neck muscles. "It's overrated."

Howie put the bagels and coffee down carefully, then did the same with the notebook computer. The smile left his face and he pushed his glasses farther up his nose.

"Hey," he offered quietly, "in all seriousness, I can talk to Mitchell. See if we can't get some slack cut and get you something that will help you rest at night."

"No. Any kind of medication leaves me groggy." She noticed the concern in Howie's eyes. "I'll be all right." God, but that was stupid. You're an admitted traitor to the United States. So you'll be healthy for the lethal injection or the firing squad.

"What about warm milk? My mom used to swear by it. I could maybe arrange a glass of warm milk for you before bedtime. Nothing there to leave you groggy."

"I'll be fine."

Howie didn't look happy.

Sam stood her ground and crossed her arms. For the last

two days, she'd felt convinced that having an agent other than Howie would have been in her best interests. Howie just came across too…honest, like he tried too hard to get along. His behavior was bringing out a guilt in her for her own subterfuge that she hadn't expected and could ill afford.

"Maybe we should get to work," Sam suggested.

Howie handed her the coffee and bagels. "Divvy. I'll get us set up." He ambled to the door and knocked. Immediately, a rolling cart and two folding chairs were passed through by guards outside.

The bag contained four lattes and a dozen bagels. Sam matched Howie when it came to caffeine, but she only kept two of the bagels. The fact that Howie could eat so much and not show it offered mute testimony to his size and dedication to fitness. The fact that he was built like a small mountain helped.

Working with obvious familiarity, Howie set up the computer, plugged in the encrypted wireless networking card that gave them access to the Agency's computers and brought the unit online.

Sam opened the briefcase and took out the discouragingly thin files regarding the master assassin known only as the Cipher. For the past four days, she'd scanned through the files looking for some clue that she and previous criminal profilers had missed before. The task was daunting. She'd only remembered the Cipher because of the unusual method of killing that he'd evidently perfected. No one had been able to advance a theory as to how the killer was able to make so many executions look accidental.

The computer peeped as the Internet service came online.

"I'm really starting to get some pressure from Director Mitchell." Howie spoke without looking at her.

"What kind of pressure?"

"He wants results."

Sam peeled the top from her first coffee. Howie always brought the best, and even stopped to microwave it before bringing it to her cell. She still felt guilty that she wasn't able to repay him or at least kick in toward the cost. She didn't like charity; she never had.

"We're working on it," she said defensively.

"I know." Howie sat in front of the computer. "I think the director is starting to come to the conclusion that maybe you're leading him on a wild-goose chase. That you weren't telling him the truth about your connection to the Cipher."

"How's he doing on thinking I'm totally innocent of everything I've been accused of?"

"Now that is a different matter. Even before MI-6 came up with digital records of you—er, someone that looked like you—the Agency had lost people over in Berzhaan. Our position there is tenuous at best because of the Kemenis and the terrorists."

Sam pinched a small piece from her bagel and raised it to her lips. "And what do you think, Howie? Do you think I'm wasting your time?"

Howie shook his head and grinned. "I love catching bad guys." He tapped the notebook computer. "And this is my weapon of choice. Bloodless and devastating, all rolled into one convenient package for the spy-on-the-go." He paused and continued staring at the screen. "However this arrangement goes, Sam, we're going to make a difference with what we're finding out. Believe me. We've already added to some of the profile that the Agency had on the Cipher."

The strange thing was, Sam did believe the big man. Now that he was working with her rather than coming after her and taking her into custody, she couldn't help responding to the positive atmosphere he constantly exuded. Howie Dunn was an immensely likeable guy.

"I do believe you." Sam popped the piece of bagel into her mouth, chewed and washed the bite down with her latte. "So you never have said what you think." As soon as she had the words out of her mouth, she regretted having asked the question. It put both of them on the spot.

"About whether or not you cut a deal with the Cipher?"

Sam hesitated, but now that she'd invested this much, she couldn't not ask the real question. "Do you think I'm a traitor?"

Howie was quiet for a short time. He studied her. "Answering that question either way might compromise my presence here," he said. "I hope you understand."

Sam nodded. "I do." Understanding dawned in her. If he said he didn't believe she was a traitor, Mitchell might pull him so that sympathy wouldn't result. If he said he believed she was a traitor, maybe the working relationship they had found wouldn't come so natural.

"I can't do my job properly if I start looking at that," Howie said. "I have to remain outside your problem and work on the one I've been given."

"I know. I appreciate that." The bite of bagel was almost tasteless in Sam's mouth. Under other circumstances, she didn't know if she'd be able to remain as neutral as Howie was. She tried to make light of the situation. "I suppose Riley McLane is the only one still holding out for my innocence. At least, where the Cipher is concerned."

"He does do that."

"I haven't seen him lately." Actually, she hadn't seen Riley in four days. Not since her awkward attempt to seduce him. She hated remembering how she'd practically thrown herself at him. But sometimes, in the night, she half dreamed and half fantasized about that encounter, and sometimes—when she felt she could safely deny control over her thoughts—things progressed much further than they had in real life.

Unfortunately, dreams like that provided a lot of discomfort later. On mornings after those dreams she'd felt the pangs of loneliness close around her like the steel jaws of a bear trap.

"Riley's not here," Howie said as he opened files they'd earmarked the previous day.

That surprised Sam and yet it didn't. She had noticed Riley's absence and wondered how he'd been able to stay away so long. Not that she believed he was so attracted to her, but he would have come by to put more pressure on her. Riley McLane wasn't the kind of man to leave a situation alone.

"Riley's not here at the Agency," Sam repeated. "Today?"

"For the past four days."

"What happened?"

"Director Mitchell gave Riley some time off."

"Because of me?" Although Howie hadn't brought it up, Sam felt certain the agent knew about her attempted seduction. She felt embarrassed and vulnerable, and she hurried on. "What happened four days ago wasn't Riley's fault. He was a…an innocent bystander. I was just trying to get him to…"

"Sam," Howie interrupted gently. "Sam."

She quieted and looked at him.

"Riley took some time off for medical reasons."

"Oh." Sam felt her face burn. She hated that. As fair complexioned as she was, her face always showed red. "Is he all right?"

"Medical cleared him. He chose to take time off."

"Why?"

"He said his shoulder was still bothering him."

That didn't make any sense. Riley had been chafing to get back into the field.

Or maybe what I did got back to whoever left the lipstick on Riley's shirt collar. If she's in the business, and she probably is, then she probably heard about it. Maybe he's off trying to save that relationship. Sam felt as if she'd been punched in the stomach. Guilt over possibly interfering with a personal relationship assailed her. The image of Riley in the arms of other woman, someone dark and sultry and exotic, filled her mind.

"You okay?" Howie asked.

"Sure," she replied. "Why?"

"You look like you ate something that disagreed with you."

"Just tired. I haven't been sleeping well."

"Yeah." Howie tapped the keyboard. A pleasant *ding* sounded. "I've got some pictures I want you to see."

Capturing her latte, Sam walked over to stand behind

Howie. She peered at the notebook computer's monitor over his shoulder.

A series of picture icons popped up on the screen with metallic pings. Howie put the cursor over one of them and double-clicked to open the .bmp file.

The picture opened, filling the screen and revealing a man's image. The man was obviously Middle Eastern, judging from the hooded eyes and large nose, but his complexion was more buttery than coffee. His beard was short, a ruffle of tight curls.

"Know him?" Howie asked.

Sam studied the face, wondering if the image was a trap of some sort. "No. Who is he?"

"A guy named Faisal Hamid. Supposed to be linked to the new arms trade that's shaping up in Berzhaan." Howie tapped keys. "Faisal is making the rounds throughout Suwan, trying to set up business with the Kemenis and the Q'Rajn."

"Those people don't deal with the same suppliers," Sam said. She knew that from the background reports she'd read.

"Only if the suppliers have political aspirations," Howie corrected. "Faisal, here, is totally apolitical. A dollar is a yen is a deutsch mark to him. Guy's totally about the bottom line." He paused. "You sure you don't know him?"

"No."

"That's strange," Howie said, "because he was one of the guys who got identified at the shootout when MI-6 filmed you in action."

Sam went very still, thinking quickly.

Howie looked up at her expectantly.

"The Cipher is very cautious about the work he's doing there," Sam said. "Most of us didn't know the others."

"So what capacity did you serve in?"

"Just support."

"Interesting." Howie turned back to the screen.

"What do you mean?"

"According to the new Intel we've gotten, a woman was arranging for the Russian weapons that were being delivered that day."

My mysterious double is the ringleader of the arms suppliers? Sam couldn't believe it. "There was more than one woman in the group."

"In a Middle Eastern theater?" Howie raised a skeptical eyebrow. "That's a chancy play."

"Berzhaan's not the typical Middle-Eastern country these days," Sam pointed out. She'd seen the country and knew that what she was saying was true. Suwan was becoming something of a crossroads of Eastern and Western business and tourist travel. "I worked undercover there for the Agency a couple times."

"Not in a high-visibility capacity."

"Selling black-market arms to a country's guerrillas and terrorists isn't exactly a high-visibility occupation." Sam remembered the digital sequence she'd seen. "I wasn't supposed to be seen at all. I was just in a support capacity."

"All right." Howie clicked more buttons, shifting through the pictures. He asked her about several other people sitting at tables in open-air restaurants or going into and out of homes and businesses.

Sam didn't know any of them. "Who are these guys?"

Howie stopped on the picture of a tall man leaning against an alley wall. The man wore khaki pants and a white shirt rolled to midforearm. His hair was black, shot through with gray, and he wore a long mustache that nearly reached his jawline.

"Sergei Ivanovitch," Howie replied. "He's a colonel in the SVR."

That made Sam curious. The SVR was the Russian equivalent of the CIA, an espionage agency that operated outside the country to collect information on potential international threats.

"Russia's *very* interested in Berzhaan's political future," Howie said. "Whichever way the political leanings and sympathies of the government in charge of the country goes, so goes the untapped oil reserves Berzhaan is sitting on."

The oil reserves promised to make a huge impact in the Middle East as well as the Western world and Russia. China was starting to make inroads into Middle-Eastern oil to answer that country's own growing energy needs. Unfortunately, with the oil reserves nearing capacity production, China's interest threatened the Western interests as well as Russia's.

"I don't recall Ivanovitch on the debrief," Sam said.

"He's not," Howie said. "He's a new addition to the Berzhaan scene."

"How new?"

"We're not certain. An…operative in Berzhaan just spotted Ivanovitch there."

Sam noticed Howie's hesitation but didn't say anything. It bothered her that Howie might not want to trust her with sensitive information. But she understood completely; she was quite certain under similar circumstances that she wouldn't have trusted her, either.

"Ivanovitch keeps a low profile." Howie pressed more keys.

The pictures on the computer monitor flickered. There were two more pictures of Ivanovitch lighting a cigarette and smoking it, then the man was gone.

"Did Ivanovitch make our agent?" Sam asked. Too late, she realized that she'd referred to the agent as *our.* There was nothing *our* about the operation.

"We don't know," Howie said.

"Did the agent get a feeling?"

"The agent didn't say."

"You're still in touch with him?"

"With the agent? Yes."

"What is Ivanovitch doing there?"

"We haven't ascertained. In the past, the SVR have actively sought an American government link to the weapons the Kemenis are being supplied with. They still contend that the CIA is supplying those weapons."

"Are we?" Sam asked.

"No."

Even though Howie sounded certain and probably believed it, Sam knew the possibility still existed. "When did these pictures come in?"

"This morning."

"Why did Mitchell decide to show them to me?"

"Because he wants results." Howie sipped his latte. "Director Mitchell also felt there might be a Russian connection."

"Why?"

"Because the first language you spoke as a child was Russian." There was no accusation in Howie's look.

Sam let out a slow breath. "Understood. But you need to know that I don't remember anything about that. I had to learn Russian again later in school." But learning that language had come more easily than any of the other languages she spoke. The spoken language was there almost instantly, but the written portion of the language had come with difficulty.

"Who are these other people?" Sam asked, watching the pictures as Howie flicked through them as steady as a metronome.

"Our agent has identified them as part of a group of weapons dealers who have been in Berzhaan for the last few months. Do you recognize any of them?"

"No," Sam answered. She grew agitated. The lie she'd told about being involved with the Cipher wouldn't hold up under stiff scrutiny for long. She didn't know enough to make the story stick. She was beginning to think Mitchell suspected that, though she was certain he wouldn't let her go, either. If anything, with the video proof he had of her guilt, the director would say she was bluffing to buy time for herself or her partners. "Let's get back to the Cipher." Despite her own predicament, she still wanted to protect the Cassandras if she could.

"Sure." Howie tapped the computer keyboard again and brought up the master file they'd created on the assassin. "Looks like we were right about the yacht crash along the Turkish coastline two months ago."

"The Cipher?"

Howie brought up the news stories they'd ferreted out at Sam's insistence. During his career, the Cipher had become a shadow, never leaving behind anything that would identify him. Ultimately, though, the leads to the Cipher came from the people who hired him.

Despite a clean murder scene and an "accidental" death, the people who had contracted the Cipher had sometimes still fallen prey to law enforcement agencies and insurance investigators. They'd talked of the mysterious assassin-for-hire who promised a death no one would investigate.

If the Cipher had only killed people without wealth or corporate stock or political influence, his crimes might never have been discovered. But killing those people didn't pay.

"I accessed the police and maritime reports concerning the crash," Howie said.

The newspapers and television media had published the yacht's sudden veering out of control as the result of the boat pilot's inebriated state at the time of the collision. The yacht had rammed two fishing vessels, resulting in four deaths besides the owner's. All three vessels had gone down.

The owner had· been a fifty-year-old man newly promoted to CEO of his father's oil concerns under development in Berzhaan. Six months previously, the man had inherited his father's controlling interest in the corporation. Upon his death, the controlling interest was disseminated among his four sons, splitting the vote and leaving the corporation open to a hostile takeover that had just happened.

That takeover had alerted Sam to the possibility that the

Cipher might have had a hand in the man's death. Usually, the assassin's targets had been men whose removal would trigger events favorable to governments, world leaders, political groups or financial empires. The man did not work cheaply.

But if that was the case, why would the Cipher murder Rainy? What was there at the Athena Academy that would interest the assassin or his employer?

She thought about the egg-mining operation that Rainy might have been subjected to while under the care of the Athena Academy staff. If she assumed Rainy had uncovered the theft of her eggs and was pursuing the truth when she was murdered, the hardest part of the whole scenario was realizing that someone from the academy might have hired the Cipher to kill Rainy.

Sam was convinced someone had. The MO fit too tightly, and the stakes were evidently high.

"Going over those reports last night after I left you," Howie said, "I found details that had been omitted from the international news." He tapped keys, and documents showed up on the monitor.

"What am I looking at?" Sam asked.

"Eyewitness accounts. One's in Farsi and the other is in Italian. I know you read Italian." Howie tapped the keys again. "I thought you might pay close attention to this section."

A highlighted segment of text appeared on the monitor.

Sam read the handful of sentences quickly. "This person—"

"One of the sexual entertainers hired to accompany the yacht," Howie said.

"—mentions that the pilot apparently had some kind of seizure just before the boat went out of control," Sam said.

"I know." Howie tapped the keys again. Both sections, one in Italian and one in Farsi, shimmered and became sentences in English.

Sam read through both sections. "The second statement confirms the first. The victim went down only seconds before the yacht slammed into the fishing trawlers."

"Right. Sounds like the Cipher's MO, doesn't it?"

Sam nodded. "Was the boat owner autopsied?"

"Yes. So were the other bodies. All of them were posted because they died a questionable death unattended."

"And?"

Howie shook his head. "The tox screens came back negative. The guy had been drinking, but not enough to cause him to pass out."

"Was there any other physical evidence that might have caused the fainting spell?"

"No, but there is this." Howie tapped keys again, and a new picture filled the screen.

The photograph on the monitor was clear, obviously taken by a professional. It showed a harbor rescue team pulling a body from the water onto a boat.

"This was shot by a travel reporter from a helicopter," Howie said. "She lucked onto the shot and it was used in a chain of newspapers. I found out about it and got a copy."

"We've seen this picture," Sam said. She remembered the picture from several newspapers and magazines they'd gone through.

"Yeah," Howie agreed. "But we never saw a copy of the original. The guy's death wasn't earth-shattering, so we only saw the reduced version. Watch what happens when I blow it up." He tapped keys again.

Sam watched silently as the image multiplied several times. The view focused on the dead man's left ankle. A shadow took shape there.

"Know what it could be?" Howie asked softly.

Studying the shadow wrapped around the dead man's ankle, Sam recognized the image with a start. "Fingers."

"Yeah. Those are bruises. Evidently somebody grabbed hold of this guy's ankle and held him under till he drowned. He must not have been completely out when he went into the water."

"The Cipher was there," Sam whispered, understanding at once.

"Right," Howie said. "He got to the pilot somehow, with some fast-acting agent, knocked the guy out, then managed to survive the wreck and made sure of the kill he'd been hired for."

"We'd assumed he didn't like to be there for the kill," Sam said.

"Everybody did," Howie agreed. "Obviously the guy doesn't take a lot of chances when he's working a contract, but when it comes down to it, he's not afraid of going head to head with a situation." He paused. "That makes this guy a lot more dangerous than anybody had ever thought."

"I know," Sam said, feeling excitement grow inside her, "but it also means that the Cipher was part of the group on the yacht. We've got copies of the film and pictures that were shot aboard the boat prior to the wreck, right?"

Howie nodded.

"Break it out. If we got this lucky, we might be able to identify him."

Riley McLane felt naked without a weapon. But getting a weapon in Berzhaan was impossible to do without drawing too much attention to himself. On guard against the Q'Rajn and the Kemeni guerrillas, the national military teams policing Suwan seemed to be everywhere. If he'd had enough cash, he could have bought a pistol from a black-market dealer. But bringing a lot of cash out of the United States and into Berzhaan was a problem, as well.

He sat at a small table in an open-air café a few blocks from the city's main tourist drag. The morning sun slanted across the street and left shadows pooled at the feet of the buildings on the east side. Inside the shadow of the café, the temperature was fairly moderate for the desert environment, but the heat of the day was coming.

"Anything more I can get for you, sir?"

Riley glanced up at the server coming over to his table. The man was young and lean, nut brown from a lifetime in the harsh sun.

"No," Riley replied. "I'm good." His sweating tea glass was still half-full.

"Of course, sir." The server retreated to the next table, asking the same question in his broken English.

Lounging in the chair and checking his watch frequently, Riley looked like a guy who was awaiting his wife's return from a morning of shopping. He even wore a wedding ring to carry off the appearance. The khaki trousers and pale blue shirt featuring exotic birds completed his disguise. Wraparound sunglasses and a four-day growth of beard subtly changed his features.

There were people in Berzhaan who could recognize him. Some of them wanted him dead, not from things that had happened there, but for things that had happened elsewhere that couldn't be forgiven or forgotten. Riley wanted some of them dead, as well.

He kept his attention on the man across the street. Riley's quarry was of medium height, of Middle Eastern origins, and—by all accounts—a dangerous man. Riley had staked the man out for the last day and a half.

Faisal Hamid, his identity confirmed through a phone call to Howie Dunn, talked on a satellite phone. He'd been caught up in his conversation for almost three minutes, doing more listening than talking.

One of the contacts Riley had used on earlier ops in the country had pointed Hamid out as a man who was setting up munitions deals. According to the man Riley had talked to, Hamid was trying to undercut the CIA sales of weapons to the Kemenis.

As far as Riley knew, there were no CIA-sanctioned sales of weapons to the Kemenis. Or to the Q'Rajn. The United States was actively supporting the present government in Berzhaan.

Finished with his conversation, Hamid drained his coffee and stood. He crossed through the tables and walked to the street.

Riley dropped money on the table to settle his bill, then followed Hamid. From what he'd been able to find out from his source, there was a woman in Hamid's organization. Riley's source had mentioned that she hadn't been around in a couple months. But the contact's description of the woman matched Samantha St. John to a *T.*

CIA involvement within Berzhaan was limited. Most of the U.S. support came in the form of troops and economic advisers and an infusion of low-interest loans garnered from American oil investors hoping to close a deal. That was why Sergei Ivanovitch's presence and operation had gone largely undetected. The military teams didn't share a history with Ivanovitch.

Hamid stayed on the street, walking under the thick awnings of shops and businesses.

Riley followed. Behind him, his hired car and driver tailed at a discreet distance. If Hamid decided to get into a vehicle at any time, Riley had that angle covered. The driver was a man Riley had used before, a guy who would stand up if things went badly, and would know enough to save himself if things turned really bad.

A short distance farther on, Hamid turned right and stepped into an alley.

An alarm bell went off in Riley's head. For the last two days, he'd tailed Hamid. Without a team to work the rotation with, Riley knew he risked exposure. Even changing his appearance every day wasn't a guarantee. During that time, Hamid hadn't done anything more than talk on the phone. Whatever business dealings he'd had, they'd remained secret.

Riley approached the alley, his mind rushing. The safest thing to do was keep moving and pass by without a second look. It was what he should have done, what every bit of training he'd had and every bit of field experience had taught him to do.

But safe isn't going to do Sam St. John any good, is it?

During the past four nights, memories of Sam in his arms had haunted him. No matter what the digital record Mitchell had gotten from MI-6, Riley couldn't buy the fact that Sam was guilty of treason. She'd been willing to put herself on the line to help her friends, even admitting to treasonous activity.

Or maybe she just wanted you to think that, his more jaded side suggested. Maybe she knew that you weren't the kind of guy to take advantage of a situation like that. Or maybe even if you had, she wouldn't have cared.

Those reasons and his own feelings about Sam St. John, as confusing as they were, had prompted him to cling to the medical cover long enough to get out of the U.S. and go to Berzhaan four days ago. Even then, the hope that the answer to the digital footage British intelligence had shot remained thin. Until he'd picked up the nearly invisible trail of Hamid and the woman who sometimes worked with him.

Pass by or turn in? That was the question Riley faced in three short strides. If Hamid was securing a weapons drop, Riley knew he needed to see that, in order to figure out who the players were. Information was hard to come by in Berzhaan of late.

Omar Razidae, the prime minister of Berzhaan, had withdrawn some of his open-arms treatment of the United States over the past couple months. No explanation was given in the news, but Riley felt certain that the British intelligence service had passed their damning record of Samantha St. John in action to the prime minister. The obvious conclusion was that St. John and the Agency were working to supply the Kemenis against the present government.

In the end Riley had no choice and he knew it. He turned at the alley and entered the long tunnel.

Smooth-sided buildings rose to three stories on either side of him. One of them had a zigzagging fire escape ladder that ran up the side. Lines of clothing hung between the buildings at ground level and at the second and third floor. The fabric drifted in the slight breeze and created moving shadows on the ground.

The alley ended in a cul-de-sac, which was a frequent occurrence in the city's design. Riley saw that from the way the buildings rose at the other end of the alley. Suwan was an old city, but had been added to and rebuilt a number of times since it had risen from the desert sands hundreds of years ago. The architecture varied throughout the different sections of the city, as well.

Riley's experience kicked into threat assessment mode as he advanced on the clothesline swaying under the weight of sheets and blankets in the slight breeze. He'd been foolish to follow Hamid. The alley would be a bad place to get caught. Even as he thought that, his peripheral vision caught sight of a slim form dropping through the lines of clothing hanging between the buildings overhead.

Chapter 12

Reacting at once, Riley spun and tried to set himself, bringing his hands up to defend himself. Instead, he caught a kick in the face that sent him to his knees with tears rushing down his face and blood spilling from his nose and split lip. The sudden, intense pain followed almost immediately, but his spiking adrenaline levels kept the discomfort muted and away from him for the moment.

The lithe form fell to the alley floor off balance, but the attacker rolled and came upright almost instantly. A gloved fist pushed a silencer-equipped pistol out toward Riley.

Surging up, Riley lashed out with his left foot and kicked the pistol. The weapon spat a single bullet that shattered brick from the wall behind Riley, letting him know the round was a heavy one. All he heard was a throaty *chuff* as the long silencer muted most of the noise of the bullet detonating.

The pistol flew from his attacker's hand and dropped yards away.

Setting himself in a martial arts stance, both hands open before him so he could grab or deflect, his feet splayed into an L-stance, Riley faced his opponent.

She wore acid-stained jeans, a solid green blouse, and had her hair pulled back. Her face startled Riley instantly, because he knew her features at a glance.

"Sam," he croaked in surprise.

She took advantage of his hesitation, stepping in and delivering a front snap kick that caught him in the center of the chest. Despite her small stature, her strength was surprising. The impact against his chest drove him back in stumbling steps to slam against the wall behind him.

Riley's mind reeled as he watched the woman go for the pistol he'd kicked from her hand. There was no way that Sam was here. Howie would have told him if she'd been released. Or escaped. And they had talked only hours ago about how things had gone with Sam that day during her quest to identify the Cipher.

Acting on instinct and out of self-preservation, Riley threw himself in pursuit of the woman. She was a half stride ahead of him. He took that away by throwing himself at her. He collided with her just as her fingertips grazed the weapon's barrel, then they rolled forward over the pistol.

She came up with catlike grace, rolling to a standing position without pause. Riley extended his hand for the pistol, but she squatted and spun with a leg fully extended. Her heel, barely an inch off the ground, smacked into the pistol and sent it skittering away.

Riley cursed as he stood and crossed his wrists to block

another kick that came straight at his face. She was amazing, deft and powerful, every move poetry in action.

"Sam!" Riley said.

The woman looked at him. Her eyes narrowed for a moment in perplexion. "Who are you?" she asked.

The voice even sounded like Sam St. John's. But there was a difference. The pitch was the same, but the cadence was a little off.

"What's going on?" Riley circled to his left, shifting to his right foot forward, taking a step, then placing his left foot forward again.

"You should have continued playing the tourist," the woman said.

"Do you know Samantha St. John?" Riley asked. Pain bit into his face where she had kicked him when she'd dropped from the overhead window.

"No. Who are you?"

Too late, Riley heard the scuff of a shoe behind him. Before he could move, warm metal pressed up against the back of his neck.

"I have two pistols, my friend," a calm voice with an accent stated. "You might be able to sidestep the one I am now holding against the back of your neck, but I promise you that I will shoot you with the other with only the slightest provocation on your part. Understand?"

"Yeah," Riley said. He froze. If the man had wanted him dead, he would have already fired. "I got it."

"Stand relaxed."

Reluctantly Riley dropped his hands to his sides and stood up. The pistol barrel pulled back from his neck.

The man walked around in front of Riley. The man's

dark, hooded eyes regarded Riley with casual disdain. His mustache gave his small smile a sarcastic twist.

"Do you know him?" the woman asked.

"He is an American CIA agent," the man told the woman. "His name is Riley McLane. I just this morning confirmed his identity."

Riley stared at the Russian. "You're Sergei Ivanovitch."

"Yes." The man gave a nod of acknowledgment, but he also frowned. "It troubles me that you know me so easily. So what is your interest here, Agent McLane? Are you protecting the CIA's arms trade with the guerrillas?"

"We're not trading with the guerrillas," Riley replied.

Ivanovitch smiled crookedly. "We must all protect our little lies, mustn't we?"

Riley kept an eye on Ivanovitch, but he stared at the woman. It was Sam St. John, but not Sam St. John.

"I must ask you again," Ivanovitch said, "what your intentions here today are."

"I was following Hamid."

"Yes. So I saw. But why?"

"Because I wanted to find her." Riley nodded toward the beautiful blonde.

No emotion touched her face as yet. If anything, she only looked curious.

"Why?" Ivanovitch asked. He stood with both pistols still in his hands. The bedding waved on the clotheslines around them, sending shadows scurrying constantly.

"A buy was made a few months ago," Riley said. "A British agent was killed. However, the support team got digital footage of the firefight that resulted when the Kemenis interrupted the arms shipment."

"I would deny any knowledge of this," Ivanovitch said.

"Go ahead," Riley said. "The fact remains that the Brits caught this woman in the footage."

Ivanovitch glanced at the woman.

"I saw no cameras," the woman said.

Ivanovitch stared at her a moment longer, then turned his attention back to Riley. "You still haven't said why you would come after someone British Intelligence was interested in."

"MI-6 gets testy when one of their own is gunned down."

"Understandable. But you are not with MI-6."

"A woman as beautiful as that," Riley said, readying himself for action, "you tend to remember. I thought if the Brits were interested in her, then I should be, as well."

The fact that Ivanovitch hadn't put away his pistols gave Riley a bad feeling. Normally when two agents of different governments confronted each other and hadn't been ordered to terminate on sight the other agent, hostilities ended and negotiations began. Ivanovitch showed no sign of doing that.

"Someone is framing the United States regarding the arms deals with the Kemenis," Riley said. "I was sent here to find out whom it is."

Ivanovitch showed Riley a shark's smile. "All by yourself, Special Agent McLane? I don't quite believe that's the whole truth."

"Believe what you want," Riley replied.

"Of course."

"If there are no further objections, I think I'll just take my leave." Riley took a step backward.

"No," Ivanovitch said. "You will stop or I will shoot you."

Riley stopped, weighing his chances.

"Russia is very interested in the outcome of the business dealings of this country," Ivanovitch said. "My government wants to build a trade agreement with Prime Minister Razidae. My superiors sent me here to get proof of American involvement in supporting the Kemenis. I admit that the task has been somewhat difficult."

"That's because it's not going on," Riley said.

"Oh, it's going on all right," Ivanovitch said. "But proving this has been almost impossible. Or, perhaps, I have no true patience. I am not a spectator, as this job so often requires. Rather, I am a predator." He smiled. "Now I see before me the perfect opportunity to meet the demands of my superiors and end my own boredom. You are here without official sanction, Special Agent McLane. Not only that, but I know that there is a woman in your group who is being held for helping transport weapons."

Riley wasn't totally surprised at the Russian agent's knowledge. In addition to the fact that intelligence agencies often couldn't keep all their secrets, they also sometimes used the same resources inside a country. Information inadvertently got swapped as a result.

"I think the case can be built that you were here to do damage control regarding that compromised agent," Ivanovitch said. "Perhaps to take over the munitions operations to the Kemenis."

"I won't tell the story that way," Riley said. He was tense. He concentrated on being loose and ready.

"You won't have to. The body of an unsanctioned CIA

agent gunned down at a weapons buy a few hours from now will explain a great number of things to the prime minister and his cabinet. I've already had a number of discussions with Razidae. I believe he would be quite amenable after seeing your body."

The woman reached behind her back. "I'll secure him." She took out a pair of disposable handcuffs from behind her back. "Turn around."

Riley stood his ground. If he let himself be handcuffed he knew he'd never stand a chance.

"Do it," Ivanovitch ordered.

At that moment the woman stepped forward. Maybe she was inexperienced, though Riley doubted that after seeing her in action earlier, or maybe she didn't see any fight left in him. Her movement effectively put her in the middle of Ivanovitch's field of fire.

Riley turned and grabbed the clothesline, holding on to it as he broke out into a sprint. He released the line with a pop and set the line of clothing in motion. By then, he was through the clothes, angling for the other side of the alley and staying low.

A brick in the wall across the alley fragmented. Another only a few feet away suddenly showed a deep score where a bullet had slid along it. Then the sharp reports of Ivanovitch's pistols exploded the lazy din from the street that filled the alley.

Ivanovitch's third shot hit the right alley wall, only a few feet behind Riley. The fourth smashed a window in front of him. Then he was out of the alley and on the street. The driver he'd hired to tail him idled just in front of the alley.

Riley waved to the man, hoping that the guy didn't jump ship to save his own skin. It was possible. Riley had been abandoned before with trouble breathing down his neck. Even if the driver didn't stay, Riley was in the tourist area. The chances of Ivanovitch or his people catching him were small. There were too many people around and too many places to hide. And Riley felt confident the Russian SVR officer didn't want to kill a civilian and risk identification later.

The driver eased the older Chevrolet sedan up as Riley reached the street. He reached across the seat and opened the passenger door.

Riley grabbed the door, opened it, and swung inside to drop into the seat.

"Go," he told the driver just as Ivanovitch and the woman who wasn't Sam St. John raced from the alley. The Russians had their pistols tucked out of sight behind their backs.

The driver put the car into motion, cutting into the heavy traffic and drawing fire from half a dozen horns behind him.

Riley watched Ivanovitch and the woman walk along the street as they shoved their weapons out of sight. Passersby already gathered timidly at the alley. Gunfire was nothing new in Suwan.

Winded, excited and wary, Riley fell back into the seat. The woman wasn't Sam St. John. He clung to that fact.

"Where to?" the driver asked. He knew from his previous association with Riley not to ask questions.

"The airport," Riley replied. As long as he remained in Suwan—even Berzhaan—without sanction, he was a target. His agent's jacket was big enough that if Ivanovitch had done what he'd threatened to do, the United States and Berzhaan's relationship would further fragment.

He needed to get back to Langley. More was going on in Suwan than their Intel had indicated. And since Sam St. John might not have been the woman in the digital footage offered from MI-6, she deserved to be released.

Besides that, he had a plan.

"St. John."

Recognizing Riley McLane's voice, Sam stopped her forms in midmovement and turned to the door of her cell. Her defenses were up instantly. When she'd last seen him seven days ago, they'd parted under strained circumstances.

"McLane?" she called.

Howie Dunn had left hours ago when they had finished for the evening. They had put in six days on the search for the Cipher, two days since the Russian connection had turned up in Berzhaan and Sam had started figuring out who the agent on the ground was in Berzhaan. If McLane wasn't there now, she had to think that maybe she was wrong.

"Are you decent?" he asked.

"Yes." Decent, Sam thought, taking stock of her perspiration-sodden clothing, but not presentable. Then she thought that assessment was stupid. She was totally not happy with Riley McLane and didn't give a damn what he thought about how she looked.

The door opened and Riley walked in with an armful of clothing.

"Are we going somewhere?" Sam's heart leaped at the possibility. In almost two months, she'd only been out of the room the one time Riley had taken her earlier. And that had only been to Stone Mitchell's office, barely five minutes of open air. Even the skills at isolation that she'd developed getting bumped from foster home to foster home hadn't prepared her for the ordeal she'd faced. A window had made a lot of difference, a constant reminder that a world existed outside of the place she had stayed then.

"No," Riley said, lifting the clothing. He sounded tired and edgy. "I'm trying to catch up on my laundry." He laid jeans, a green turtleneck and a black jacket on the made bed. A clear plastic bag contained white, French-cut panties and a bra.

"Well," Sam said, "I'll have to question your taste."

Riley had three boxes of footwear and dropped those on the bed as well. "C'mon. We haven't got all day."

She was surprised at the amount of angry rebellion that flooded her. "No."

He looked up at her and scowled irritably. "What do you mean, no?"

"No means no. I'm not going. I'm a prisoner here. Not someone you can check in and out like a library book."

Riley growled. "We've got a mission briefing and a plane to catch. We really don't have time for this."

Sam's thoughts reeled. A mission? A plane? For a moment she thought she needed to pinch herself, to see if she would wake up.

"What are you talking about?"

Rolling his wrist over so that he was looking at the inside of his wrist, Riley said, "We're losing time. We didn't have enough time as it was."

"I'm not going until you tell me what's going on."

"I was over in Berzhaan," Riley said. "I found the woman who was in the digital recording MI-6 gave us. Mitchell knows it wasn't you. I took pictures of her with a minicam I wore."

Sam felt like she'd been hit by a bus. She'd just about been able to get her mind wrapped around the idea that her incarceration was going to last a really long time after her "confession" so she could get a look at the files concerning the Cipher. Now she was free?

"Who is she?" Sam asked.

"I don't know," Riley answered.

Anger burst free inside Sam. Someone—some stranger—had taken her life away from her. Only, that wasn't true. She'd seen the pictures of the woman in the digital footage. The woman had looked enough like her to be a sister.

Sam struggled with her voice, striving to sound normal. "Does she?"

"Does she what?"

"Look that much like me?"

Riley hesitated only a moment. "Yeah. She does. MI-6 made a mistake. *We* made a mistake." He hesitated. "We know that now."

Sam's eyes burned with frustration and anger and hurt. She refused to cry. She wouldn't let him see her cry.

"Two months, McLane," she said in a voice made hoarse by strain and surprise. "Mitchell took almost two months of my life and I spent them in here. After I promised myself I would never be locked down like this again."

All the times she'd been sent to her room or a corner in

foster homes, not to be seen or heard, had haunted her. She had felt powerless and helpless in a way she hadn't felt since she was a child. No one should have to go through what she'd gone through, then and in the past two months.

Riley looked at her. Pain echoed in his eyes. "Sam, I can't do anything about that. I've fixed what I could."

Her voice broke, and she didn't speak until she was under control again. "I missed Rainy's funeral. I wasn't there with my friends when they needed me. No matter what you do, you can't fix that."

"I know."

"I want out," Sam declared. "You can't come in here after two months and tell me everything has been taken care of, but now we have a mission. My apartment has been taken by this time, and my personal property has either been thrown out on the street, locked in storage or auctioned off."

"Your apartment is still there," Riley said. "I made the last two payments for you. I took care of your utilities, as well. You don't have any credit cards. Your car is out in the parking lot here at the Agency." He looked at her. "Your life is intact, Sam. So is your job."

"I'm free?" She stated that as if she couldn't believe it.

Riley nodded. "Free."

"And what the hell makes you think I want my job back?"

He looked at her. "Maybe you don't, Sam. I don't know how I would feel if I were you. I don't know how you feel right now. However you feel, I'm trying like hell to understand and I'll help you any way I can. But I need you." He pushed his breath out. "This woman that looks like you, she's tied up in the arms shipments in Berzhaan somehow. I've convinced Mitchell that I'm the right guy for this job. That *we're* the right people for this job." He paused. "I need you to make this work. The same likeness that exists that landed you in trouble can be used against her."

His words echoed in the room. The honesty in them was so real they cut like a knife. She discovered that she liked having heard him say that. *I need you.* Simple and direct, and she was surprised at how good it made her feel. Yet, at the same time, his words and his need—so apparent in him now—scared the hell out of her. *I need you* was also a trap, a commitment that she didn't want to have to make.

"Where were you when I needed you?" Sam asked in a ragged whisper. If he saw that what he was asking was more than he had given, surely he would just go away.

He eyed her steadily. "I was here, Sam. Then, when I couldn't be here anymore, I was in Berzhaan. Maybe if I hadn't been the one to bring you in I wouldn't have stuck around. But I was. And I did." He paused. "I'm also the one who found the woman in Berzhaan."

Sam crossed her arms and shook her head. "I can't go. I want to see my friends. I *need* to see my friends." I want to be around people who don't want to lock me up, she thought. Not around someone who might change his mind at any moment. Not around someone I embarrassed my-self with.

"I understand that. Let me show you something." Riley reached into his pocket and pulled out a portable DVD player. "You and Howie were working on the Cipher killing."

Sam stood her ground. She wasn't going to be lured into Riley's trap. What she wanted to do, *all* she wanted to do, was get back to Arizona and check in with Kayla, Alex, Darcy and the others.

"Howie told me you guys got close to discovering the Cipher's identity," Riley said.

"Maybe."

"Howie told me about the boat," Riley went on. "About how you picked that 'accident' as a contract hit." He opened the DVD player. "You narrowed it down to what? Fifteen guys?"

"Eleven," Sam said, still not moving. "There were eleven men on that yacht. Provided the Cipher isn't a woman with large hands."

"He isn't. He was onboard the yacht when it slammed into the docks."

"Probably not then, but shortly before," Sam agreed. "He must have dived out of the boat just seconds before the impact. That's the only way he could have gotten close enough to grab his victim's foot and hold him under till he drowned." She studied his features. "We can't prove that the Cipher was there."

"Take a look at this." Riley pushed the DVD player in her direction.

Reluctantly Sam looked. Image after image scrolled through the DVD viewer screen.

"After you nailed down those eleven faces," Riley said, "the Intel databanks went to work crunching known assassinations carried out by the Cipher. And deaths that potentially related to him. Nearly everyone the Cipher killed was someone high profile. Cameras, media as well as security, cover a lot of those incidents. Computer programs searched thousands of hours of video. We kept coming back to one face. One of those eleven potential faces you identified."

Then a man stepped into front and center of the view screen. He stood at the edge of a crowd inside a large metropolitan building. At least six feet tall, he was broad and powerful looking. He looked to be in his midfifties, fit and muscular. His head was shaved, gleaming occasionally as the smooth skin reflected light. He passed by the sequence like a man on a mission. He wore a lab coat and carried a small PDA. He could have been a doctor or an intern. The security footage was good, but the man never quite looked at a camera.

"He knew where all the cameras were," Riley said. "See how he moves? Maybe he mapped them out ahead of time, hacked into the security system and familiarized himself with the layout."

"Do you know who he is?" Sam asked.

"No."

"Why did you look into this?"

Riley was silent for a moment. "Because I thought you were right about your friend being murdered. I wanted to believe in you."

"That was a big change. You didn't want to believe in me at first."

"No," Riley admitted. "But that was when I was remembering what I'd seen in that file MI-6 had sent Mitchell. A week ago I saw you lay everything on the line in an effort to help your friends."

Sam felt herself go cold inside with anger and humiliation. She knew what had happened between them a week ago. Not a night had passed that it hadn't haunted her.

"What?" she asked in a flat voice. "You're talking about my offer of sex?"

Riley's eyes slitted and his mouth turned down. "Don't," he whispered.

"That's all it was, right? An offer to have sex? That's what you called it." Sam couldn't stop the anger she felt. Two months of being locked down, having her attempt at seduction thrown back in her face; it was more than she could take. And Riley McLane had the nerve to walk into her prison cell and expect her to act as if none of it had mattered, that she was just supposed to forget that any of it had happened.

Riley's face turned neutral. "Yeah. That's what I called it. That's what I thought it was. My mistake." He turned and walked to the door.

"Where are you going?"

"Out."

"What about me? Am I still free to go?"

Riley stopped at the doorway. "You're out, St. John. Free to go. Free to stay. Free to do whatever the hell you want to do." He stepped outside and the door closed behind him.

Sam listened to the hollow click of the door closing. This time, the sound of the lock activating didn't follow. Emotions swelled within her, almost overcoming her. She tried to push the pain and uncertainty away, but every time she did it seemed to roll back over her and attack her from another position. She couldn't get away.

He didn't deserve that, she told herself as she stared at the closed door. He'd only been doing his job.

She drew a shaky breath and looked at the clothes on the

bed. Doing his job didn't excuse him completely. He'd doubted her, and he'd hurt her. She'd shown him her vulnerable side, and he'd cast it away as though it was nothing.

You should have expected that, she chided herself. You can't leave yourself open to anyone. They're strangers, not family. They will hurt you if they get the chance, and sometimes even when they don't mean to. They're not family— Riley isn't family. He doesn't know the first thing about you.

Hesitantly, afraid of what she would find and preparing herself for the worst, Sam approached the door and tried the knob. It really was unlocked. She pulled the door open and felt the slightly cooler air in the hallway push in against her. No one was in the hallway.

She drew a breath of fresh air, then pulled her head back inside the room. She stripped off her workout clothes and showered, turning the spray up so hot she felt certain she was going to be scalded, then switching to cold needle spray.

She toweled off and dressed quickly. She left her prison garb behind in the room. As she strode down the hall, she considered her options. She wanted to return to the academy, to talk to Kayla, Alex, Darcy, Josie and Tory.

Rainy's possibly mined eggs figured into the mix somewhere, but that also put the Cipher into events, as well.

He killed Rainy. The thought slammed into Sam. He killed her and he's getting away with it. Before she knew it, tears ran down her face. She wiped them away with the back of her hand. She was mad and hurt and confused.

Going back to the academy sounded good, but it meant

relying on the friendships there instead of standing on her own. She'd been locked down for two months, unable to do anything to avenge her friend.

Are you going back to them like this? she asked herself. All busted up and broken? Is that how you want to go back? Let them see that you never really made it out of all those foster homes? Is that what you want, St. John? The sympathy vote? Damn you. You were never a quitter. Not then. Not now. You're going to finish this.

She shut off the tears and wiped her face by the time she reached the security checkpoint. The young agent manning the security desk looked up at her.

"I need to borrow the phone," Sam said.

He hesitated for a moment, then set the phone unit on the top of the counter. "Punch nine to get out."

Sam took the handset and dialed Mitchell's office.

"Mitchell," he answered in a calm voice.

"It's Sam St. John."

"Hello, Agent St. John. What can I do for you?"

"Does McLane have a cell phone?"

Mitchell hesitated. "Yes."

"I need the number."

"Why?"

"Because I changed my mind."

"You turned him down?" Mitchell didn't sound surprised.

"You bet your ass."

"I told him you would. I also told him that wouldn't be your final answer." Mitchell read off the cell-phone number. "You're not someone to leave something unfinished, and the Cipher is unfinished business. So is the woman you were mistaken for."

Sam tried to respond to that, but nothing came to her.

"Good luck, St. John." Mitchell broke the connection.

Pushing through the surreal feeling of the moment, Sam punched in the numbers for Riley's cell phone.

"McLane," he answered. His voice sounded gruff and rushed.

"Me," Sam said. Silence filled the line for a moment. "I want the Cipher. He killed my friend. I'm not going to let him get away with that. Where can I meet you?"

Chapter 13

Less than an hour later, Sam was aboard an air force jet transport winging out of Langley Air Force Base. The rest of Commander Novak's SEAL team was waiting when they arrived. The SEALs were working security and covert ops on the mission.

All of the Navy Special Forces men were young, lean and hard. They exuded confidence and efficiency, but they could have passed as college students or young business executives. They were a mix of white, black, Asian and Middle-Eastern.

Seated at the conference table bolted to the floor, Sam felt the vibration of the jet's powerful engines.

While en route on the helicopter, the SEAL commander and Riley had stayed busy on cell phones making arrangements. Howie had worked on the notebook computer. Absolved of any duties and not able to hear what Riley was saying because he'd cut her out of his communications loop, Sam had forced herself to sleep for the half hour the trip to Langley Air Force Base took. Sleep was her oldest retreat from events that were out of her control, and from unhappiness that had been too much to bear. She'd woken as soon as the helicopter had begun its descent.

The air force jet was large and set up for handling meetings in-flight. The interior was almost set up like a conference room, complete with coffeemakers, a well-stocked refrigeration unit and a kitchen area.

Novak's SEAL team members were quiet and efficient, much like their commander. They all ate and sat attentively around the table as Riley provided the briefing.

"Gentlemen," Riley said, "for almost two years, the United States, particularly the Central Intelligence Agency, has been under intensive scrutiny by Prime Minister Razidae and his cabinet. We are providing arms and acting in an advisory capacity to Berzhaan's military, but several of that nation's citizens as well as our own people have gotten suspicious of our efforts there."

"We will continue in that capacity," Novak said, "while we follow through on this mission. Our primary mission is to keep Agent McLane's team alive and in good health while they follow through on their assignment."

"That assignment is going to be risky," Riley went on. "We've got limited resources, a definite risk of exposure, and know for a fact that our intelligence sources have a leak."

One of the SEALs raised a hand. He was young and lean and earnest. "How exposed is the operation going to be, Agent McLane?"

"For the most part, we'll maintain a stationary post," Riley answered. "However, going into the situation, we're going to attempt to take down a Russian agent who is probably guilty of arms dealing with the Kemenis and, possible, the Q'Rajn. We expect a lot of resistance to that part of the plan. If we're caught."

"Take down?" one of the SEALs asked. "Do you mean, terminate?"

"No. I mean we'll take the woman into custody." Riley nodded at Howie, who tapped buttons on his keyboard.

The monitor at the front of the conference area juiced and filled with an image of the mystery Russian woman. Unfortunately, the SEALs thought Sam was the one on the screen. They turned to look at her.

"Wrong woman," Riley said. "Everybody makes that mistake." He looked at her, then changed his focus back to the SEALs. He pointed at the image on the screen. "We haven't identified this woman yet, but we know she's working with a Russian SVR officer named Sergei Ivanovitch."

The images on the screen changed again, showing Ivanovitch in a montage of scenes around the Eastern European countries.

"Ivanovitch is currently stationed in Berzhaan with orders to prove that the CIA is delivering weapons to the Kemenis," Riley went on. "We've confirmed that through Intel networks. Until a few days ago, no one knew Ivanovitch was in the area." He frowned. "Be advised that Ivanovitch is not above doing whatever it takes to prove that the CIA has dirty hands in the arms deals taking place in Berzhaan. If Ivanovitch finds you, he *will* compromise you and this mission."

"Is that why the Russians had plastic surgery performed on the woman you showed us earlier?" another SEAL asked. "To compromise the CIA's presence there?"

"We don't know," Riley answered. "Our first stage of this mission is to take this woman and allow Agent St. John to pass herself off as this woman for a few hours. When she's successful, we can plant a computer virus in their machines that will give us a second look at some of their incoming and outgoing communications. Hopefully by then we'll know more about the Russian activities in Suwan."

"Sir," another SEAL spoke up, "you're talking about putting your agent into a guaranteed hostile situation. We can't protect her there."

"No," Riley said. "We can't. But if things go wrong, we will go get her."

"Second thoughts, St. John?"

Sam glanced up from the sandwich she was making in the jet's small kitchen area. Riley stood in the doorway to the kitchen area. Concern touched his face, but Sam guessed that he was probably worried about the success of the mission, not her. He'd come back to Langley to get her because she was a better means to finish his mission in Berzhaan. She made herself face that fact, and she embraced it. Getting used for something had been a way of life for her for a long time.

"I'm fine," she said. She finished assembling the sandwich, then took out a knife and cut it into triangles. She wasn't particularly hungry, but eating and sleeping were important factors in living through a bad situation.

"You look tired."

"Look," Sam said, unsheathing steel in her voice, "you don't have to worry about me. I didn't crack for two months while Mitchell kept me sequestered away."

"You didn't crack because you didn't have anything to tell. You weren't guilty."

Then why don't you cut me some slack? Sam wanted to know. But she didn't ask the question. Instead, she said, "I'll come through with what I'm supposed to do."

"What you're supposed to do," Riley growled, "is infiltrate a top-notch SVR unit that is trying to undermine CIA ops in a foreign country with an undeveloped oil field. That's a lot of responsibility."

"Is that what this is about, McLane?" Sam seethed. "That I might screw up your mission?"

"Damn, but it's hard to talk to you." Riley crossed his arms over his chest. "You don't have to take on the world by yourself."

"I'm the only person I trust," Sam said. "While I was locked up, I looked around every day. I didn't see anyone else locked up with me."

"One of your problems is that you don't open up. You like being the loner."

Being the loner is safest, Sam thought. Memory of how Riley had turned her away filled her stomach with shards of glass. The thing that hurt her most was how much she'd gotten into the role of seductress. Everything had felt so right, so natural, like some of the chemistry Darcy and the others had talked about from time to time. Sam got as angry with herself as she was with him. She'd been the bigger fool. She should just get over it and be done with it.

"I open up just fine," Sam said. "A lot of times I've found the results just aren't worth the trouble."

Riley took in a deep breath.

"I'll get my part done," Sam said. "You still haven't made a believer out of me that the Cipher is in Berzhaan."

"If he's not there, Ivanovitch's team will know how to get in touch with him."

"What makes you think that?"

"After you and Howie ID'ed the hit off the coast of Turkey, Howie dug into who would profit from the murder. Turns out that one of the brothers is deeply in bed with a Russian investment company. He's a compulsive gambler, and they're blackmailing him. Agency Intel knew about that, but no one put the brother's death into the mix. Until you and Howie developed the investigation, everyone believed the man's death was accidental."

"What company?"

"It's a front for the Russian *Mafiya*," Riley said. "A shell company. The investors are Russian organized crime members with an eye toward expansion. Howie's efforts turned up some possible links to American organized crime. A meeting of criminal minds."

Sam considered that, not surprised. Since Russia had declared Communism dead after the Berlin Wall fell in 1989, the whole country had gone into the business of free enterprise. Crime families there had already made giant strides in the black market, drugs, white slave trade, and illegal weapons sales.

"The day of the murder," Riley went on, "one of the criminal families the CIA has been monitoring regarding arms sales moved a hundred thousand dollars into a private account in the Cayman Islands," Riley said. "Howie lost the trail there, but the money was obviously a payoff for the murder."

"That's thin," Sam pointed out.

"You're the one who brought up the fact that Intel has placed the Cipher in Berzhaan lately. Seems like that angle bears investigation." Riley shifted.

"There's more," Sam said.

Riley crossed the room and helped himself to a cup of coffee. Then he leaned a hip back against the counter. "Sergei Ivanovitch is more of a wild card than we thought."

Sam took a bite of her sandwich. For the first time she saw how tired Riley was. The last week hadn't been kind to him, either.

"Ivanovitch has been linked to the crime families," Riley said. "One of the double agents we use for information has indicated that lately Ivanovitch has decided to use his position to influence events in Berzhaan to help the *Mafiya* gain a foothold in that country."

"For the oil?"

Riley nodded. "The oil is a big draw for anyone. But Berzhaan is something of an open market. Gain Prime Minister Razidae's trust and confidence, and you can move a lot of product through the city. Any kind of product you want to move."

"Does it matter whether Ivanovitch is there for the Russian government or the *Mafiya*?"

"Yeah, it does." Riley squinted and didn't look happy. "He's in the same boat you are, St. John. He doesn't trust anyone. He's going to be looking ahead and over his shoulder at the same time. Someone like that, they're going to hurt someone before they even know it." He paused. "If we're successful in putting you inside Ivanovitch's operation, you're going to be stepping inside a viper pit. The only plus we have is that you look so much like the woman in his operation."

Enough to fool Ivanovitch? A cold chill slid down Sam's back. Even if she could make herself up to look like her doppelganger, there were a thousand things that could go wrong. Maybe even a million. Any one of them was enough to get her killed.

"You still don't know who the woman is?" Sam asked.

"Not yet. We will. We're going to flip a source in Suwan that Intel has identified as one of the assets Ivanovitch has had in the city. We're going to own him. Then we'll find out enough to get this operation up off the ground. In the meantime, we know where to find the woman."

Riley turned to rinse his coffee cup out in the sink. For the first time Sam saw the days-old bruise that still lay faded and yellow under his cheekbone and across his nose. Before she could stop herself, she reached out to touch his face.

He turned into her touch so that her hand lay along his face. His gaze consumed her, stirred up those memories that had haunted her for the past week. She throttled those feelings and took her hand back.

"Where did you get the bruise?" Sam asked.

"The woman," Riley answered. "Like I said, she's good at hand-to-hand. That's another thing the two of you have in common."

One of the Navy SEALs stepped into the kitchen area, then quickly stopped. "I'll come back later."

"No," Sam said before Riley could point out that nothing was going on between them. "I was just leaving." She gathered her plate and bottle of water and did just that, returning to the main conference room where Novak's men continued briefing on the mission.

Sam took a seat at the back, listening but not hearing. Seated in the middle of the men, she was effectively alone. She'd learned how to do that in public school before she'd gone to the Athena Academy.

Riley came out of the kitchen area, gazed at her for a moment, then took a seat near Novak. The briefing continued and Sam tried to keep from thinking that the plane was hurtling through the night toward certain death. She just hoped whatever disaster waited ahead didn't take any of them. Let it be someone else's death, she thought. Someone like Rainy's killer.

Chapter 14

"There she is. I've got her."

Sam stood in front of a shop a block from the hotel where the mysterious woman who looked like her was staying. Sam put a hand to her face to cover her communications. She wore a radio earplug to stay in touch with the rest of the team.

"Which way?" she asked.

"North."

Sam turned and started walking, threading through the tourists and shopkeepers scattered along the street. Cross streets surrounded the hotel as if it were the center square of a tic-tac-toe board. Down the street fronting the hotel, the main drag was apparently into the shopping area where Sam was. North was toward the Old City, and it was also toward Riley McLane.

"I've got her," Riley said.

"Careful," Novak advised. "Everything we've seen on her suggests that she's decisive, quick and deadly."

"Affirmative."

Sam put more haste in her steps. Twilight closed in over Suwan, bringing up pools of neon lights where the city had started a slow conversion to Western decadence. There were few of those, but that was where most of the tourists went in the evenings.

They do *not* head into Old City, Sam told herself. Not for any good reason.

"This might not be a good time to pick her up," Riley said.

"We might not get another chance," Sam said. "She could vanish and we'll never have this opportunity again."

"I know."

Howie Dunn had broken into the hotel's guest records and discovered the woman had been staying for more than two weeks. She was also a frequent visitor under the name Elizabeth Harris and had traveled to Suwan a number of times. Looking back over the times, Howie had discovered matches to several instances when incriminating evidence against the CIA had been discovered, or when the Kemenis had gained increased firepower, causing more damage to government buildings and carrying through assassinations.

"It's your call," Novak broke into the communications link. "We're in position."

"She could be heading for a meeting with someone," Riley said.

"I'm not going to get inside their organization without

meeting people," Sam said. She put more effort into her stride.

"She has a point," Novak replied.

"Damn it," Riley said. "I know." He paused. "You're ready?"

Sam knew he was talking about her. "Yes."

"Then let's do it."

Sam reached into the shoulder bag she carried and closed her fist around the S&W .40-caliber pistol there. She slid the safety off with her thumb and stepped across the street.

Riley's heartbeat picked up speed as he saw the woman walking toward his position. Even knowing that she wasn't Sam St. John, that she was a Russian agent whose real name they still didn't know, he couldn't believe the similarity. They even had the same kind of aggressive walk, complete with a hip roll that was mesmerizing.

"Watch her," Riley advised the young SEAL who flanked him. They stood in the alley outside a small café that had been constructed in the building's basement. A nearby window stood a little above ground level. "She's deadly at hand-to-hand. Don't underestimate her."

The SEAL grinned. "I was top of my class in unarmed combat. And I'm more than twice her size." He stood leaning against the building, arms crossed over his chest. "The trick will be to take her down without hurting her."

"She knows me," Riley said, turning away from the approaching woman.

"It's okay. I've got her."

In the multi-paned café window Riley watched the

grayed-out reflections of the young SEAL approaching the Russian agent. His stomach tightened. The woman was stepping into exactly the kind of trap he was going to push Sam into in just a short time.

"Hey, Elizabeth," the young SEAL said in a pleasant voice.

Riley watched as the woman swiveled her head up in the SEAL's direction. She smiled, but the effort never reached her eyes.

"Bill," she said, veering toward him, acting surprised and puzzled at the same time. "Is that you?"

It was a good act. For a moment the SEAL must have questioned if he had the right woman, because he hesitated.

At that instant Riley knew the wheels had come off the operation. The woman hadn't been fooled for a moment. He started to turn, reaching for his pistol at his waistband.

The young SEAL was caught flatfooted. He hadn't been disarmed by her smiling approach so much as he had by her delicate appearance. With the SEAL standing between the woman and himself, Riley couldn't see exactly what she did, but the SEAL jerked back, his face suddenly a mask of blood. Then he flew backward and crashed into Riley. Outweighed by the bigger young man, Riley went backward as well. Both of them crashed through the café's window and went down across a table in a shower of splintering wood and shards of glass.

Riley shifted the SEAL's unconscious bulk from him and tried to get his feet under him as the café's patrons scattered. The woman looked at him through the window. Interest showed on her beautiful features but no fear. Riley knew she had to be trying to figure out who had given her up, and how much the CIA knew.

"Man down," Riley called over the earplug. He pointed his weapon at the woman. She moved immediately, as elusive as a ghost. "Man down. Confirm?"

"Affirmative," Novak's calm voice replied. "How bad?"

"He's still breathing." Riley clambered through the window. "She's getting away. I'm in pur—"

The woman hadn't run. She stood just to one side of the window. When Riley turned to face her, she kicked the pistol from his hand, then, in an extension of the same movement, kicked him in the face hard enough to drive him back against the window frame.

"You should have stayed away, Special Agent Riley McLane," she said in a voice that sounded so much like Sam St. John's. "Now we're going to have to talk more intimately." She reached out and caught hold of his hair, yanking with enough force to cause agonizing pain. She was surprisingly strong.

Riley surged up from the café, intending to bowl her over before she could set herself. Instead, she dodged to one side and swept his legs out from under him with one foot. He went down hard, smashing his chin against the paved surface of the alley so hard he almost blacked out. The coppery taste of blood flooded his mouth. He struggled to focus his double vision.

"Why did you come here?" the woman demanded. She still had hold of his hair. She glanced around quickly.

"We're coming," Novak said. "Close the perimeter, Red Team. Close the perimeter."

There were eight points of confrontation spreading out

from the Hilton, a circle set within a circle, all designed to stick with the woman and overwhelm her. If Ivanovitch had put anyone on the woman to back her up, the SEALs wouldn't have been able to get that close to her.

Curious men and women lined the two windows of the basement café. Heads poked out the broke window. None of them, Riley saw, belonged to the young SEAL.

Riley tried to get up. The woman pushed his face back into the alley floor. Pain exploded throughout his skull.

"No," she chided. "Now that you have begun this little sortie, we'll do things my way. Answer my questions or I'll snap your neck."

Riley believed her. He flailed at her as she seized his chin and the back of his head in her hands. She stood with a foot on his hand nearest her, pinning it to the ground and staying too far back for him to reach her with his other hand.

Metallic *tings* sounded overhead. Then Riley spotted a lithe shadow moving amid the twilight darkness gathered on the alley floor. The woman responded to the sound and the sight, as well, dropping his head and turning to face the latest threat.

Sam St. John reached the second-floor landing on the metal fire escape she'd evidently used to climb down from the rooftop, then she launched herself over the railing.

Sam was already in the air before the woman holding onto Riley McLane glanced up. When the woman did look, moonlight played over her pale face. The fact that she did look so much like her in person surprised Sam. Then she hit the woman in a cross-body block that took them to the alley floor.

Ribs aching, bruised if not broken, Sam rolled and came up on her feet. She lifted her hands before her automatically and came set in a defensive position, feet set in the L.

Amazingly, even after taking out two opponents, her look-alike did the same. Their martial arts styles were different, Sam noticed. The woman's looked more like a Korean style, tighter and more aggressive. Sam's was Chinese, loose and flowing. Only a true expert would have known the difference.

"Who are you?" the woman demanded. Surprise widened her eyes.

Sam circled to the left, shuffling her feet and never crossing one foot over the other so she could be caught off balance. The woman mirrored her, moving her feet with the same caution.

Sam said, "Surrender." Only after she'd spoken did Sam realize they were both speaking Russian.

"No." The woman's eyes narrowed. Then she attacked.

Sam gave ground immediately. Kung fu was a discipline that taught a fighter to use an opponent's strength against him or her. The look-alike tried to drive her blows through Sam's defenses, relying on muscle and speed. Matching her kicks and punches with her opponent's, Sam turned aside the flurry of blows and had her own blocked. Her arms and legs ached with the forceful impacts immediately.

The woman threw a right-handed punch at Sam's head. Sam automatically stepped outside the blow, slapped at the back of the woman's wrist with her left hand to throw her off balance, and stepped around to the side in an attempt to hit her with a spinning back fist. Instead, she caught a whirling back kick full in the face.

Staggered, Sam stepped back, giving ground immediately. Her opponent gave no quarter, dropping into another attack form and coming at her instantly. Sam batted aside a side kick with a sweeping forearm, ducked beneath a roundhouse kick that would have taken her head off, and met a front snap kick with one of her own.

Without warning the woman broke off from the fight, turned and ran.

Sam hesitated just a second, thinking it was some kind of trick. Then she realized that Commander Novak and his SEAL team were quickly surrounding them. She ran after the woman.

One of the SEALs tried to intercept the woman as she streaked for the same fire escape Sam had leaped from. When she'd first taken up pursuit, Sam had claimed the high ground, thinking that the vantage point would allow her to keep up with the action better. After years of *la parkour,* she was at home on the rooftops, and the alleys were narrow enough to leap from building to building.

The SEAL set himself to block the woman, then punched at her. She swept his punch away, then came forward with the same arm she'd blocked with and slammed an elbow into the SEAL's face, stunning him. She twisted around to the side, grabbed a handful of the man's hair and evaded Riley's sudden lunge at her. Then she ran up the SEAL's back even as he was falling. She caught hold of the fire escape and pulled herself over the railing.

Another SEAL leaped after her, but he was too late. His hands slammed together just as she pulled her feet out of reach. She threw a chain around the ladder that would normally slide down at a pull, effectively blocking the way up. There wasn't another fire escape till the next block.

"Riley." Sam ran at Riley. "Help me up."

Realizing what Sam intended to do, Riley gathered his hands into a stirrup, bent over, caught her foot in his hands and helped propel her up. Sam caught the edge of the landing railing as her look-alike sprinted up the stairway, turning and yanking herself up. After she pulled herself over, Sam hurled herself in pursuit.

They gained the rooftop within a heartbeat of each other. The look-alike glanced back over her shoulder as if calculating her chances of confronting Sam, then obviously thought outrunning her would be the better choice.

"South," Sam said over the radio frequency as she ran after her quarry.

"Affirmative," Commander Novak responded.

From the corner of her eye, Sam caught the movement of the SEALs below in the alley. Two of them helped the man the woman had flung through the café to his feet.

At the roof's edge, the look-alike didn't hesitate, flinging herself over the alley and landing on the next rooftop. She dropped and rolled, coming at once to her feet.

Sam followed, throwing herself over, as well. She noticed at once that she was better at the rooftop travel than her double, and she leaned into the race. Evidently her doppelganger was an expert in hand-to-hand, but she lacked skills in urban racing.

They ran across three more rooftops, going up a floor on a taller building. Sam leaped forward and caught the building's edge, trying desperately not to think of the three-story drop below her. She pulled herself up and continued the chase.

"East," Sam called when her quarry broke and ran in that direction. She continued calling the changes to guide the SEALs rushing through the alleys below. Chayton stayed in touch, his voice calm and neutral. From below, they could never have tracked the woman.

Her breath burned the back of her throat. Her legs began to feel like lead. She pushed through the fatigue, noting with grim satisfaction that the chase was wearing on her double as well. Still, for all the skills Sam had at *la parkour*, she knew her double was in better shape than she was. The two months of being incarcerated had taken some of her endurance edge away. It had been hard to use large muscle groups in an aerobic activity while in the room.

Sam concentrated on putting one foot in front of the other, letting her instincts and her skill give her the edge. Gradually she started overtaking her double.

"North," Sam shouted hoarsely, throwing herself over the side of the next building. Her feet thumped solidly against the rooftop, then she regained her balance and kept running.

"Affirmative," Novak replied, sounding exactly as he had long minutes ago when the chase had first begun. "We're close to your position now, Sam. Just keep her moving."

Sam leaped another alley, losing sight of her double for just an instant. She hit the other building's rooftop and sprinted forward, not seeing the woman's leg come shooting out of the darkness around the side of a HVAC unit on top of the building until it was too late.

Raising her hands to at least partially block the kick, Sam grabbed the leg, tripped herself and went back and down. She hung on to her opponent's leg and twisted violently, bringing the other woman down with her. Rolling away, Sam shoved up to her feet. She was winded and hurting. A small cut over her left eye wept blood down into her eye, and part of the world turned black.

The woman attacked, using everything she knew. It was all Sam could do to keep her face from being broken up and to stay upright. She swept her arm out, blocking a punch, then came back with a reverse punch that slammed into her opponent's face at the same time a back kick hammered her stomach. Her breath left her lungs in a rush. Black rimmed her vision.

"Are you finished then?" the woman asked.

Using everything she had, Sam straightened. "No."

"You are." Her double grinned confidently and wiped blood from the corner of her mouth. "If you make me kill you, I will. Don't doubt that."

"I don't." Sam stared into that face that was so much like her own. The whole experience was too strange. If the pain hadn't already numbed her to anything else, the surreal quality of the situation would have.

"They have blocked the way ahead of me, yes?"

"Yes." From the corner of her eye, Sam saw two shadows leaping across the rooftops in their direction. Evidently two of the SEALs had found egress to the rooftops.

"I can still get away," the woman said. "I will go through you if I have to."

"You haven't been able to so far."

"How did you get my face?"

"I was going to ask you the same question," Sam said.

"It's a pity," the woman said. "You're almost as pretty as me. This will almost be like destroying myself."

Too late, Sam realized that the woman's words weren't egotistical. They were said to distract her, to work on any hesitation that she herself carried, and to enhance any insecurity.

The woman feinted, then launched into an all-out attack that drove Sam backward. Sam fought defensively, staying as small and as pliable as she could, trying not to stand forcefully in the woman's way. Getting a broken arm or a leg or a skull fracture wouldn't just end the fight, it would also effectively end her chances of doing any real good going undercover in the Russian operation.

It would end her chances of finding the Cipher. The assassin would get away with Rainy's death.

For a time Sam held her ground. Knowing that all she had to do was hold her ground because the clock worked against her opponent. Every second, the SEALs got closer, the net grew tighter. Then, a foot seemed to come from nowhere and landed against her jaw. Sam's head whipped around and a nova erupted inside her skull.

"I've got her in my sights," a man's voice said over the ear transceiver. "I've got the shot."

"Take her down," Novak ordered.

"No," Sam yelled weakly. An image of the woman's face exploding from a bullet filled her dazed mind. She didn't want to see the woman who wore her face die. The thought sickened her in ways she was not prepared for.

Sam's double hit her again, knocking her to the ground. Then the look-alike was off like a shot, sprinting for the nearest side of the building. Two steps from the building's edge, she stumbled but kept going. Sam pushed up and threw herself after the woman.

"I hit her," the SEAL radioed.

"Damn it," someone else said. "She's headed for the edge."

The look-alike stumbled again as she tried to leap from the building. Her legs turned rubbery and she fell over the side, her legs dragging.

Sam threw herself down and reached for the woman. The four-story drop promised nothing but sudden death or a trip to intensive care.

Blindly, guided by instinct and desperation, Sam caught the woman's foot as she fell. When the weight hit the end of her arm, Sam felt certain her shoulder was going to be torn from its socket and the sudden impact with the roof's edge was going to crush her chest. If nothing broke, she was still in for heavy bruising. She cried out in pain. She knew she wasn't going to be able to hold on long. The woman was dead weight at the end of her arm. She could feel the woman already sliding from her grip. Managing to get her other hand around the slim ankle she held, Sam only forestalled the inevitable.

Then Riley was there, dwarfing her with his size. He reached down and took hold of the woman. Immediately the look-alike's weight lessened. Sam kept hold with both hands.

"It's okay, Sam," he said. "You can let go. I've got her."

"Don't drop her," Sam pleaded. What would it be like to see the woman dead? Would she still look like her, or would she look like someone else?

And how the hell did she get my face?

"I'm not going to drop her," Riley promised. "I've got her. Let go."

"No."

"Damn, but you're stubborn."

"I can't," Sam whispered. "I can't let her go. I can't let her fall." She didn't know where that impulse came from, but she knew it was true.

"All right, then, let's pull her in. On three." Riley counted quickly. On three, they pulled the woman to the rooftop just in time for a SEAL with a short tranquilizer rifle to kneel down and put disposable plastic handcuffs on the woman.

Sam finally let the woman go then. She sat with her back against the rooftop and ached all over.

"Don't get too comfortable, St. John," Riley said. "We've got to get you up and running. Someone's going to miss her soon. Either you're in place or we scratch this phase of the mission."

Minutes later in the back of the truck the SEALs used as a command vehicle, Sam unbuttoned the woman's shirt and started stripping her. The unconscious state the woman was in made handling her and getting the clothes off almost impossible. She had to cut the disposable cuffs from her.

"What are you doing?" Riley asked.

"I need her clothes," Sam said. "If I return to the hotel in a different outfit, someone may notice."

Riley swore. "I didn't think about that."

"I thought you were the one with the plan," Sam stated

sarcastically. "Did you think maybe we were going to co-
ordinate outfits for the kidnapping?" She tugged on the
shirt again. "Help me."

They worked by flashlight. Once they had the
woman's shirt off, Riley handcuffed her again, putting
her hands in front of her this time and securing the cuffs
to an eyebolt set into the metal frame of the truck's
cargo area.

Sam knew that Riley was uncomfortable and embarrassed by the way he handled the sleeping woman's body.
At first Sam enjoyed that, watching Riley totally out of his
depth as they took her double's pants off, leaving her clad
only in a silky emerald bra and bikini panties that emphasized her slender figure and milky pale skin.

"Damn, St. John," Riley whispered hoarsely. "She really could be you."

Sam silently agreed. The woman was a match for her,
so it might as well have been her lying there nearly naked,
unprotected and vulnerable. She suddenly felt everything
she was certain the woman would have felt if she'd woken
and seen them looking at her. Riley stared at the woman,
and Sam didn't know if it was her double's nakedness or
likeness that kept him glued to the sight of her.

"And you know we look that much alike because you're
seeing her nearly naked?" Sam started to ask when he
could have possibly seen her naked, then she remembered
the constant surveillance she'd been under in her cell. The
thought of Riley watching her through the cameras with
the night-vision capability made her angry, but the possibility also unexpectedly excited her.

And if he'd been interested in watching her in the

shower, the fact that he'd been able to spurn her attempted seduction said a lot.

Riley looked up at her with a guilty expression that quickly disappeared. "I'm just saying that the resemblance is even more noticeable now."

"I'm going to do us both a favor and not ask what makes you think that." Sam took an army blanket from the supplies the SEALs had in the truck and covered the sleeping woman. She used a sanitized cloth to clean the blood from the woman's face.

"I've seen the inside of your lip," Riley said. He had helped her clean up after the fight. "I think you need a couple of stitches."

Sam had felt the cut on the inside of her lower lip with her tongue. Her lip was puffy from swelling and the edges of the wound felt raw and jagged. She agreed with Riley's assessment, but she knew medical help was impossible.

"We can't," she said as she continued her ministrations. Although they'd been opponents only moments ago, the act of helping the tranquilized woman brought Sam an unexplained peace. The beating she'd taken was going to be noticeable. Medical attention would be immediately suspect.

"She'll be all right," Riley said. "She's sleeping because of the drug. Not because of something you did."

"I know."

Riley stood and walked a few steps away. Trying hard not to be noticed, he checked the time. Full night had sprung upon the city outside the truck. They still didn't know if her double had been going somewhere important when they'd intercepted her, or merely out for dinner and drinks.

Aching and battered from the fight, Sam stood as well. "Do me a favor, McLane. Let me change clothes and I'll get to the mission."

Riley turned to look at her. "What you're about to do, Sam…" He hesitated and looked at the drugged woman lying on the cot against the wall. "It's dangerous."

"That's hardly a news flash."

"I know. But if you want to pull out of this thing, now would be the optimum time."

"Is that what you want me to do?" Sam stared at him.

"I don't want you hurt."

"Is that the real answer?" Sam asked. "Or are you just more afraid that I'll screw up your operation?"

"This is risky, Sam. It's more than you've ever been asked to do. More than you've been trained to do."

"Stepping into potentially hostile situations where I can't count on anybody but myself?" Sam arched a brow. The effort hurt and caused her headache to pound. "That's what I've been doing all my life, McLane. You've seen my background. You know that. I only thought things had changed when I signed on with the Agency." She paused, knowing she'd scored with her barbed comment. "I'll be fine. I'm back where I belong, not trusting anyone and suspicious of everyone I come in contact with."

"Hell of a way to live your life," Riley growled.

"I didn't pick it. And, just so you know, getting locked up by you and Mitchell just reemphasized something I should never have let myself forget."

Sipping a long, slow breath, Riley nodded and said, "I had that coming."

"Yes."

Riley looked at her. "You changed your life for a while. You had—have—your friends from school."

"Yes."

"You might want to rethink risking all of that."

Sam looked at him, uncomfortable with his attention now. "Tell me the truth."

"What?"

"Is the Cipher really connected to the Russians? Or is he just the carrot you dangled to get me here?"

Riley gazed at her. "He's connected to this, Sam. Just like I said he was."

"Then I'm going," Sam said. "The Cipher killed one of my friends. I'm going to shut him down." She paused. "Now give me some time to get dressed." She turned away from him and picked up the woman's clothing.

A moment later she heard him walking toward the end of the truck. Taking a deep breath, she pushed aside her fear over what she was about to step into, and she boxed the hurt that Riley had caused her. When she was safely in neutral, where she was aware of the pain in her body but not truly feeling it anymore, she pulled her top off and started getting undressed.

Stepping from the back end of the truck parked in an alley on the other side of Suwan, Riley joined Novak against the alley wall. The SEAL team commander looked ready and alert.

The SEALs kept a tight perimeter on the alley. Few of them were in sight. They had a way of blending in with their surroundings. Riley's past experiences with the special forces warriors had taught him that.

"She's going," Novak said. It wasn't a question.

"Yeah," Riley said, confirming the SEAL team commander's suspicion.

"We wouldn't have caught her double if it hadn't been for her."

"I know."

"You're worried about her."

"Hell, yes."

"She's good at what she does. She took that woman on after she put two of my guys down. Thomsen's going to have to be medi-evaced out of here."

"Sam's good, but she hasn't ever gone undercover before." Then Riley remembered what Sam's files had revealed to him. Actually, she'd been preparing for undercover work all her life.

"She'll do all right," Novak said. "If not, she has us. All she has to do is hit the panic button."

"Yeah, well, the cavalry sometimes gets there too late."

"Not in my movies," Novak said.

A few minutes later, Sam stepped down from the back of the truck. If Riley hadn't handcuffed her double in the truck, he would have sworn the woman had somehow escaped.

Riley walked over to her and studied her face. She was bruised and bloodied, her face swollen. He checked her eyes. Both pupils looked the same size, so there was a good chance she didn't have a concussion.

"How are you feeling?" Riley asked.

"Like I was hit by a truck."

Riley hesitated, not knowing what to say.

"I don't have time for a long goodbye, McLane. Neither of us do."

"I know."

"Then I'm going." Sam shouldered the bag they'd recovered that the woman had dropped, back when the young SEAL had first confronted her. She turned and started moving.

"Be careful," Riley admonished.

She stopped for a moment. "I will." She turned around to look at him. "If I call for help, don't be late."

"Bet on it," Riley said.

"I am." Without another word she walked to the end of the alley.

"That," Novak said, walking over to join Riley, "is one hell of a woman."

"I know."

Out at the street, Sam flagged down a taxi, got in the back, and was gone in the space of a drawn breath.

The hotel suite was exquisite. The bath had an old-fashioned claw-foot tub, a shower and a whirlpool, settled into Italian marble the color of coffee with cream. The bed was a four-poster affair with a white linen canopy. The desk contained a notebook computer that, unfortunately, gave no clue to what Elizabeth Harris was up to. Or who she was doing it with. The kitchen area was well stocked and contained fresh vegetables and fruits.

Sam hadn't been able to tell what room her double had been assigned from the computer keycard, and the information Riley had gotten from Fayed hadn't revealed that. Before entering the hotel, she had thrown the keycard in the trash across the street, then told the desk clerk that she'd been mugged and had lost her key.

The desk clerk had no problem believing her story and had promptly re-encoded a fresh set of keys. The hardest part had been keeping the man from calling the police.

She'd spent the first fifteen minutes checking the room over, making certain that there were no bugs. Satisfied, she'd gone to the bathroom, stripped out of the clothes and showered. She'd wanted a bath more than anything, but she wouldn't allow herself the luxury, afraid that she'd climb into warm, soapy water and not crawl out again.

She focused on the Cipher, remembering how the man had looked in the pictures she and Howie Dunn had found and the video footage from the Athena Academy. If Riley wasn't lying to her, the assassin was out there somewhere in the city.

She dressed from her double's closet, taking out a pair of khaki cargo pants and a sky-blue shawl-collar T-shirt. She wasn't too surprised to find that her double's closet was filled with the same kind of active wear she favored herself. She had definitely been going for the tourist look.

She had just finished pulling on a pair of canvas-colored cross-trainers that fit as well as her own shoes when the phone rang.

The strident, two-bell note startled her. She crossed to the phone and started to answer, then made herself remember to speak in Russian. "Hello."

"Where are you, Elle?"

Elle. Sam hung on to the name instantly. Her double's name wasn't Elizabeth. It was Elle. The two names were close enough.

"At the hotel," Sam replied. She had trouble speaking with all the damage that had been done to the inside of her mouth. "I was mugged."

"By who?"

"I don't know." Sam swallowed. The voice sounded like Sergei Ivanovitch, matching the audio files the Agency had access to. "They were young men."

"You?" Ivanovitch didn't sound as if he could believe it. "Common muggers?"

"There were a lot of them." Sam knew her garbled voice could cover a lot of the speech patterns she might have different from her double, but the best thing was too keep as quiet as she could. All she had to do was get near Ivanovitch's computers long enough to slip the spyware into the machine.

And find the Cipher.

"They did not steal anything from me," Sam went on.

"Were the police involved?"

"No. But the desk clerk knows."

"Will he be a problem?"

"I don't think so. I told him I didn't want the attention. Besides, I couldn't identify the men who attacked me. It would be wasted effort."

"Did you leave any bodies behind?" The question sounded serious, not sarcastic or teasing.

"No."

"I am in the lobby. I'll be up in a few moments."

Before Sam could reply, the phone clicked dead in her ear. Her heartbeat sped up and adrenaline flooded her system. She knew her masquerade was only going to last for a short time, but at the moment she didn't know if she was going to get out of the hotel room alive.

She retreated to her double's purse on the desk and brought it over to the wet bar area. While she'd changed clothes, one of Commander Novak's men had installed a pick-up microphone in the purse. The range was short, and a concealed button in the strap allowed her to switch the device off to avoid detection. It was the only lifeline she had.

She hoped it would be enough.

Chapter 15

"Sergei Ivanovitch is in the hotel. He's on his way up to Special Agent St. John's room."

Riley nodded at the radio operator sitting at the communications array the SEALs had set up in a secret basement below a warehouse the CIA used to conduct operations. During regular hours, the warehouse shipped goods all over Europe, conducting a profitable import/export business consisting of Western entertainment in the form of DVDs and video games, and Eastern rugs and handcrafts that shipped back the other way.

"I heard," Riley said. "Have the support teams there verified Ivanovitch's presence?"

"Yes, sir," the SEAL said, tapping the video monitor the network fed. The current image showed the hotel's lobby. "Ivanovitch is on the premises."

Riley forced himself to relax. They knew where Sam was; the SEALs were there. But he also knew they could still get to her room too late to save her if Ivanovitch discovered the subterfuge they were attempting to run.

"How many men does Ivanovitch have with him?" Riley asked.

"Ivanovitch is alone. He has a car waiting outside."

The image on the monitor changed, revealing a long, sleek sedan parked in front of the hotel near the courtesy vans.

"Do we know what he's doing there?" Riley asked.

"No, sir. We only know that he seemed concerned over Special Agent St. John. I mean, the woman Special Agent St. John is currently impersonating."

Riley touched his headset. "Put me into the communications loop on what goes on inside that room."

"Yes, sir." The communications technician tapped the keyboard.

Riley heard a couple of clicks, then the white noise coming from the headset changed frequencies.

"You're inside the loop, Special Agent McLane."

"Thank you." Everything's going to be all right, Riley told himself. Sam's sharp, and she's a quick study. But he had his doubts. And he had his guilt. He'd been responsible for helping lock her down back at Langley, and getting her here now was entirely his responsibility.

He turned his thoughts away from all the bad things that could happen in the next few minutes and focused on the good that could be done. Ivanovitch's presence, especially during the time that the American espionage services were being blamed for supplying guns to Berzhaan's rebels, was too convenient. Judging from Ivanovitch's Agency jacket, the man had to be involved somehow. He was too good not to be aware of the situation.

And then there was the Cipher. The assassin was somewhere nearby, as well.

Riley still didn't know where the events surrounding Lorraine Miller Carrington's death fit in.

He walked to the rear of the hidden area below the warehouse. Years ago, when the basement had first been built, the excavated dirt had been shipped out as cargo with no one the wiser.

The woman who was Elizabeth Harris—Elle, as Sam had informed them over the radio hidden in the woman's bag—lay on a hospital gurney. The hidden facilities had a small OR for life-or-death situations that arrived there.

The Russian agent was still under the effects of the tranquilizer dart, but she was starting to come out of it. She occasionally thrashed and fought against the restraints that held her down. She wore a gown, handcuffs and ankle cuffs.

Evidently, the drugs had triggered a nightmare that kept repeating. She spoke Russian in the voice of a small child, alternately begging and pleading, then angry. Three of the SEALs spoke Russian and had translated. She'd spoken some names.

Riley had written them all down, not missing a chance to get any information. A family name, Leonov, was repeated several times. Three names—Natasha, Mother and Father—were constantly repeated, in Russian, as if the woman were calling out to them.

The satellite phone in Riley's pocket vibrated for attention. He answered it. "McLane." The connection was heavily encrypted and there was no danger of anyone breaking the security coding.

"Riley."

Recognizing Director Stone Mitchell's voice at once, Riley said, "Yes, sir." The first thought that flashed through his mind was that the director was calling to scrap the mission.

"Something interesting turned up on the background discovery you asked for," Mitchell said.

Otherwise you wouldn't have called, Riley thought, but he said, "Regarding what?"

"I was told you still have St. John's double in custody."

"Yes."

"And that you were running names she was mentioning while under the effect of the tranquilizer."

Riley waited.

"The name Leonov popped up with some serious baggage attached to it," Mitchell said.

"What baggage?" Riley looked at the legal pad he'd been taking notes on. He'd circled Leonov.

"Boris and Anya Leonov," Mitchell said. "Log on to the FTP site. I'm sending you a file. Your eyes only. Commander Novak and his team get this information only on a need-to-know basis."

Curious, Riley opened the notebook computer on a stainless steel table next to the gurney. He'd been working on the computer, which was connected to the heavily encrypted satellite-connected network provided for espionage teams using the facility. He opened the FTP connection and watched as the file Mitchell sent was uncompressed and opened. Several documents and photographs opened in separate windows.

"As it turns out, Boris Leonov and his wife Anya were double agents for Britain decades ago," Mitchell said. As he spoke, a picture of a young man with ice-blue eyes and a beautiful, petite young woman with startling blond hair floated to the top of the computer screen.

Riley stared at the screen. "Double agents?"

"They were both KGB," Mitchell said, "but neither of them bought into the Communist party line. Anya Leonov, under her maiden name Petrov, was a gymnastics competitor in the 1968 and 1972 Olympics. She didn't medal either time, but she was a serious contender."

The next picture showed the blond woman in a leotard doing a one-handed handstand atop uneven bars. The woman's petite build and obvious athletic ability immediately reminded Riley of Sam St. John. It also reminded him of the woman lying on the gurney.

"After their marriage and activation as KGB agents," Mitchell continued, "MI-6 flipped the Leonovs, employing them as double agents. They were good at what they did, and good at walking the thin line dictated by life as a double agent. Their handler offered to bring them in, but they weren't ready to leave their families. They felt that the Communist regime couldn't last much longer and wanted to do everything they could to hasten that end. But that started to change when Anya Leonov gave birth."

Another picture floated up, showing the Leonovs at home as proud parents. They held two babies.

"Once their twin daughters, Elle and Natasha, were

born," Mitchell said, "the Leonovs wanted to come in. An arrangement was made, but something happened."

Twins, Riley thought. His mind reeled against the implications. Twin girls. White-blond hair from their mother, and ice-blue eyes from their father. Sam's first language was Russian.

The monitor changed, showing the wreckage of a bomb-blasted car.

"Unfortunately," Mitchell said, "the Leonovs didn't get clear of Moscow. The KGB was already tracking them down. Their car was hit by an RPG-7 anti-tank rocket."

Riley's throat went dry. He'd seen firsthand the kind of damage an anti-tank rocket could cause. And whoever had fired the rocket had known the Leonovs had children.

"The girls weren't killed," Riley whispered.

"No. Apparently not. The Leonovs had already taken steps to get the girls out of the country and were hoping to smuggle them to America. Although, only one of them was thought to have survived a secondary attempt to kill the children. One of the girls was believed to have been killed. The other was adopted by a Russian family. To further hide her, the baby took the surname of her adoptive parents. Her name is Elle Petrenko."

Riley felt a featherlight touch at his back where he kept a spare S&W .40 caliber pistol that matched the one under his left arm. He started turning, knowing already that he was too late. From the corner of his eye, he saw official Russian SVR identification pop up on the monitor screen. The face in the ID belonged to the woman on the gurney.

And it could have belonged to Sam St. John.

"Elle Petrenko is an SVR agent," Mitchell said into his ear.

Riley looked at the young blond woman standing behind him next to the gurney. The restraints lay open on the bed. She held his second .40-caliber pistol, peering at him over the open sights with those ice-blue eyes.

"Bang," she said softly in English. "You're dead."

A knock sounded at the hotel door.

Sam crossed the room, took a deep breath to settle her nerves, and opened the door.

Sergei Ivanovitch stood in the hall with his hands clasped behind him. He wore an elegant white suit that made his dark hair and goatee stand out. A half smile that never touched his eyes curved his lips.

"May I come in?" he asked.

"Of course." Sam stepped back and allowed him to enter. She closed the door after him.

Ivanovitch reached for her face. She flinched. He held back his hand.

"Are you all right, Elle?" he asked.

"I have been better," Sam said, her voice distorted by the swelling.

"May I examine you?"

"I would prefer not to be touched."

"And I would prefer to know how much I can rely on an agent," Ivanovitch said with a trace of irritation. He reached for her again.

Sam forced herself to stand still. Ivanovitch's touch was surprisingly gentle. He pushed her face and checked the thin bones surrounding her eyes.

"You don't appear to have a concussion," he said.

"Just a headache," she told him.

"I'm not surprised. Open your mouth."

Reluctantly, Sam did as she was told. Ivanovitch inserted a finger into her mouth and checked her lips, gums and teeth.

"Your lower lip needs stitches," he announced, withdrawing his finger. "I'll have a medical kit brought up."

"I'll be fine," Sam said.

"Nonsense. The matter is simple enough. I can attend to it." Ivanovitch took out a cell phone and ordered someone to bring a medical kit to the hotel room. He crossed over to the wet bar and poured himself a drink. "In the meantime, I've rearranged our delivery."

Delivery? Sam didn't let her surprise or curiosity show. What delivery? "Was it because of me? Because of what happened to me?"

"Yes."

"I apologize."

Ivanovitch shrugged and smiled. "As if you had a choice in your own mugging."

"You could have kept the appointment."

Ivanovitch sipped his drink and frowned. He adjusted his twin shoulder holsters. "Not without you. I've told you before, the man we're dealing with here is very dangerous. He's killed a great number of men in his time." He looked at her. "And women."

A thousand questions slammed into Sam's mind, but she knew that the real Elle wouldn't have asked any of them. She hoped that Riley and the SEAL team were hearing everything that was being said.

She asked the only question that she could. "When is the new appointment?"

"In an hour."

"Perhaps we should go."

"We have time. I will attend to your lip, then we will go. The Cipher will keep until we are there."

Sam's breath caught in her throat. She struggled to show no reaction. Rainy's killer was there. And he was part of the Russian operation. But where did he fit in?

Her train of thought was interrupted by a knock at the door.

Riley met Elle Petrenko's gaze evenly. She looked totally cold, totally in control. He didn't blame her.

He made no move for his other pistol, knowing she would put a bullet through his heart if he made the effort. No one else was in the room. He cursed his own reluctance to take one of the SEALs away from a support position to watch over the woman full-time. With Thomsen out because of injury and himself recognizable to Ivanovitch and potentially all of the Russian SVR team, he'd undertaken the duty himself. Only, he hadn't been as attentive as he should have, and he'd underestimated the woman's abilities.

The pistol in her hands never wavered, locked on target with the center of his chest.

"Sir," Riley said calmly to the phone he held against his ear, "something's come up. I'll have to let you go. I'll call you back as soon as I can." He broke the connection while Mitchell was asking questions he knew he couldn't answer.

"You know he will call your team immediately," Elle said. "He will have someone check on you."

"Probably."

"Then we'll need to move quickly. Turn around."

Riley stood his ground. "If you're going to shoot me, get it done."

"I will."

"Fine by me," Riley said. "That pistol isn't silenced. The men in the next room will at least be warned. I owe them that for not paying closer attention to you." As tight as his throat was, he hoped he sounded normal. Even if he didn't sound normal, he knew he meant what he said.

"You're a fool," she said.

"Earlier," Riley agreed. "For underestimating you. But not now. I'm not going to die with someone else's blood on my hands."

Elle's eyes narrowed. "Where did you find her? The woman that looks like me?"

"She's a CIA agent," Riley said. "Like me. Her name is Samantha St. John."

Elle paused. "I have never heard of her."

"She's never heard of you."

"Impossible," Elle snapped. "With all the plastic surgery she's had done, she must have at least known who she was being made to look like."

"No," Riley said. "I didn't know about you until a few days ago. Everyone thought you were Samantha St. John. She's been locked up for the last two months for an arms deal that you did a few months ago. MI-6 got video of that encounter."

She remained silent.

"Look," Riley said reasonably, "I wouldn't mind the opportunity to stand here and talk you through this thing, but I know we don't have the time. I'm sure my director has already notified the SEAL team commander I'm here with." He raised his voice. "Are you out there, Chief Marshall?"

"Yes, sir. I've got her in my sights." The SEAL sounded totally relaxed.

Elle started to look over her shoulder at the darkened doorway, then caught herself and didn't.

"I apologize, Chief," Riley said. "This is my fault."

"Yes, sir," the SEAL said. "I didn't think she'd come out of that trank so quick myself. I should have checked on her, too. Water under the bridge, sir. We're in the soup now, so we'll just see which way it goes."

Riley looked at the woman before him. "What do you think? Maybe you'll kill me and maybe you won't, but I can testify that Chief Marshall won't stop shooting until he knows for sure you're dead."

"That would be correct, sir."

"If it was left up to me," Riley said, "I'd rather see both of us live."

"What are you doing here?" she asked, not giving an inch.

"I'm trying to find out who's setting up my government regarding the arms shipments the Kemenis are receiving," Riley said.

"I was assigned to find proof that the Americans were supplying those weapons."

"I know."

Elle sipped a breath. "I also know that the CIA is not responsible for those shipments."

Riley waited.

"There is a man," Elle said, "a very dangerous man named Lee Craig who is involved in those shipments."

"I don't know who he is," Riley admitted.

"Tch." Elle shook her head slightly. "Then there is much you don't know." She ejected the pistol's magazine, popped the round in the chamber out, and left the slide open. "You have put my double in with Ivanovitch?"

Riley took the pistol. "Yes."

"Then she is in much danger," Elle said. "If Ivanovitch does not find out that she isn't who she says she is, then Lee Craig will kill her."

"Why?"

"Because Lee Craig knows that I am not what I seem," Elle said. "I was undercover with Ivanovitch. He represents the interests of certain crime families in Russia—the *Mafiya*—and is here dealing with Lee Craig and his associates on their behalf. The *Mafiya* and the concerns Lee Craig represents are trying to go into business together."

"If you're telling the truth," Riley said, "then I've really underestimated you."

"When you intercepted me, I had found out from my control that Lee Craig had penetrated my cover story. Perhaps he has even told Ivanovitch. One of my contacts was killed. He didn't die quickly or peacefully. I was warned only minutes before you tried to take me down in the alley. I thought you were Lee Craig's people."

Riley cursed. "Sam's with Ivanovitch now."

"If she is not already dead," Elle said, "then Ivanovitch will kill her when he finds out I have betrayed him. Perhaps he will save her for Lee Craig. Lee Craig lives to murder people."

"Who is he? The way you talk about him, I feel like we should know him."

"Perhaps you know him by his other name. He's also called the Cipher. He's an assassin."

Riley felt as if the floor had opened up beneath him. If Sam wasn't already dead, then she might as well have been. And it was his fault.

"Are you doing all right?"

Seated in a chair in the kitchen area, Sam stared into Ivanovitch's dark eyes. "Yeth," she said, because it was hard to talk with her lip numb and him holding on to it while he stitched the cut closed. He was on the fourth stitch, taking time to make them small and neat. The anesthetic took away all the pain but she felt the pulling and the pressure.

"One more stitch and I'll be finished." Ivanovitch was as good as his word. He finished the final stitch, gazed at her lip to admire his handiwork, and released her. "There. Good as new." He grinned. "Are you surprised?"

Sam tentatively touched her lip. "Yeth." Having her lip released didn't completely fix the speech impediment. With the anesthetic in her lip, the flesh was even more puffy and unwieldy than before.

"You shouldn't be surprised." Ivanovitch picked up his glass and drained his drink. "I'm a man of many talents."

Sam glanced at the watch on her wrist. "We're running out of time."

Ivanovitch nodded. "Yes. We are. But I have a feeling the people we're meeting are going to be willing to be patient a little longer. I think they're going to be surprised to see you." He put his empty glass to one side. "Get your things and we'll go."

Sam walked to the bedroom and got her bag. She didn't know if the SEAL team had heard the conversation. Returning to the kitchen area, she asked, "Has the meeting place been changed?"

"Yes," Ivanovitch told her. He adjusted his jacket, hiding the twin pistols once more.

Just yes? Sam felt frustrated. She knew better than to ask a question that could be answered so conveniently.

"Let's go," Ivanovitch said, opening the door.

Sam stepped out into the hallway. Two men stood there waiting on her and Ivanovitch. The SVR colonel took the lead, walking toward the bank of elevators down the hall. He took out a satellite phone and had a quick conversation that she couldn't hear. When he finished, he was smiling.

"It appears the American CIA is foolishly trying to follow us around again," he said. "Perhaps even more, they may be trying to intercept us. Like the agent we encountered a few days ago, remember?"

Sam thought furiously, remembering that Riley had told her how Ivanovitch had gotten the upper hand on him while he'd been looking for her double. She nodded and regretted the action immediately.

"I remember," she said.

"Your head pains you?"

"Very much."

"Only a little longer." Ivanovitch pressed the elevator buttons. "Then you'll be able to rest all you want."

Sam stood as the elevator dropped smoothly. Evidently Ivanovitch had a specially coded keycard because the elevator cage dropped without interruption, not stopping till it reached the basement. The doors opened and revealed the underground parking garage.

"I thought you had a car out front," Sam said.

"I do. But that car is merely bait. The CIA agents were spotted before my arrival."

Sam didn't think that was true. She'd seen Commander Novak's men in action; they didn't make mistakes. Of course, Riley had insisted on deep security for her. It was possible they had been seen.

Ivanovitch led the way to a Russian sedan. Situated as close to Russia as the country was, Berzhaan had a number of Russian vehicles. The sedan would be almost invisible out on the streets of Suwan.

When Ivanovitch opened the door to the rear seat, she hesitated. She was about to disappear off the SEALs' radar and she knew it. No one was stationed down in the underground parking garage, and the heavily tinted windows and the lateness of the hour would guarantee that no one would see her inside.

"Elle," Ivanovitch prompted. He gazed at her, one hand idly touching his shirt front.

"A moment of dizziness, that's all," Sam said. She climbed inside the sedan and slid across the seat.

Ivanovitch got in after her and closed the door. The driver put the vehicle into motion at once and they slid through the electric dawn of the underground parking garage and out onto the dimly lighted streets.

Riley stood watching the computer monitor over Chief Marshall's shoulder. Elle Petrenko stood at his side. Despite her obvious injuries and the fact that she'd been heavily drugged, she was surprisingly alert and capable.

On the monitor, Commander Novak led his team through the switchback stairs that made up the hotel's emergency escape routes. Every man of the team had a small video camera built into the baseball caps they wore. The caps not only served to carry the video equipment, but also to provide instant identification for the team. The video units connected to belt battery packs and sending units.

All of the SEALs carried pistols and knives. Assault rifles inside the hotel hadn't been possible.

"St. John's first language was Russian?" Elle asked quietly.

"Yes," Riley replied. He knew the woman was struggling with the information they had received from Mitchell.

"Do you think she is my sister?"

Despite the tension of the moment, Riley looked over his shoulder at the woman. Even though she projected a tough exterior, he knew she was hurting and confused inside. How the hell do you react to something like this? he wondered. Then he realized that Sam didn't yet know.

"I don't know," Riley answered. "But I know there's no way the two of you can look so much alike without some kind of family connection. You'd have to get DNA testing to confirm it."

On the monitor, Novak and his team had reached the floor Sam's borrowed room was on. They paused at the door, then Novak waved his point man through.

"I was told she was dead," Elle said. "My adoptive parents told me all of my family was dead. I had pictures of them, but that was all. Not even memories." She paused. "At least, I didn't have memories until I saw St. John."

"That triggered memories?" Riley asked.

"I don't know. Not at the moment. But later, when I was drugged, I dreamed of playing with a little girl who looked exactly like me. That was before I knew that no cosmetic surgery was involved in St. John's features. I thought she was just a double the CIA had created, though why they would go to such lengths, I had no idea."

"She doesn't remember you, either," Riley said. "But seeing you troubled her."

"If I had known that my parents' attempt to get us out of the country had worked, at least halfway, I would have gone to her," Elle said. "I believed her to be dead. All my life I have felt that half of me was missing. Did St. John ever mention anything like that?"

"No."

A vague look of disappointment touched Elle's face but it quickly vanished.

"You knew you were a twin," Riley said. "Sam didn't. She still doesn't. Seeing you has raised some questions for her, but she's a professional." He knew that was true now because he'd seen her in action. Maybe she was still green in some areas, but she was learning quickly. "Once we closed out this mission, I've no doubt that she would have investigated you."

"Does she have a family?"

Riley watched as the SEALs closed on the hotel room. Thankfully, no other guests or hotel staff were out. "Sam was raised in foster care."

"She was never adopted?"

"No. She never had a family."

Elle was quiet for a moment. "That is sad."

"Yeah," Riley agreed, thinking about his own large family.

On the monitor one of the SEALs shoved a silenced pistol at the lock. No one had seen Ivanovitch or Sam or one of his men come through the lobby. If the Russians were still inside the room, things were going to get bloody. Riley only hoped the SEALs had arrived in time.

The SEAL squeezed the trigger. The pistol jumped in his fist. Sparks left from the metal plate as the lock disintegrated under the assault of two more shots. The audio dampened the dulled thumps of the silenced pistol, the shattering metal and the splintering wood.

Then the SEALs kicked the door open wide and barreled through. They went left and right, splitting up into designated groups. Their voices came clear and quick as they secured each room in the suite.

Novak came on the line less than twenty seconds later. "They're gone. She's not here." He ordered his team out of the suite.

A cold chill seized Riley's heart as the statement sank in. *We've lost her.*

Chapter 16

Sam stared out at the rolling black expanse of the Caspian Sea east of Berzhaan. White curlers rode the tide into the expanse of sand and rock that barely supported the gnarled trees and scrub bushes along the coastline. Suwan butted up against the sea, spilling old and new docks and pilings out into the water.

A number of fishing boats sat at anchor with their sails furled. Powerboats and a few pleasure craft, mostly belonging to business executives and successful entrepreneurs, shared harbor space with freighters carrying oil, industrial goods and cargoes of food.

From her previous missions into Berzhaan, Sam knew that the Caspian Sea was misnamed. The body of water was actually the world's largest lake. The surface was ninety feet below sea level, and was reportedly shrinking every year. Much of the water was dependent on the flow from the Volga River, which accounted for three-fourths of the water supply, but the many dams built of late along the Volga had been steadily shutting the water flow down. The Caspian was literally drying out.

The driver turned and followed the gradual descent of the street from Suwan's downtown district to the docks. Suwan was constructed on a large, rolling hill.

Sam felt certain that none of the SEALs had followed them from the hotel. She'd tried to be circumspect in her interest, and felt certain she'd succeeded but she'd seen no sign of Novak's team. Also, she didn't know if the transmitter concealed in the bag worked clearly enough to record her voice and send it.

"What's wrong?" Ivanovitch asked.

"Headache." Sam answered. "Changing from the darkness to the lights out here isn't a pleasant experience. Also, some of the feeling is returning to my lip." That was true enough, as well. Her eyes ached with the intensity of the lights, and her lip felt like a bee had stung it. When her tongue explored the stitches, they felt rough and alien.

"I thought, just for a moment, that you looked…nervous."

Sam studied the SVR colonel in the corner of the back seat. Ivanovitch sat like a pampered cat, content and full of himself.

"We're doing this now," she said, "when I'm not at my best. I *know* I'm not at my best."

"I have every confidence."

That's not what you said earlier, Sam thought. But she sat quietly.

The driver evidently knew where he was going. Once he arrived at the docks, he wound through the shipping-and-receiving warehouses and parked at a dock where a sleek motor sailer was tied up. Sam didn't miss the six men stationed around the dock area in obvious security positions.

"And now," Ivanovitch said, "we do business. Come along." He got out of the car.

Sam got out on her side and joined the SVR colonel. She fisted the MR-443 Grach 9mm pistol her double had carried in her bag earlier but hadn't been able to get to.

"Go easy," Ivanovitch advised.

"He is dangerous," Sam reminded.

"I know."

Sam continued walking at Ivanovitch's side until they reached the dock where the motor sailer was tied up. A man stepped out of the shadows aboard the boat and stood waiting. He wore a black turtleneck, a black windbreaker and black trousers, looking like he was a shadow that had stepped out of the darkness. Even though he was wearing a black watch cap against the chill that came in with the tide, Sam recognized him at once.

He was the man she had tentatively identified as the Cipher in the pictures from Turkey. Her heart thundered and blood pulsed in her ears. This was the man who had killed Rainy. Her fist tightened around the pistol in the bag. She thought about killing him, but she didn't think she could do it. Not in cold blood. She remembered what it had felt like to shoot a man when she was in Munich, the guilt that had been attached even though she'd done it to save her own life. That was the only way she'd thought she would do that again. She wasn't a murderer.

Wait, she advised herself. The Cipher is a hired gun. Someone else wanted Rainy dead. This guy just cashed the check. She made herself breathe out. You want whoever hired him. Not just him.

"Come aboard," the Cipher called in English.

"Thank you." Ivanovitch stepped into the boat's bow. Sam followed him, feeling her footing go soft and mushy and uncertain.

The Cipher glanced at Sam, studying her briefly, then apparently dismissed her. She stood behind and to Ivanovitch's right, leaving herself a clear field of fire.

"You have my weapons?" the Cipher asked.

"Of course," Ivanovitch said. "Do you have my payment?"

The Cipher grinned. He led them down into the motor sailer's living quarters belowdecks. The quarters were spacious and expensive but didn't look lived in. The boat wasn't a place where the Cipher spent a lot of time; it was just a borrowed place to conduct business.

Sam found herself staring at the man, feeling herself get tighter and tighter inside. She couldn't tear her eyes from the Cipher.

He turned on her. "Do you have a problem with me, miss?"

"No," Sam said.

"You're watching me rather closely."

"I was told to. Colonel Ivanovitch says you're a dangerous man."

The Cipher grinned. "You mean, he acknowledges that I am a dangerous man."

Sam nodded.

"I'm flattered," the Cipher said. He turned his attention back to Ivanovitch and snapped his fingers.

One of the men who had followed them belowdecks stepped forward with a briefcase. He put the briefcase on a large table in the galley and opened the locks. Inside, the briefcase was filled with diamonds, a sparkling deluge of them.

"Some of South Africa's finest," the Cipher stated with a trace of pride.

Ivanovitch ran his hand through the glittering gems. The facets caught the light as they trickled through his fingers.

"All right," Ivanovitch said. "I'll take you to your weapons now."

They returned to the motor sailer's deck. Ivanovitch asked to pilot the boat and took over the controls. The engines started smoothly and he pulled the craft out into the water.

Sam stood at Ivanovitch's side, but she scanned the coastline and harbor for any sign of Riley McLane or the SEALs. She saw none of them.

"Are you all right?" Ivanovitch asked over the sound of the wind and the dulled roar of the engines.

"Yes," Sam said, but she felt sick. The anesthetic had completely worn off. Her whole face hurt, but the pain seemed localized in her lower lip.

"It won't be much longer," Ivanovitch promised.

Sam nodded. She kept hold of the Grach 9mm inside the bag. If the transmitter in the bag didn't work, there was always the pistol.

Riley sat in the back of the sedan and talked with Mitchell in an effort to secure another CIA team that was on the ground in the city. The agents operated within a skeletal framework, gathering information instead of responding to threats. Military security at the American Embassy took care of open threats, and getting them out into the operation to recover Sam St. John would leave the embassy exposed to the Q'Rajn terrorists. Sam had the only fireteam in-city. As it turned out, even a few of the CIA agents were impossible to reach.

Mitchell couldn't say how long those agents had been offline because they had random contact times. They were supposed to be so deep in the city's infrastructure that they were invisible.

Riley was getting a bad feeling about the missing agents. The people they were up against, the people Lee Craig represented as well as the Russian *Mafiya* and Ivanovitch's SVR unit, knew far more than the Agency could guess.

Elle Petrenko spoke Russian rapidly into a borrowed satellite phone.

Riley didn't understand the language well enough to follow the conversation. Russia had never been a main theater of operations for him. He stared through the front windshield, watching the other vans in front of him and the dark mass of the Caspian Sea even farther out.

Elle said she knew where Ivanovitch would be. Riley chose to believe that. Thinking anything else, with Sam St. John out there and exposed to hostile guns, was too much. He had no choice but to believe they could save her. He caught the eyes of the SEAL driver in the rearview mirror.

"Do you speak Russian, sir?" the driver asked.

"No," Riley admitted.

"She's talking to her control. A man named Khukhlov."

Riley had heard the name and recognized it from Ivanovitch's files. Pitor Khukhlov was one of the old spymasters from the KGB days. He had a good reputation as a man who could be dealt with, one who kept his country's interests close to heart. But he was also one who had fiercely embraced Communism and still believed in it.

"Khukhlov doesn't have any teams in the area," the SEAL said. "Too much chance of exposure to Ivanovitch's troops. He kept his people pulled back, but they're en route now. They should be here in the next ten or fifteen minutes."

Turning to the woman at his side, Riley said, "I don't want Khukhlov putting his people into this operation."

Elle looked at him and stopped speaking.

Riley heard the man's voice at the other end of the phone connection.

"This is our operation," Elle said. "The SVR's."

"No," Riley said. "Not as long as I've got one of my people on the ground inside a potential bloodbath."

"You put her there," Elle accused.

"And I'll get her back," Riley said. Or die trying.

"And what will you do to achieve that?" Elle arched an eyebrow at him, and Riley was instantly reminded of Sam St. John. "Fight with us, as well?"

"If I have to."

The man at the other end of the conversation spoke English. "Let me talk with the agent, Elle."

"Of course." Elle handed the phone over.

"General Khukhlov," Riley said as he put the phone to his ear.

"Special Agent McLane." Khukhlov had an old man's

voice, brittle and dry. "We have a scheduling problem it seems, no?"

"No," Riley agreed. "I've got an agent inside. I'm going to bring her out before she gets caught in a cross fire."

"I understand your concerns," Khukhlov said, "but I have my own problems in this matter. A rogue agent like Ivanovitch can do a lot of harm if he is allowed to go free."

"I understand that," Riley said. "I know that he was acquiring American-made weapons on the black market and selling to Lee Craig and his associates."

"Some of those weapons," Khukhlov admitted. "There are a great number of weapons that Craig's associates brought in before Ivanovitch became involved."

The driver directed the car along the winding, uneven two-lane road down to the sea's edge and the harbor proper. Elle took a pair of night-vision binoculars and scanned the wharves.

"We're going to get there before you," Riley said.

"It would be best if you waited."

"I can't."

Khukhlov sighed. "Because you put her in place, into this dangerous situation."

"Yes."

"The responsibility of leadership is never an easy burden to bear. I have put plenty of my own people in harm's way, and I have lost some of them over the years."

Riley's hand tightened on the phone. "I don't want to lose this one."

"I understand. But when you and your fellow agents invade Craig's operation, you could scatter them. I want them all in one spot."

"I'm not traveling with CIA agents," Riley said. "I've got a squad of U.S. Navy SEALs specially trained in counterterrorist tactics. We've got orders to terminate with extreme prejudice anyone who stands in the way of getting Sam—our agent—back."

"Even so, you're talking about a high-profile operation. There will be a lot of fallout involved in this. Either way, your government and mine are going to be dealing with the presence of dead agents and soldiers in Suwan, of operations conducted without the permission of the prime minister. In addition to a large shipment of weapons."

"That's your mess."

"True, but your government will be viewed dimly for not notifying Prime Minister Razidae and allowing him to police his own country's affairs."

"We're prepared to deal with that."

"Of course you are." Khukhlov sounded somewhat sarcastic. "These days the United States pursues the course of the champion to the world every given moment."

"We have a difference of opinion," Riley said. "I just see it as us doing a job that we're ready, willing and able to fulfill."

The car rolled to a stop at the sea's edge.

"I've got to go," Riley said.

There was a moment of silence, long enough that Riley started to suspect Khukhulov had simply hung up and the sound of that hadn't touched his ears. Then Khukhlov asked, "Is this woman of yours Elle Petrenko's sister?"

Riley hesitated. "Given everything that I understand about the situation, I believe so."

"Thank God. All those years ago, I thought we had lost her. The KGB killed Boris and Anya, ordered their deaths as double agents, and they almost intercepted the children as they were ferried through the lifeline Boris had set up. There was much confusion, much death. I was with the squad that recovered Elle, and later I placed her with her foster family. Her parents were friends of mine. But we had no way of knowing that little Natasha had survived the attack."

"You attacked those children?"

"The people who were trying to get out of the country with them, yes." Khukhlov paused. "I have carried the guilt of Natasha Leonov's death for many years. I am glad that it can be eased now."

"You didn't try to find her?"

"No. We believed she was dead. And the Americans who took her would not have trusted us, anyway. We had reported the Leonovs and both their children dead. Those days were very…strained. Then, during the confusion when Communism was rejected in my country, there was no time to follow up on Natasha Leonov. She was just gone. Until tonight. Does she remember her sister?"

"I don't think so. Sam's had a hard life. She was raised pretty much as an orphan. No family. She didn't have what Elle obviously had."

"That is too bad." Khukhlov paused. "I will do this for you, Special Agent McLane, seeing as how I am also trying to rectify an old wrong—and I am near to retirement anyway if my government does not approve of my choices in this matter. I will hold my people back until you are able to get Elle's sister out of harm's way. Then we will descend upon Colonel Ivanovitch with all the wrath of the Old Testament."

"I understand, General," Riley said. "Thank you."

"Should this turn out all right," Khukhlov said, "I will stand you to a glass of vodka."

"As long as I buy the second round." Riley broke the connection and followed Elle out of the car.

Elle peered out at the sea. "It's gone," she said.

"What's gone?" Riley asked.

"The ship. The ship Ivanovitch had moored here."

"What's the name?"

"*Fisherhawk*. She's a cargo ship out of Ekerem, Russia. Much construction is going on there these days to revitalize the port."

Anxiety shot through Riley as he relayed the news to Commander Novak and the SEAL team. Riley looked out across the harbor, feeling the enormity of the task before him. The harbor was filled with ships, and not all of them bore names that were easily legible or at all. And he didn't know what *Fisherhawk* looked like in the Cyrillic alphabet.

"The ship must have been moved," Elle said as she jogged along the wharves and looked at the ships. "We'll need a boat to search for them out on the water."

"Wait." Riley walked to the back of the sedan and opened the trunk. He removed a duffel that contained gear Novak and his SEALs had parceled out. The duffels contained assault rifles and other gear that equipped the men for a full-fledged battlefield. He took two packs out of the trunk and passed one over to Elle. "Weapons."

Elle accepted the duffel with a nod, checked inside and quickly slung the bag over her shoulder.

"Now let's find a boat." She set off at once.

Riley followed her down to the water, trailed by the SEAL who had driven the car. Glancing around, he saw that Novak had assigned his teams to acquire boats, as well. Thankfully, the time was late enough at night that most of the owners were gone and no one hailed security.

Elle stepped aboard a luxury powerboat that had seen better days. The SEAL cast off the lines from the mooring cleats as Elle hot-wired the engine, then he hopped aboard as she got underway.

Riley stood near the pilot's wheel beside Elle and unpacked the M4A1 assault rifles, Kevlar vests and extra ammunition. Then he scanned the harbor with the night-vision binoculars.

"Do you love her?" Elle asked over the roar of the engines.

Surprised, Riley turned to face the Russian agent. "What?"

"Do you love her? Do you love my sister?" Elle spoke the term as if still trying to get used to it.

"I care about your sister. We haven't seen eye-to-eye on a lot of things." Riley remembered the night in Sam's cell when she'd attempted to seduce him. There had been a lot of sleepless nights and sweat-soaked sheets in two countries since that time. But he'd never forgotten how it felt to cup Sam's flesh and claim it as his own.

Looking at him, her hair flying around her head in the wind, Elle nodded in satisfaction. "You do love her. Or you will. I can see it in your face. Russian women, we know these things. Love is one of the greatest tragedies of life. You never get to truly choose those you fall in love with. Or when. It can all be so inconvenient." She spoke as though she knew firsthand what she was talking about.

"It wouldn't matter anyway. Sam St. John can't get rid of me fast enough."

"Don't be so quick to judge. When I was going to kill you in the alley, she threw herself to your rescue."

"It was one agent coming to the rescue of another," Riley said. "I'm doing the same thing for Sam St. John now."

Elle showed him a brief smile. "Exactly my point. And since you are able to love her, I have hopes that I, too, can love her. These things do not always work out like that. Especially when facing more than twenty years of separation."

And all that depends on whether we can save her, Riley thought. But he didn't give voice to his doubts and fears. He pulled the night-vision binoculars back to his eyes and resumed his search.

After only a few minutes, Ivanovitch guided the motor sailer to a small cargo ship anchored out in the harbor. The ship was old, covered with barnacles and peeling paint. Her running lights were dim. Sam knew the ship would hardly have rated a second glance in Suwan's harbor.

Ivanovitch cut the engines and expertly guided the motor sailer up along the cargo ship. Crewmen aboard the cargo ship threw lines down and quickly tied the boat alongside. Afterward, they threw down a rope ladder.

The Cipher went first, then Ivanovitch followed. Sam went after that, feeling her body ache and resist the demands she made on it. The rough hemp of the rope ladder bit into her hands.

"The weapons are stowed below," Ivanovitch was saying as she gained the deck. "The explosives have already been set."

Explosives? A warning tingle shot through Sam. What explosives? But she made herself remain silent. She gazed around the ship, noting that the crew was in excess of a dozen members, which was quite large for a ship sitting at anchor in a harbor. All of them were armed with pistols, and a few of them carried assault rifles and shotguns.

Ivanovitch led the way belowdecks. The darkness in the cargo hold was held back by electric lanterns. The ship held a musty stench, like old death mixed with foot odor.

Crates occupied a lot of the ship's cargo area, but not all of the space was filled.

"You have what I asked for?" the Cipher asked.

"Of course." Ivanovitch stepped toward the nearest crate and took a crowbar from a wall mounting nearby. He put the flat end of the crowbar under the nearest crate and pried the lid off.

Inside the crate, packed in silicon pebbles, a row of M-16A2 assault rifles lay neatly stacked. The sheen of gun oil clung to the barrels.

Ivanovitch continued through the crates, opening them up one after the other like a salesman eager to show off his wares. Sam stood in stunned wonder as LAWs, light anti-tank weapon rocket tubes, M-60 machine guns, American grenades and other weapons were revealed.

"Very good," the Cipher complimented.

Sam stood her ground, feeling the roll of the sea echoed in the slight movement of the cargo ship fighting the anchor and the tide. She kept her fist around the butt of the 9mm. Despite his ease around her, she got the definite feeling that the Cipher knew she was holding a weapon. The pain in her lip was distracting, but she remained focused.

"All United States military hardware," Ivanovitch declared. "Gleaned from the first Iraqi War as well as action against the Taliban in Afghanistan. The Americans flood areas with weapons, but they don't always keep count of them."

"You mentioned you had mined the ship," the Cipher said.

Ivanovitch reached inside his jacket and took out a micro-miniaturized electronic device. "Yes. It is mined. After you mentioned what you had planned for the ship, I took the liberty of having the work done for you."

"Very good." The Cipher snapped his fingers. Two of his men walked the length of the ship, shone their lights around and returned.

"Everything looks good," one of the men said.

"I leave the timing in your hands," Ivanovitch said. "You can control all the detonators with the device I gave you, or you can control individual bombs."

The Cipher pocketed the device. "Good enough, when the ship crashes into the harbor, I'll set them off. Not everything will be blown up in the resulting explosions. Plenty of identifiable military hardware will remain to point the finger at the United States. But the damage all along the harbor will cost millions of dollars to rebuild. Since trade is such a big part of Berzhaan's economy, they will be impacted financially as well as politically. I'd say that will set back negotiations with the United States for years if not decades."

"At which point," Ivanovitch said, "my superiors will

offer me a commendation, at least, and a promotion almost certainly."

Sam thought about the kind of damage the Cipher planned to wreak. She felt sick. Simply running the boat into the public areas would have caused a tremendous amount of damage, but the explosions that would follow would kill or maim dozens of people.

"No," the Cipher said, "I'm afraid those days are behind you."

Ivanovitch looked wary. "What are you talking about?"

"You've had a traitor in your midst, Colonel," the Cipher said. "I've no doubt that she has already informed your superior about your secondary career."

Ivanovitch's eyes tracked to Sam. After all, she was the only female in the cargo area. She started to pull the pistol from the bag. Instead, she froze as a cold pistol barrel bumped up solidly against the back of her neck.

"Here, now," a soft voice with a British accent said, "I'll be after having that."

Sam released her hold on the pistol and the man took it from her.

"And I'll be wanting you to put your hands on top of your head," the man continued.

Cautiously Sam put her hands on her head. She didn't lace her fingers, leaving her hands free.

"What are you talking about?" Ivanovitch demanded.

"Agent Elle Petrenko," the Cipher said, "is working undercover for the SVR. Whatever she told you to get you to bring her inside this operation isn't true. Her loyalties lie with the SVR. Not you. Not to the profits that she could be making working with us."

For some reason, Sam took pride in that. Perhaps it only had to do with the fact that her double looked so much like her. Unfortunately, she was left to bear the consequences of her double's integrity.

"As thorough as you are in your weapons delivery," the Cipher said, "I'm just as thorough in checking out the people that I work with."

The lights in the cargo hold suddenly dimmed. The cavernous roar of starting engines swelled to life.

Knowing that she had no choice, that her life was forfeit if she didn't take chances, Sam lowered her left arm and spun backward. Her estimate of the man's height behind her was dead-on. Her backfist caught him in the temple and turned his legs wobbly.

She caught the man's pistol with her other hand, stripping it from his grip by pinching a nerve cluster between his thumb and forefinger. Still moving toward the exit from the cargo hold, she slid the pistol into her hand and swiveled around to shove the weapon at the Cipher and Ivanovitch.

Both men and the guards around them were in motion.

Sam squeezed off two shots, anyway, letting them know that she meant business and that she was definitely armed. The bullets smashed into the wooden crates containing the assault rifles and bricks of C-4 plastic explosive. She didn't worry about the C-4 exploding; it would take a detonator to trigger it.

She stayed moving, flattening up against a stack of crates. Bullets slammed into the wooden surfaces. She felt the vibration of the impacts against her back.

"Hold your fire!" the Cipher ordered. "I can handle her!"

Sam looked at the metal stairway leading out of the cargo hold. I can make that, she told herself. Once I get topside, I can escape into the sea. She braced herself and started to launch herself across the distance.

Then everything went black.

A series of flat cracks caught Riley's attention. He touched Elle's arm. "Cut the engines."

Elle did. "What is it?"

"I thought I heard gunshots."

"I didn't hear anything."

Riley strained his hearing, hoping for a repeat of the sound. Noise traveled farther and faster across a body of water than it did across land.

He didn't hear anything.

"Let's go," he said.

Elle restarted the engines and got the boat underway again.

C'mon, Sam, Riley thought as he scanned the night-vision binoculars across the clusters and lines of ships and boats. Give me something.

Chapter 17

When Sam's senses returned, she had a blinding headache that mirrored the deep throbbing basso booms of the cargo ship's engines. Instinctively she tried to get to her feet only to discover that she had been handcuffed to a crate. She pulled at the short length of metal between the cuffs but only succeeded in acquiring fresh bruises around her wrists. The chain ran through a space in the crate, effectively tying her down to it.

"Who are you?"

Sam looked up at the Cipher standing before her. He no longer looked complacent.

Without seeming to move, and quicker than she could move, the Cipher slapped her face hard enough to turn her head.

"You were speaking English while you were out," the

Cipher said. "Not Russian. You mentioned a woman named Lorraine Carrington. Rainy. How did you know her?"

"You murdered her," Sam said. She tasted fresh blood inside her mouth, and her whole face stung from the slap. Beneath her, the cargo deck quivered as the ship's engines throbbed and continued to power up. Judging from the changing pitch and yawl of the cargo ship, the pilot was continuing to change directions, getting the vessel set up to ram into the harbor where its deadly payload could be set off to incriminate the United States in the clandestine munitions deliveries coming into Berzhaan.

"How did you know her?" the Cipher demanded.

"She was my friend," Sam said before she could stop herself. Evidently whatever had caused her to black out was still impairing her judgment to a degree.

The Cipher shook his head. "The Carrington woman was never a friend of Elle Petrenko's. The background checks I saw would have revealed that."

Sam felt nauseous. She gagged and almost threw up.

"Don't feel so good, do you?" The Cipher grinned. "It can have that effect on some people."

"What did you do to me?" Sam asked.

The Cipher extended his hand and showed her a small electronic device. It was no bigger than a penny and only three times as thick. One side had an adhesive strip.

"I used a neuro jammer," he said. "When my guard took your weapon, he put one of these on your back as insurance."

Sam hadn't even noticed.

"The neuro jammer emits a high-frequency pattern that

causes a reaction in the brain that looks exactly like a narcoleptic attack." The Cipher held the device between his thumb and forefinger. "I jimmied the Carrington woman's seat belt, then I put one of these in her car. I triggered the device to knock her out, and she left the road. She hit a tree and died on impact."

Sam couldn't believe how callously the assassin talked about her friend's death. She kept her tears back with difficulty.

The Cipher looked up at Ivanovitch. "Evidently Petrenko's espionage jacket had more left out of it than I believed. I don't recall it mentioning that she trained at the Athena Academy. Or anywhere in the United States."

"She didn't," Ivanovitch said. He frowned. "Something strange is going on here."

The Cipher's satellite phone rang. He took it out of his pocket and spoke quickly, then put it away and looked up at Ivanovitch. "The pilot has the ship in position and on course. It will reach the harbor in minutes."

"Then we should go," Ivanovitch said, gazing at Sam. "We could take her, ask her more questions."

The Cipher shook his head. "I keep thinking about those CIA agents that you said turned up at her hotel. If they were there watching her, they could still be out there. I don't want to try to juggle a hostage if that's the case. They could even know to look for this ship."

"Then they're wasting their time," Ivanovitch said. "After Elle told me she had been mugged, I had the ship moved to this location. She didn't know that until we arrived here."

"That's bought us some time."

"Not enough," Ivanovitch said. "Not if this thing works out the way you want it to. We should go. If they're still out there, we'll find them when we need to."

The Cipher looked around. "You have the other packages we agreed on?"

Ivanovitch used his crowbar again. He opened a large, upright crate, then stepped back as four male bodies crumpled to the floor.

All four men were dead.

"These four men are all CIA agents?" the Cipher asked.

"They were on the list that you gave me." Ivanovitch looked at the corpses. "I've had dealings with two of them while I've been in Berzhaan."

"Good. When their bodies are found in the debris and the wreckage of the ship, it will look even more like the CIA was behind this." The Cipher looked at Sam and smiled. "And you will be the poor Russian intelligence agent they caught and were ruthlessly interrogating when the ship went out of control, rammed into the harbor and exploded." He paused. "We'll still get a lot of use out of you. Don't know if the explosions down here will kill you, or if you'll drown. Either way, you're in for a short, interesting time."

Sam didn't say anything as the Cipher and Ivanovitch left. As soon as they were out of sight, she started working on her cuffs, finding them too tight to pull her hands through. Her lip throbbed with pain as she considered her next move.

While training at Langley, Sam had heard of agents who had successfully escaped from handcuffs by breaking their thumbs so they could squeeze their hands through the cuffs. She braced her feet against the crate, folded her left thumb into the palm of her hand, and pulled with all her strength.

The throbbing engines grew louder. The deck trembled as the vessel surged forward.

Crying out in pain, wishing she could stop, Sam kept pulling. Her mind worked busily, planning past her point of escape.

The Cipher had killed Rainy. He'd admitted that, and he'd even told her how he'd done it. Nowhere in her research and training had Sam ever heard of a neuro jammer. She also didn't think the Cipher had invented the device. The guy was an assassin, not a tech specialist. That meant he was working with someone, and that someone must have ordered Rainy's death.

It had something to do with the eggs that Rainy had been robbed of twenty-two years ago. Sam didn't doubt that for an instant.

She was trembling, on the threshold of having to deal with too much pain. Her hand wasn't coming through, and her thumb wasn't breaking. She wasn't certain if she was going to pass out or simply not have the stomach to subject herself to any more pain. She wanted to give up, but she couldn't.

She pulled again, shutting out the pain, thinking about the way Rainy had died, and about all the innocents who were going to die along the harbor in the next few minutes. Setting her feet again, she lunged back, putting all of her weight and strength into the effort.

Her thumb snapped loud enough to be heard over the drone of the ship's engines. Sam cried out. The pain almost made her pass out.

Hanging on to her senses, Sam pulled the handcuffs through the crate and stood up. Her left hand throbbed horribly, swelling visibly by the second. She'd had broken bones before, so she knew she could still function.

Standing unsteadily, Sam walked to the crates of weapons. She was tempted to take an M-16, but she was afraid that she couldn't handle the assault rifle's weight for long with her injured hand. Instead, she took four Beretta 92F, the standard sidearm carried by American Special Forces. Loading the magazines for each of the weapons was hard and she ended up scattering 9mm shells across the cargo deck.

Once the pistols were loaded, she thrust them into her pants pockets and waistband. Turning her attention to the crate of C-4, she found electronic detonators and quickly thrust them into the bricks of plastic explosive on top, set them to receive one signal, and picked up a detonator complete with a battery that took only an instant to install.

The detonator cycled, then blinked green, indicating that it was ready.

As an afterthought, Sam picked up two of the LAWs lying in a nearby crate. She slung one over her shoulder, then telescoped the other one into a long tube so that it was ready to fire.

You're going to wish you'd killed me, Sam thought as she started up the metal stairs. The engines droned on.

At the top of the stairs, she pushed open the door with her injured hand. Pain exploded through her thumb, but she ignored it. Glancing to the west, she saw the harbor less than five hundred yards away. Lights in buildings and on ships marked the geography.

"Hey!"

The voice drew Sam's attention at once. She glanced toward the cargo ship's wheelhouse and raised the LAW to her shoulder. Men were in the process of abandoning the cargo ship and climbing down into the motor sailer the Cipher had been waiting on.

Muzzleflashes tore holes in the night's darkness.

Sam stayed low, watching sparks strike near her to let her know how close her opponents' bullets had come. She took hold of the LAW's pistol grip, slid her finger over the trigger, aimed for the center of the wheelhouse, and squeezed.

The LAW shoved back against her. Muzzle burn vomited from the rear of the long tube, throwing a cloud of heated air over her that warred with the cold brine wind that cycled over the sea.

The 94mm warhead struck the wheelhouse squarely and exploded. A whirling orange and black gout of flames wrapped around the wheelhouse. All of the men around the wheelhouse were thrown to the ground. Glass shattered and emptied from the superstructure's windows.

Okay, Riley, Sam thought desperately as she tossed away the disposable LAW tube, *if you're anywhere in the area, you've got to see that.* She pulled the second LAW from her shoulder, telescoped it, and aimed the weapon at the motor sailer. Whoever was piloting it was already pulling away from the cargo ship. Bits and pieces of flaming debris drifted down through the air and landed on the uneven surface of the sea.

Sam drew a breath and let half of it out, held the rest. She led the motor sailer slightly, then squeezed the LAW's trigger.

The rocket *whooshed* from the LAW, streaked across the sea trailing fire and smoke, and impacted against the motor sailer's bow. Part of the coaming blew away and a pool of fire washed back over the motorsailer's windscreen. More flames caught in the folds of the furled sail and climbed the mast.

Glancing at the coastline, Sam saw that less than two hundred yards separated the cargo ship from the harbor. Time was running out. She took the detonator from her pocket and readied it. Before she could trigger the C-4 bricks in the cargo hold, a line of bullets smacked into the deck in front of her, chewing through the wooden deck.

Sam dodged to one side. The impact of landing against the deck jarred the detonator from her hand and sent it spinning away. She drew one of the Berettas and focused on the figure behind the muzzle flashes ahead of her. She steadied herself, tried not to think of the bullets that would cut through her in a heartbeat if they hit, and squeezed the trigger steadily.

On the seventh shot, leaving seven in the magazine and one under the hammer, the man fell. Sam didn't know how many times she had hit him; she was just glad he'd gone down. She pushed up with her good hand and pursued the sliding detonator. She trapped it against the deck with her injured hand, then used her fingers to send the signal.

Immediately she felt the earthquake that shivered through the cargo ship. The tremendous avalanche of booms followed a heartbeat later. The cargo ship immediately stopped nearly dead in the water, letting Sam know the chain of explosions had ripped out a large section of the vessel's bottom.

The ship started sinking at once.

On her feet and running now, Sam crossed the deck to the port side. At least one or two of the Cipher's or Ivanovitch's men still lived. They fired at her, but their marksmanship was off or she was just too quick for them. Reaching the ship's side, she hurled herself over, shoving both hands out in front of her so she could cut through the dark water deeply. Reflections of the burning cargo ship reflected on the sea's surface.

Then she struck the water and went under.

Riley raised the M4A1 assault rifle to his shoulder and targeted the two men standing at the railing of the sinking cargo ship. As soon as the first explosion had ripped into the ship's wheelhouse, Elle had steered for the vessel.

They were only eighty yards out from the ship and closing fast. He'd spotted Sam St. John firing a pistol at one of the men who had survived the rocket attack on the wheelhouse. By that time he knew there was something seriously wrong with the cargo ship because it was settling into the sea all wrong.

The men at the cargo ship railing fired at Sam as she struck the water. Then Riley squeezed the trigger and swept three-round bursts across the two men. Both of them stumbled and went back and down.

"McLane," Colonel Novak called over the headset Riley wore.

"Here," Riley said.

"We're taking fire from support vessels. Evidently Ivanovitch or Craig had teams in the water. We're trying to keep the civilians clear and open communications with the local law enforcement," Novak said.

"General Khukhlov can aid with that," Elle said. "He has many contacts in place here."

"Affirmative. Call him and let him know we'll patch him through to our frequency."

Elle took out the satellite phone she'd borrowed and punched in a number as she powered the boat down. She spoke in rapid Russian while peering over the side of the boat.

At that moment, Sam's head broke the surface of the water. She came up holding a Beretta in both hands, pointing the weapon at Riley.

"Sam," Riley called out, lowering the assault rifle. He felt the boat shudder beneath him and knew that the sinking ship was creating a strong undertow. If Sam didn't get out quick, the ship would pull her down.

"Riley," she called up.

The flames still burning aboard the ship illuminated the area. Her pale face took on an orange tint.

Riley reached down into the water. The SEAL that had accompanied Elle and Riley reached down into the water, as well. Sam caught Riley's hand first, then grimaced in pain. Her grip wasn't strong.

"What's wrong?" Riley asked over the roar of the fire aboard the ship.

"I broke my thumb," she replied. Her other hand came up out of the water. A pair of handcuffs hung around her other wrist. "I had to."

Elle spun around and brought the assault rifle to her shoulder as a row of bullets smashed through the boat's Plexiglas cowling. "Hurry," she said.

Riley and the SEAL hauled Sam from the water. She stood drenched and shivering.

"Go," Riley told Elle.

Elle powered the boat up and sent them speeding away.

Riley took a lockpick from his pocket. "Let me see those cuffs."

Sam lifted her right hand to let the cuffs dangle. She still held the pistol. She stared out across the sea toward the harbor.

Riley picked the hand cuff lock, pulled it off and threw it into the sea.

"That boat," Sam said, pointing with her injured hand. "Ivanovitch and the Cipher are aboard it." In terse sentences, talking loudly enough that her voice carried over the wind and the noise of the boat's engines, Sam explained what Ivanovitch and Lee Craig, though she didn't know his name, had planned with the ship.

"There's still going to be a lot of explaining to do," Riley said.

Sam nodded.

Looking at her standing there, Riley couldn't help being amazed at everything Sam St. John had been through over the past two months. Most people would have cratered after losing a close friend, being locked up for two months, and having to hit the ground running on an operation that had turned bloody within hours. And yet, she still somehow seemed indomitable.

Elle kept the boat powered up, swiftly closing the distance between themselves and the yacht with the flaming prow.

Ivanovitch had aimed his boat at the closest dock, navigating between other boats. Elle kept the power on, never slacking. Twice the boat traded paint with other vessels hard enough to shudder from the impacts. Hardly slowing, Ivanovitch ran the boat up onto shore, ripping out the bottom and turning the boat over onto its side as it careened into stacks of cargo.

"Hang on," Elle warned.

Men scattered from the burning yacht. Dock workers fled the scene immediately. In the distance, sirens ripped through the night and whirling lights sped along the twisting roads as Suwan security teams arrived.

Two men fired from cover behind the overturned yacht. Their muzzle flashes marked their positions.

"I need the Cipher alive," Sam yelled over the roaring engines. "He admitted to killing Rainy." She looked at Riley. "He killed her, Riley, but someone hired him to do it. I need to talk to him."

Personally, Riley didn't think Lee Craig would talk. With the reputation the man had, with the clientele he served, he couldn't afford to. Someone would kill him.

Elle didn't let off the throttle. The powerboat hit the shoreline and shot toward the overturned yacht, scattering the gunmen behind the vessel. The other boat shattered and went to pieces, some of them still flaming.

Riley felt as if his arms had gotten wrenched from their sockets by the time the powerboat smashed up against a stack of crates and came to a halt. He turned to check on Sam but found that she had already bailed over the side of the powerboat and was in motion.

A flash of movement caught Sam's eye and sent her to ground behind a small fishing boat that someone had pulled up onto the sand. Bullets chopped into the sand only inches from her head. Sand kicked into her eyes and brought stinging pain. She'd also landed wrong on her broken hand and the sudden agony almost swept her senses.

She fisted the Beretta and came up firing, putting three rounds into the center of the mass that confronted her. Already dead on his feet, the gunman fell to the ground. By then, Sam was already running again.

She kept the Cipher under observation, watching the man dodge in and out among pallets of cargo that were obviously still being loaded or unloaded.

Someone stepped into place beside her.

Sam whirled, bringing up the Beretta at once. Elle blocked her movement with a forearm.

"It's me," Elle said. "I will help you bring this man down." She glanced at Sam's broken thumb. "You're not whole."

Sam nodded, glancing back down the incline and seeing Riley trading shots with Ivanovitch, who managed to keep each other pinned down. Sam swapped the partially expended pistol for a fresh one. The wind off the sea blew so sharply cold through her wet clothes that she felt as if she was getting cut in two.

"How did you get my face?" Sam asked.

"Our parents gave it to me," Elle said. "The same as they gave you yours."

"Parents?" Sam couldn't believe what she'd heard. "We have the same parents?"

Elle nodded.

"Where are our parents?" Suddenly a thousand questions filled Sam's mind.

"They're dead." Elle looked sad, but the emotion was an old and weathered one. "They were murdered a long time ago."

Sam looked at the other woman. "You're my twin sister?"

"Yes."

For the first time, Sam realized they were talking in Russian as if they had always done that. Emotions broke loose inside Sam and she had to force them away. If they lived, there would be time to explore everything that lay between them.

"Are you ready?" Elle asked, setting up on the other side of the cargo they took shelter behind.

"Yes." Sam listed the pistol beside her head.

"Go."

Sam whirled around the corner of the crates and balanced the Beretta across the back of her left hand. She moved her feet deliberately, never crossing one over the other and remaining in a half crouch to make a smaller target. She caught occasional glimpses of Elle on the other side of the row of cargo and saw that the woman—my sister!—moved the same way with her weapon held in the same fashion.

Tension mounted inside Sam. Had the Cipher gotten away? He had a reputation for doing that.

Metal gleamed in the sand under her feet.

She looked down and spotted the metal disk that was the same circumference as a penny but was three times as thick. Remembering how quickly the device had knocked her out earlier, Sam kicked the device away, watching it spin into the water line.

"Elle." Sam wanted to warn her sister, but when she looked across the way, she saw Elle drop to her knees. Her eyes rolled up into her head, showing only rolling white.

Then the Cipher was there, stepping out of the shadows with a big pistol in his hand. He pointed the pistol at Elle's head.

"Two of you," the Cipher mused with a tight smile. "And when I pull this trigger, there will be only one."

Sam looked at him. She wanted him alive. She wanted to know who had ordered him or paid him to kill Rainy. And why.

"Put your weapon down," the Cipher ordered. "Put your weapon down or I will blow her head off."

Elle remained passed out, helpless and exposed.

"Do it," the Cipher growled. "Do it now."

Sam remembered all the nights and days she'd spent alone in the homes of strangers, how she'd always wanted a family, how she'd always wanted to know where she came from and why her parents would give her up.

Elle had the answers to at least some of those questions.

In a split second Sam made her decision. The Cipher must have seen it in her eyes, because he pulled his pistol up and tried to shoot her. His bullet burned the air by Sam's ear.

Feeling the Beretta bounce against her broken thumb, Sam put three bullets through the Cipher's head. His features destroyed and the back of his head blown away, the man dropped to his knees, then fell face forward.

Epilogue

"I didn't have a choice. I had to kill Lee Craig." Sam St. John paced in the shade of a palm tree while she talked on the satellite phone. The cast on her broken thumb felt awkward and heavy.

At the other end of the connection, Kayla Ryan said, "You did what you had to do, Sam. And the Cipher wouldn't have stopped with just killing your sister. If he'd gotten the chance, he'd have killed you, too."

"I know."

"Your sister is all right?"

Sam thought that was still strange to hear. "Your sister" sounded unnatural in a way, but it was one of the best things Sam had ever heard. "Elle is fine. She arranged a couple days in Suwan to handle some of the other information she turned up while she was undercover in Ivanovitch's organization."

"That will give you guys some time to get to know each other a little more."

Sam stood still and stared across the beach at the volleyball game underway. Although Suwan was primarily a Muslim nation, a lot of Western ways had crept into the country as entrepreneurs pandered to the tourist dollars. Of course, some volleyball players on the hill were American military personnel on their off time.

"Yeah, it will give us a little more time," Sam said. "I think we're both looking forward to that."

"You've already got a lot in common," Kayla said. "The whole spy thing."

"Different sides of the fence, though."

"Russia and America? Not so much on different sides of the fence these days."

"There are a lot of differences, though." Sam stared up the hill and saw Elle—her sister—in the thick of an enthusiastic volleyball game.

Elle was dressed in a barely-there thong bikini and showed her body off in ways that Sam could never have done. She took two quick steps forward, then leaped up and spiked the ball back across the net, driving it into an open area between two young Marines who could not get to it in time. Elle lifted her arms and celebrated.

"How are you doing?" Kayla asked.

Sam turned away from her sister and peered out at the harbor. Salvage boats, from Russia and from the United States, worked the area of the sea where the cargo ship had gone down two days ago.

"I'm fine," Sam said.

"You've been through a lot," Kayla said. "Losing Rainy

and not having any of us around you to help you through it. Spending two months as a prisoner of the CIA. Finding out everything you have about your sister. None of that was easy."

"No. But I'm getting through it. I've been able to get through everything I had to."

"I know," Kayla said. "I've seen you do it. But you need to remember that you don't have to do that alone now. When you get things cleared there, after you've had a chance to visit with your sister, come back home for a little while." She paused. "And it's not just for you, Sam. It's for us, too. We need you."

Tears burned the backs of Sam's eyes. Unable to stop them, she pulled her sunglasses from the top of her head and slid them into place.

"I know," Sam whispered. "I'll be there as soon as I can."

"There's more going on here than just Rainy's murder," Kayla said.

"We still don't know why she was killed."

"At this point, we have to assume it was because she was investigating the theft of her eggs twenty-two years ago."

"This is really getting weird."

"I know. Did I tell you that Josie thinks she may have a way to follow up on the Cipher?"

"No." Sam was immediately intrigued.

"Her sister, Diana, is in Army Intelligence. Josie's going to ask Diana to check around and see if she can turn up anything now that he's been identified."

"You'll let me know?"

"The minute I find out anything. Take care of yourself, Sam."

"I will. You, too." Sam punched the end button on the phone.

On top of the hill, the volleyball game slowed down for a while. Elle sat down with the two Marines and started talking. Sam's partner, Riley McLane, came down the hill.

As she looked at the man, watching the way he moved like a big cat, everything working together, Sam felt her insides turn liquid. She wrinkled her nose. She could deal with finding a sister she never knew she had, getting locked up for two months through no fault of her own, going head to head with a world-class assassin…

But there was something about Riley McLane that just kept her on edge.

"Hey," he greeted. "Finish your call?"

"Yes."

"Everything okay?"

"It's getting there. Rainy's still gone. There's no getting around that."

"No. I suppose not." Riley wore athletic shorts. His body was already turning nut brown, and perspiration helped define his musculature. The only things that jarred were the old scars and the new pink ones that wrapped his shoulder.

Sam found herself taking a deep breath and feeling itchy all over.

Riley pushed his sunglasses up on his head. "That's some sister you've got there, St. John. She plays volleyball like you play racquetball."

"I've noticed. You guys are beating the hell out of the Marines."

"True, but I don't think they mind so much."

"There is that matter of the spoonful of bikini she's wearing."

Riley grinned. "I'm sure that has a lot to do with it."

Sam walked over to the cooler they'd brought to the beach and took out two bottles of water. She gave one to Riley.

"Thanks." He twisted the top off and took a long drink. "You've told your friends about Lee Craig?"

"Yes. They're working on some other leads."

"Taking him down wasn't a bad thing."

"I know. It just would have been better if I'd taken him alive."

Riley shook his head. "Guys like Lee Craig, they don't get taken alive."

Sam looked at him, remembering how she'd tried to seduce him that night in her cell. They hadn't talked about that night since.

Glancing back up the hill, Riley said, "I think we're done with the volleyball game for a while." He grinned sourly. "Matter of fact, I know we are. Elle told me to come down here and take you for a walk."

"She's awfully pushy for a new sister," Sam said.

"I guess maybe she figures she missed out on a lot of years of pushing. So she's trying to catch up." He looked at her. "So I'm asking—would you like to go for a walk? There's a little café not far from here. I'll even buy lunch."

"Because my sister told you to?"

Riley walked over to her, put his fingertips up under her chin and tilted her head back. Then he bent down and lightly touched her lips with his. "No. Because I thought talking over lunch would be a good way to get to know more about you."

Sam still felt the kiss tingling on her lips. "Sure," she said. "I'd like that. A lot."

Books by Meredith Fletcher

Silhouette Bombshell

Double-Cross #14

Silhouette Books

Femme Fatale
"The Get-Away Girl"

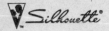

Silhouette®

BOMBSHELL™

COMING NEXT MONTH

SBCNM1004